About the author

Katheryn Thompson is currently studying for A-levels at a sixth form college in her home town of Warrington. She wrote *Brown Leather Shoes* at the age of just fifteen, while working towards her GCSEs, and its sequel is well under way. Katheryn has always had a passion for writing, and hopes to pursue a career in English.

BROWN LEATHER SHOES

Katheryn Thompson

Book Guild Publishing
Sussex, England

First published in Great Britain in 2014 by
The Book Guild Ltd
The Werks
45 Church Road
Hove, BN3 2BE

Typesetting in Sabon by
Ellipsis Digital Ltd, Glasgow

Printed and bound in Great Britain by
CPI Group (UK) Ltd, Croydon, CR0 4YY

A catalogue record for this book is available from
The British Library.

ISBN 978 1 909716 30 8

Prologue
Brown Leather Shoes

Large droplets of rain fell from the charcoal grey sky onto the equally grey pavement and bounced upwards again as if trying to return to the sky. Andrew could hear the bullets of rain hitting the ground and if he closed his eyes, he could smell that memorable smell of rain, which, in his mind, was at its best on a hot day straight after a shower. Andrew had seen shops selling water-scented candles and he had often wondered what the manufacturers imagined water smelt like; when he imagined its smell it was *this* smell of rain. However, the candles never seemed to smell like that to him. Maybe it just wasn't possible to recreate that specific scent synthetically. How could chemicals and factories possibly recreate such a pungent fragrance and all of the memories which went with it? Floral air fresheners never quite managed to capture the essence of summer's beauty and her fragrance nor did, Andrew supposed, water-scented candles conjure up that indescribable yet tangible smell of rain, that precious rain on a humid day, or the rain of his childhood when he would carelessly splash through puddles in his shiny wellington boots, which always had at least one hole in them however new they were.

Andrew reluctantly pulled his eyes away from the rain outside and away from his reminiscences of childhood and back to reality – whatever that was. He sighed deeply and his brow furrowed in concentration as he tried to wiggle the fingers on his right hand and then on his left. Both attempts were futile and Andrew felt frustrated: an emotion that wasn't new to him. He was worried about Margaret. The rain was getting heavier outside; the strength and speed of the rain were so much that Andrew was surprised there weren't holes in the pavement. Yet Margaret wasn't home. He didn't know where she was, although he never did. She always claimed to have told him – he just didn't listen – so he waited and when she returned simply smiled and nodded and pretended that he knew where she had been and why; pretended he had listened when she had gone off on yet another tangent. Andrew chuckled briefly, his large, boulder-like shoulders rising and falling. Then the smile faded. The weather was growing worse outside and he was worried about Margaret. He knew that she could take care of herself and that she always scolded him for worrying. Although, she never quite managed to fully conceal the smile, because his anxiety meant that he cared, which he did; he just wasn't very good at showing it, but she was more delicate than she liked to admit and he was worried that she would catch a cold. If only he could go out to find her and bring her home, or just be with her. Ironically enough, whenever Andrew was anxious or nervous, he would feel a deep pang for Margaret; he knew that she would know what to do and even if she didn't it would still make it all better somehow.

Andrew inwardly scolded himself; what was he doing, sat here becoming all emotional? He inhaled deeply but then angrily blew the air back out of his mouth in a short, sharp blast. He could feel his nerves tickling his stomach and panic pacing up and down his mind, just as he wanted to do in this room. He always paced when he was trying to concentrate or when he was frustrated, angry, nervous or simply impatient. Margaret was always dismayed at him and warned him that he was going to wear the carpet thin. He never did, though, probably because of all the Turkish rugs covering the floor, or whatever they were called, that Margaret was so fond of. Andrew looked around the room and remembered with a grin on his face how Margaret had tried to get him involved in decorating the house when they had first moved in, before Aziza and Caley were even born. In the end she had given up and made all of the decisions on her own; when Andrew tried to give his opinion she simply sighed and disagreed anyway and Andrew had simply 'ooh'ed and 'aah'ed in what he hoped were the right places.

Andrew surveyed the living room with its deep red Turkish rug (or maybe it was somewhere else near Turkey? Iraq perhaps?) covered in intricate swirls and patterns, its burgundy sofa, the colour of Margaret's favourite wine (which Andrew always kept stocked in crates in the cellar, unbeknownst to Margaret), and the threadbare armchair which Andrew loved so much (and the fact that Margaret allowed him to keep it – and on show – showed just how deep her love for him was). Andrew chuckled once more, but then fell silent as he noticed a pair of trainers carelessly thrown on the floor in front of their bronze fireplace. Andrew automatically began to stand up and tidy away the trainers before Margaret returned and moaned at him, and it was only when he realised that nothing had happened and he was still sat in his favourite armchair that he remembered that he couldn't move. Andrew furrowed his brow so much that his eyes all but vanished, yet still nothing happened. Resolved to staying in his chair, Andrew studied the trainers and began to wonder why they were there in the first place. Margaret's compulsive tidiness meant that although Andrew's office at work and study at home (which Margaret never went in: not because Andrew didn't allow her, because Margaret would simply ignore him, but because she respected his privacy; it was an unspoken agreement and Andrew never went into Margaret's study either) were an absolute disgrace to all things neat and tidy, he automatically took off his shoes before stepping into the house, hung up his jacket instead of tossing it carelessly over the banister and had adopted various other habits around the house to save Margaret's nagging. So why *were* his battered running shoes sat in their living room?

He only ever wore those shoes for his morning run, but then he always took them off in the hallway and put them away. He would then go upstairs, get showered and get dressed for work. Andrew looked down at his clothes. He was wearing his running clothes which, if he concentrated, he could remember getting changed into that morning when he awoke. His memory, however, was fuzzy, which baffled him as his memory was usually so reliable and precise; this was one of the reasons that he was so good at his job. He continued to concentrate on searching his memory, but it was too blurry and lots of different memories and images – some of which he was sure were fabricated – moulded into one another. It was impossible, like trying to catch smoke. Andrew couldn't understand why he was still dressed in his running clothes.

Suddenly, a thought jumped into his mind, like a light bulb flicking on in the cartoons that he grew up watching, when a character had a brainwave. If he was wearing his running clothes, but his running shoes were on the living room floor a few metres away from him, then what was he wearing on his feet? Andrew looked down and scowled. On his feet were a pair of hideous, brown leather shoes that no doubt were designer, not to mention ridiculously expensive, and no doubt Aziza would coo over them like a new-born baby or a puppy, or something else equally ridiculous, which turned perfectly intelligent women such as his daughter into simpering idiots.

Andrew had no idea where the shoes had come from or why he was wearing them. He wished he wasn't wearing them, but because he seemed to be somewhat frozen it was impossible for him to remove them and consequently, he was stuck with them. The brown leather shoes were one of a few things that Andrew couldn't fathom; along with his running clothes, which he shouldn't still be wearing, and his running shoes, which were

4

misplaced, why was Margaret missing? Why was his memory distorted? Why couldn't he move? And why was there an extremely annoying, high-pitched beeping noise continually repeating in the background somewhere. The latter was annoying Andrew greatly, especially since he couldn't find the source of it. It wasn't a doorbell because they didn't have one (they had an old-fashioned brass door knocker which Margaret had, naturally, chosen and which Andrew secretly loved), and it was distinctly different to a car or house alarm. The incessant beeping, however, whatever it was, was annoying Andrew almost as much as the fact that he couldn't move from his armchair, and almost as much as those hideous brown leather, designer shoes currently on his feet.

Whatever Andrew's feelings were towards the shoes, however, he couldn't shake the feeling that he had seen them somewhere before, and recently, and that they were important somehow.

1

A Deep Deep Sleep

Caley paced up and down the room, the flat base of her shoes clicking against the mint green tiled floor as she walked, up and down, up and down. The door behind her slammed shut and she span around on her heel, immediately tense, but when she saw her mother she relaxed.

'No news?' Caley asked, although the lack of hope in her voice made it sound less like a question and more like a statement.

'No news,' Margaret repeated, although the hope in her voice made it sound more like a question than a statement.

Caley continued to pace, until Margaret couldn't stand it anymore.

'Caley, sit down,' she snapped and then took a deep breath and added, 'Please, you are driving me crazy.'

Caley sighed deeply and walked over to where Margaret was sitting and stood next to her.

Margaret laughed exasperatedly. 'You are just like your father; he could never just sit and wait either. You are as impatient as each other.' She let out a half-laugh and then pressed her lips together and let out another; this one sounded more like a sob than a laugh.

Caley sat down in the cheap plastic chair next to Margaret

and laid her hand on Margaret's knee. Margaret pressed her lips together harder, so hard that when she stopped her lips were almost fully white, and looked upwards towards the off-white ceiling, blinking back tears determinedly.

Caley sighed again and leapt back to her feet. 'I'm sorry, I just can't sit still. Why don't I go and get us some coffee or something?' she suggested. 'It would walk off my frustration and besides, I'm starting to get thirsty'.

Margaret nodded. 'That is a good idea, thanks.'

Caley strode out of the room, the door slamming shut behind her, leaving Margaret alone in the empty waiting room with only the silence and her own thoughts for company. A single tear rolled down her cheek and she added in an undertone, 'Besides, we could be here for a while.'

Hearing footsteps in the corridor approaching the waiting room, Margaret hurriedly brushed the tears off her face and lowered her head so that she was staring at her lap where her hands were resting, fingers interlocked, displaying her dainty, silver engagement ring, with strands of diamond-studded silver interwoven around it, and her equally dainty wedding ring. She forced back the tears which threatened to fall once more and pinched the bridge of her nose with long, slender fingers while inhaling and exhaling deeply.

The door opened once more, but this time it was pushed open gently and when it closed, it did so with only the slightest of noise. The woman who walked through the door moved so elegantly and gracefully that she practically glided, despite the four-inch heels that she was wearing. Her shoes were a light blue: the same shade as her suit, which consisted of a knee-length pencil skirt with a slight split at the back, and a jacket with three-quarter length sleeves with a slight cuff folded back to reveal light-blue silk lining. Her blouse was also silk but cream to match the dainty (and genuine) pearl studs in her ears and pearl necklace resting on top of her blouse, which formed a bow at the base of her neck. Her glasses were as elegant as the rest of her outfit, with their bronze rectangular frames and arms with intricate designs weaving around one another in gold. The woman's handbag was also cream and leather and was in the hands of the man standing behind her.

'Aziza,' Margaret smiled. Yet somehow it was a sad smile and although she only said one word, she communicated many more. She pressed her lips together again, once more on the verge of tears.

Aziza returned the sad smile, tears rolling down her own face, and rushed towards her mother.

When Caley returned she found Aziza and Margaret embracing in the centre of the room. Ray stood awkwardly behind them, Aziza's handbag in one hand and an umbrella in the other. The latter was creating a large pool of water on the tiled floor. Even though the door slammed shut behind Caley, neither Aziza nor Margaret moved. Ray, on the other hand, turned to face Caley.

'Hi,' he smiled awkwardly, shifting his weight onto his right foot and then his left and back again.

'Hi. Thanks for coming,' Caley replied.

'I couldn't leave Aziza to come on her own,' Ray replied. 'I've taken the day off work.'

Caley nodded and for a while they stood in silence, until Aziza and Margaret walked over to them.

'Honestly, Ray,' Aziza sighed. 'You're going to flood the place in a minute,' she added exasperatedly and shook her head, but when she looked up at Ray (even in her heels she was only 5 foot 8 and Ray was 6 foot 7), there was a smile on her face. She took the umbrella from Ray, went over to the corner of the room where there was a cloakroom of sorts and placed the umbrella in a large box where another umbrella was already residing.

'If I'd known you were coming, I would have got you a coffee,' Caley said to Ray, holding out a takeaway cup wrapped in corrugated cardboard for Margaret and an identical cup for

Aziza. The third cup was on a chair near the door.

'I'm fine, but thanks anyway,' Ray replied.

'Is this tea or coffee?' Aziza asked, holding the cup up to Caley.

'Coffee,' Caley replied. 'A latte to be precise; they didn't have any herbal tea and I wasn't sure what you would want.'

Aziza smiled and began to take a sip, but then stopped. 'Is it–?' she began.

'Skimmed milk and decaffeinated. Yes,' Caley finished, smiling.

Aziza returned the smile. 'Thanks,' she replied, lifting the cup to her lips. 'You know me too well,' she winked.

Silence invaded the room and the two Arlings, one Peter and one Peter-to-be (but currently an Arling) silently moved over to the chairs and sat down.

'So what happened?' Aziza asked delicately, her voice wavering slightly. Ray noticed her hesitation and wrapped a long, muscular arm around her slender waist.

Caley put her own black coffee onto the floor beside her chair and began her report, for that was how she thought of it, how she forced herself to think of it so as to not get upset. Her voice was as empty of emotion as when she usually stood before her commanding officer to give her report, for she – like her father – had become a police officer, and it had been just the same earlier that day when she had given her statement to the police.

'As you know, Dad and I always go for a run together in the morning. We meet at the entrance to Domsville Park at six thirty and jog around the park together. This morning I was late–'

'Another quality you inherited from your father,' Margaret added in an undertone, a wry smile on her face. 'He was even late to our wedding.'

'And when I got to the park gates it was twenty to seven, but Dad wasn't there. I waited, figuring that he might be late, too. After all, it is Monday, but quarter to seven came and he still wasn't there and I began to grow worried. It was raining so I wondered if he had gone to wait somewhere drier, so I headed over to the bandstand, but he wasn't there either. I didn't know where else he could be because it's the only sheltered place in the park really, and I knew he wouldn't jog round without me. I checked my phone, but he hadn't called, so I decided to call him instead. I was just about to call when I heard a woman scream. The inspector inside me was on alert.' She smiled briefly, but then returned to her expressionless poker face which she had learnt, along with many of her other policing skills, from her father. 'So I went out to see what was happening but it was just some woman panicking because her child went too close to the edge of the water. I was about to head back to the bandstand to call Dad when I saw a pair of shoes sticking out of a bush by the boating lake. As I got closer I recognised them as Dad's running shoes, so I ran over to find Dad lying in a clearing in the trees by the boating lake, unconscious.'

Margaret was staring at something evidently fascinating on the bottom of her shoe, blinking rapidly and pressing her lips together firmly. Aziza, on the other hand, had abandoned all pretences and was crying freely, tears rolling down her face, and leaning into Ray, her dainty, manicured hand inside his large hand covered in scars and bruises, most from rugby, which he played professionally.

When the doctor, whose name no one seemed to remember, walked into the room a silence fell upon it abruptly. Caley froze mid-pace, one foot hovering slightly above the ground; Margaret leapt to her feet, immediately demanding respect, something which her very presence caused and which always amused Andrew because she only actually stood 3 inches above 5 foot; and Aziza shifted her body away from Ray so that she was sitting up in her seat, her back ruler-straight, but her hand firmly gripping Ray's. The doctor was used to this reaction, so she simply stood waiting, patiently, a small understanding smile evident on her face.

'I take this to mean that there is some news?' Margaret asked, all heads turning towards her as she spoke, struggling to keep the hope and fear out of her voice.

Despite her many years of telling friends and family bad news, sometimes even the very worst and seeing their reactions of sorrow, pain and sometimes even anger, it never got any easier.

'I'm afraid that your husband,' the doctor replied addressing Margaret, 'and your father,' she added, acknowledging Caley, Aziza and Ray, 'hasn't yet regained consciousness. His heartbeat is strong, however, and he will hopefully come round soon.'

Caley replaced the foot that had been hovering above the ground onto the tiled floor, which was painted in the same, slightly faded shade of mint green as the walls; it was supposed to be a soothing and pleasant colour. Margaret swayed slightly but remained standing, her head high as if she was determined not to get emotional.

'What does that mean exactly?' Margaret asked as the doctor reeled off several medical terms which, naturally, were completely beyond the comprehension of all present: an inspector on the police force, a professional rugby player and two business owners, one of a clothes shop and the other of an antique shop and jewellers.

'It means that Andrew is in a coma.'

The silence in the room was tangible, as was the pain.

'Then there is still hope, surely?' Caley asked. 'I've known lots of people to come out of comas,' she added, not mentioning, nor daring to think about, all of those whom she had known who didn't.

The doctor nodded reassuringly and sympathetically. 'Yes, there is definitely still hope. After all, like I said, his heartbeat is strong and his blood pressure is normal.' As an afterthought, she added with the trace of a smile playing around her lips, 'And he's a fighter.'

Margaret smiled exasperatedly. 'That he is, not to mention extremely stubborn.'

Caley, who had also inherited these traits, smirked to herself.

'Can we see him?' Aziza asked quietly, instantly recreating the tension which had been broken with the moment of humour.

The doctor nodded softly. 'Of course you can.'

As they followed the doctor through the door, down the corridor and to the door of Andrew's room, Caley secretly wondered whether she had nodded softly out of sympathy and sensitivity, or whether it was to prevent her deep crimson hair from tumbling out of the loose bun at the nape of her neck, secured only by a single, jewelled hairclip.

The doctor, whose name was actually Rose, pushed open the door and entered the room, stepping over to one side so that Margaret, Aziza, Caley and Ray could all fit into the room too.

When Margaret saw Andrew lying in the bed she gasped and her face became visibly paler: almost as white as her lips, which were firmly pressed together, despite herself. A heart monitor stood next to him, clearly registering his strong heartbeat, the heartbeat of a fighter, with a loud and incessant beeping and a single neon green line. His face was slightly bruised where he had hit the ground and slightly scratched for the same reason; the ground of the clearing was covered with twigs and leaves as autumn arrived, trailing her long coat of burgundy red and burnt orange behind her, scattering leaves in her wake, but other than that he looked surprisingly healthy and, well, normal. His eyes were shut, but his face looked rested so that he appeared to be sleeping, and his face didn't show the pale pallor of an ill man, but his usual golden brown, weathered from years spent outdoors.

'He just looks like he's sleeping,' Aziza whispered, clutching Ray's hand like a life ring.

'He is in a way. A coma is the body's natural defence, to rest him while he heals. It's just like a deep sleep,' Rose replied, tucking a stray strand of hair behind her ear, which had escaped from her bun.

'A deep, deep sleep,' Caley mused as she watched Andrew breathing in and out, oblivious to the pain of those around him or perhaps even their presence. 'Can he hear us?' she asked.

'It depends on the person, but quite often people in comas can hear what's going on around them, yes,' Rose answered. 'I've got other patients to see to so I'll go now and leave you in peace with him,' she added.

'Thank you, Doctor,' Margaret said, automatically taking charge.

Rose nodded in reply and headed towards the door. Just as the door was about to shut, she wedged the tip of her grey plimsolls between the door and the wall and added, 'If you need anything just give me a shout, and if there's any change' – she nodded her head at Andrew when she said this – 'someone should come automatically, but please do alert us using the button beside his bed.' She smiled around the room once more – the sad smile not quite reaching her eyes, which were older than her actual age and spoke of the tragedy and pain which she had seen – and removed her foot from the door which closed quietly behind her as she walked away. For a while, the only noise was the beeping of the heart monitor, until Margaret spoke, resuming her position of authority.

'There are only two chairs here. Why don't I go and get two more?' she suggested.

'No, it's fine, Mum; I'll go. Why don't you stay here with Dad?' Aziza replied.

'I can go if you want,' Ray volunteered.

Margaret shook her head. 'It's fine; I can manage.'

When Aziza opened her mouth to argue, Margaret shook her head softly. 'Please, you stay; it will give me something to do and I will feel like I'm helping.'

Aziza smiled sadly and nodded, as if she understood.

While Margaret left the room, Aziza walked over to one of

the two chairs beside Andrew's bed and collapsed into it, her piercing light-blue eyes, so much like her mother's, brimming with tears. Ray automatically headed over to her, but then hesitated.

'Would you like to sit down?' he asked Caley, gesturing to the remaining chair next to Aziza.

Caley shook her head. 'No, thank you. I'm fine standing. Besides,' she added as Ray cast a worrying glance at Aziza, who was now sitting with her elbow resting on the arm of the chair and her head resting in her hand, 'you should console her. I wouldn't know what to do,' she smiled.

While Ray comforted Aziza, Caley knelt down next to Andrew and wrapped her hand around his, immediately comforted by the familiar, coarse skin.

'I'm sorry,' Caley whispered. 'I'm so sorry I was late.' Yet, as Caley knelt next to her dad, all that she could think of was the irritating beeping noise emitting from the heart monitor beside her.

Hearing footsteps in the corridor, Caley wiped the tears from her face and was about to stand up when she noticed something written on Andrew's hand. She remained kneeling, but removed her hand from Andrew's and turned it over gently so that she had a better view of the palm. There, in the centre of his palm, was written the single word: 'Genesis.'

Caley could hear alarm bells ringing in her head over the sound of the heart monitor and slowly pushed herself to her feet.

'Aziza, do you have any wet wipes?' she asked.

Aziza blinked through her tears up at Caley, a puzzled expression on her face. 'Sure, one minute.' She rummaged through her handbag and produced a single wet wipe.

'Thanks,' Caley said, taking the wet wipe from Aziza and wondering why some women, such as her big sister, always carried everything but the kitchen sink around with them in their handbags. Caley then rummaged in the pockets of her battered, beloved, black, leather jacket (which William argued was really more of a coat as it reached her knees) and found her mobile phone, her debit card and some chewing gum. She then searched the pockets of her faded jeans, as she didn't have a handbag with her – she didn't actually think she owned a handbag at all – and discovered her house keys, car key, a ripped five pound note and her police identification badge. Shrugging in bewilderment at what else someone would possibly need with them, Caley knelt back down and took her phone out of her pocket. She then quietly took a picture of the word 'Genesis' on the palm of Andrew's hand, and then rubbed gently at his hand with the wet wipe until it had completely vanished. She then pocketed the wet wipe, turned his hand back over so that it faced downwards and got back to her feet just as Margaret walked back through the door. Margaret wasn't carrying any chairs, however, because she had gone for some air and discovered Caley's colleague Sergeant William Aaron smoking outside. He, instead, was carrying three spare chairs into the room, while Margaret walked next to him complaining about the fact that she wasn't carrying anything. William, naturally, ignored her and placed all three chairs, piled on top of one another, at the foot of Andrew's bed.

William surveyed the room and acknowledged both Aziza and Ray with a friendly nod of the head. When his eyes met Caley's, however, she widened her emerald green eyes and glanced at the door. William, taking the hint, walked over to Margaret and said, 'I'm just going for a cigarette.'

'What, again?' she asked, the look of repulsion evident on her face. Andrew had smoked once, until he had met her that was.

'It's just, well, seeing him like that,' William explained, gesturing to where Andrew lay.

Margaret smiled softly and nodded. 'I see.'

As William headed out of the door, Caley waited a moment and then approached her mother, laying a hand on her arm.

'I'm just going to go with him, check that he's okay. Besides, I could do with some air myself,' she admitted.

Margaret nodded once more and watched as Caley followed William out of the room and into the corridor.

'Come on, let's go for a coffee. They have a coffee shop here. The coffee's pretty disgusting, but it's better than at the station. We need to talk.'

William nodded impassively while Caley filled him in on what had happened to Andrew, but when she reached the part about Genesis his eyes widened. Noticing, Caley paused and looked at him questioningly but he motioned for her to continue. It wasn't until she was finished that he spoke.

'I suppose there was always the threat of something like this happening. Andrew may have been popular amongst his friends, family and colleagues, but throughout his career he has made lots of enemies. It's cliché, but it's true, especially in the criminal world. He has solved lots of cases and puts lots of people behind bars. Sooner or later, someone was bound to want revenge.'

Caley nodded, her eyes alone speaking of her pain and sadness, the rest of her face remaining expressionless. Even her eyes were difficult to read, but William had worked with her for many years and was one of the few people who could read them.

'People have threatened him before, attacked him even, but this . . .' Her voice trailed off.

William placed his hand over hers, 'I know.' He paused while she composed herself and then added, 'What do you want to do?'

'My job.'

2

The Search Begins

To say that Caley's office was small was an understatement; it was practically a cupboard. William had given up trying to ask why she didn't move into a larger office. As an inspector, she was entitled to one, but she seemed to like not being able to move in her office. She simply smiled and shrugged and said that she liked her office the way it was whenever William tried to ask.

Caley's office had a single, narrow window, about 3 inches wide, on the wall opposite the door, which opened outwards (otherwise it would fill up the entire office). Pushed up against the wall with the window was a scarred, leather chair on wheels which were never used, because to get the chair out of the office you would have to lift it over the desk that was wedging it against the wall. How Caley managed to get in and out of the chair was a mystery to William. The desk was very wide and filled the remainder of the office with the exception of a gap running the length of the office (which wasn't very far), which was about half a foot wide. Two filing cabinets were squeezed into this gap leaving a narrow escape route to the door. On the back of the door was a dartboard which is why William always knocked before entering. Caley often used it when she was frustrated, mainly because there wasn't room to pace in her office. Her desk was currently covered in information relating to Andrew's attack. All of her other work was stacked underneath in mountains reaching up to the underside of the desk.

William and Caley had arrived at the station about fifteen minutes ago and had spent about ten minutes making notes on the large whiteboard that they often used in cases. The whiteboard was on a stand, on wheels and was usually kept in the large, open-plan work space where Caley's colleagues in the Cold Cases department worked, including William. It also contained a long table, which was kept propped up against the wall the rest of time, so that the room could double as a meeting room. Caley's office was off this room. They had spent the other five minutes trying to get the whiteboard into Caley's office. The whiteboard was currently wedged between the two filing cabinets, which were opposite each other and consequently, the door was completely blocked. William had asked Caley how they would get out of the office when they were finished and was rather worried when Caley told him that they would cross that bridge when they came to it, which was one of Caley's favourite sayings as Caley never seemed prepared for anything and would instead simply 'wing it' (another one of her favourite sayings). If necessary, they could use the window.

'Right, I think that's everything,' Caley commented, stepping back from the board, which meant that she was perched on the edge of her desk.

'So what does this mean?' William asked, unsure of what Caley wanted out of this meeting, raking his hand though his thick, perfectly styled, chocolate brown hair as he spoke. However, unlike Caley, whose hair, after she had just raked her hand through it, appeared even more tousled (merely a euphemism for messy) than usual, William still looked as suave and as stylish as ever.

'It means that we start investigating, just like any other investigation that comes our way. Our notes are done.' She gestured towards the board. 'And so the search begins,' she finished, her fists clenched in a way that made William almost feel sorry for the person who attacked Andrew – almost.

'So, let's talk it through,' William replied, gauging Caley's reaction to see whether or not she was too upset to follow their usual procedure when solving a crime.

After a brief internal struggle Caley nodded and William began.

'So we can presume that Andrew went to the park to meet with you as usual and that either before he got there or after he got there, he met up with someone and went off with them.'

'Right, because Andrew was strong and in good shape and because of where he was found, it's unlikely that he was taken by force, which implies that he met someone he didn't think of as a threat,' Caley agreed.

'Unless he got a phone call from someone asking him to meet up,' William suggested. 'Was his phone on him when he was found?'

'No, which is highly unusual because he rarely went anywhere without his phone. We should probably check, though, just in case.'

'I agree,' William nodded, taking a whiteboard pen off Caley's desk and making a note to check Andrew's house for his mobile phone.

'Of course, there's always the option that whoever Andrew went off with knew him,' William suggested.

Caley visibly winced and William nodded. 'I know, it's something we hope isn't true but it is a possibility.'

Caley nodded in somewhat reluctant agreement.

'Of course, it could be someone who was a threat. Andrew *has* been known to take risks before,' William reminded Caley.

'I know, but he isn't stupid. He wouldn't have gone off with someone he was afraid of or that he thought that he couldn't handle. I think it's more likely, because he didn't alert anyone else of his whereabouts, that he met up with someone that he wasn't afraid of.'

'I have to say that I'm inclined to agree,' William replied. 'Do you know if the police have searched the house?'

'Yes they have. They haven't found anything yet, though. I have a contact in the department dealing with Da . . . Andrew's attack,' Caley said, forcing herself to refer to her dad as Andrew to make it less personal.

'I have a friend in Forensics. Do you want me to give him a call and ask him to keep us informed?' William asked.

'Yeah, that's probably a good idea,' Caley nodded. 'But make sure that this stays as quiet as possible, us "interfering",' she said, using her fingers to make sarcastic quotation marks, 'may not be appreciated. After all, this isn't our case and . . .' she added in a quieter voice, 'it's personal.'

William dug his phone out of the pocket of his jeans and was about to step outside when he saw the whiteboard barring the door. 'I'll just make the call in here,' he decided.

While William was on the phone, Caley made a few finishing touches to the board and then began to study it. She waited until William had hung up before she spoke.

'Any problems?'

'No, he said that he will be happy to keep us informed and understands why we're investigating and more importantly, why we want to keep our investigation quiet,' William replied and then added, 'Everyone is more than happy to help; Andrew was well-liked by everyone who knew him.'

Caley studied the board and murmured, 'Evidently not by everybody.'

William tossed his phone onto Caley's desk and stood beside her, his thumbs in the front pockets of his suit trousers, surveying the board. 'Any more thoughts?' he asked.

'I was wondering how he, or she, managed to carry whatever they used to hit Andrew in and out of the park without being noticed.'

William thought for a moment. 'It would help if we could track down people who were in the park too that morning.'

Caley nodded and added it to their to-do list down one side of the whiteboard.

'It will help, of course, when we get a medical analysis of Da ... Andrew and we have a better idea of what was used to hit him, but it had to have been heavy to take him down with one blow.'

'Or well-aimed,' William added.

Caley looked at him, her eyes narrowed. 'Are you suggesting that this was a professional hit?'

William shrugged and leant back against the edge of the desk, which Caley was also resting against. 'I don't know but for one hit to do this much damage . . .' He trailed off, unsure of what else to add.

'It had to be someone who knew what they were doing,' Caley finished.

'It helps to point towards the theory that Andrew trusted his attacker enough to turn his back on them or at least enough not to be on guard,' William pointed out.

Caley's computer suddenly beeped loudly, interrupting their train of thought. Caley cocked her head towards the source of the noise and froze momentarily, her brow creased in bewilderment, and then she suddenly leapt up excitedly.

One of the great questions of life, according to William, was answered when Caley reached her office chair, currently wedged between her desk and the wall, by placing her hands on her desk and swinging her legs over her head and over the desk. She did this efficiently and effectively, landing gracefully on the other side, as though she had done this many times before. Ignoring William's amused expression, actually ignoring William altogether, Caley all but jumped into her chair and fixed her eyes on the computer screen.

After a few minutes, William coughed subtly and when he was completely ignored, coughed more loudly. Eventually, he banged his fist on the desk and Caley looked at him questioningly.

'Hi, I'm William,' he smiled sarcastically, holding his hand out to shake hers.

Caley smiled exasperatedly. 'I've found out what Genesis is. Although I'm not sure how it fits in or if it helps at all actually,' she told him, her brow furrowing as she reached the end of her sentence. 'Come and have a look,' she added, gesturing to the computer screen. 'I ran a search in our database on Genesis hoping that it was the name of a case, which it was. That's what the beeping was; the search was finished.'

'Good idea. I'd completely forgotten about Genesis,' William replied and leant forward on the desk earnestly. 'Well?'

'You'll never be able to see from there and it's easier to explain if you just have a look,' Caley replied, gesturing to the computer once more.

William was about to enquire as to how he would get around the desk, not being as accustomed as Caley to simply jumping over the desk, when Caley interrupted him.

'Before you come, could you just do me a favour and add "check Andrew's study" to our to-do list? If this has any relevance to his attack then maybe it was something he was investigating, in which case his notes will be at home in his study, because it's non-work related. Although, I suppose it wouldn't hurt to search his office at work too.'

William nodded and added to the list using a whiteboard pen that he had hunted for and eventually found sticking out of his trouser pocket. When he returned to the desk he looked at Caley enquiringly. 'How exactly am I supposed to get onto the other side of this desk?' he asked.

Caley looked at him for a moment as if he was incredibly stupid and then her expression suddenly changed as if she had just understood his dilemma and she said, 'Oh sorry. I'm so used to it. It's just habit to jump over automatically.'

William shook his head at her, amused, while she looked around the office as if searching for a secret passageway to the other side of her desk. Finding none, she simply shrugged and informed him that he would have to simply jump over. 'You can't get underneath because it's completely blocked with paperwork, so it'll have to be over.'

William sighed and sat on the desk, swinging his legs around and then sliding down the other side. It was nowhere near as impressive as Caley's route over the desk, but at least it didn't result in him making himself look like a total prat by knocking himself out with his own feet; William highly doubted that he could vault over the desk as Caley had without doing something of the sort.

'Okay, so I thought that the fact that Andrew had "Genesis" written on his hand probably wasn't a coincidence and I wondered if it was the name of a case,' Caley recapped.

William, who was standing snuggly beside Caley, as there was only one chair behind the desk and limited room, nodded. 'You thought that he might have been investigating another case "unofficially".' William used his hands to make quotation marks. 'And *that* case was the one which resulted in him being attacked and we can presume, left for dead.'

Caley nodded. 'Exactly. After all, he wasn't really working on anything at the minute. Because of how high he is in the police force he doesn't really investigate specific cases anymore. Although I do know that he is a lot more involved than he is supposed to be; he loves his job and he just can't help himself from becoming involved.' The edges of Caley's mouth curved upwards as she spoke.

'So what have you found?' William asked. 'What *is* Genesis?'

'I can't believe how many people have been already,' Aziza exclaimed as yet another person left the hospital room, the card which they brought now added to the artistic display of cards on Andrew's bedside table, courtesy of Margaret and Aziza. 'I mean, look at all these cards,' she continued, gesturing towards the bedside table where a wide range of 'get well soon' cards stood. 'And all these flowers, too,' she added, gesturing to the window-ledge table in the corner of the room and the table at the foot of Andrew's bed, both of which were covered in flowers.

Margaret smiled. 'They really brighten up the room.' Her smile disappeared, however, as she added in a quiet voice that was practically a whisper, 'I just wish that he was awake to enjoy them.'

Aziza smiled sadly and wandered over to where Ray was sitting, a giant teddy bear at his feet, which had been brought by Andrew's tearful secretary who had been with Andrew for many years and had risen with him up the ranks. She had recently given birth to a baby boy and admitted that she had seen the bear and loved it so much that she had bought it for her son, despite the fact that he was not old enough to enjoy it. When she heard about Andrew she had rushed out and bought another, identical bear for him.

Aziza sat down lightly on Ray's knees and watched as Margaret wandered around the room aimlessly, fighting back tears as she fussed over the arrangements of various bouquets of flowers. She paused at a large bunch of lilies and admitted defeat as tears fell helplessly down her face. 'We had lilies at our wedding,' she whispered to no one in particular. She then turned to face Aziza and Ray and continued in the same quiet voice, such a contrast to her usual loud and (truth be told) bossy voice. 'I had told Andrew to leave everything to me which he did, gladly, and I told him that all he had to do was turn up on time, which he didn't manage of course,' Margaret laughed. 'He was about half an hour late. I had chosen lilies because they were my favourite flower and I always think that they're so elegant, and when we were on our honeymoon he gave me a single lily that was from my bouquet. It had been treated with some chemicals of some sort so that it would never die.' Margaret's voice trailed off as she fingered the lilies thoughtfully, her vision completely obscured by tears so that she could only make out blurs of colours and shapes.

Aziza got gently to her feet, walked over to Margaret and

wrapped her arms around her. 'I never knew that,' she said softly. 'Do you still have it?'

Margaret nodded. 'He can be so romantic and thoughtful sometimes, but then other times he is about as subtle as a sledgehammer,' she laughed. Her laughter, however, soon turned to tears and as she stood embracing Aziza, she caught sight of Andrew lying in the starched hospital bed and sobs racked her whole body. She buried her head into Aziza's shoulder and Aziza began to cry. Ray began to stand up and go over to them, but then he decided against it and sat down again. Unsure of what to do, he had awkwardly got to his feet and indecisively returned to his seat five times before Aziza, despairing, beckoned him over to them. Ray stood behind Aziza, his thick, muscular arms wrapped around her tiny waist, taking the weight of both Aziza and Margaret as they cried into one another.

Several minutes passed before Margaret pushed herself gently away from Aziza and Ray, and dabbed at her eyes with a cream, lace handkerchief, visibly embarrassed by her outburst of tears.

'Thank you,' she smiled at Aziza, who had remained in Ray's arms and clasped her hand, their rings clinking against one another. She sighed deeply and tucking the handkerchief back away into the pocket of her ankle-length cream skirt, she strode over to Andrew and brushed his hair out of his eyes, hair which had been dark brown when they first met, but which over the years had turned steel grey. However, it had never thinned, so he still had a thick head of hair. Margaret's hair, on the other hand, was still very light-blonde in colour without a single grey hair in sight. As she raked a hand through his hair she shook her head softly and sighed in amused exasperation. 'I must have been nagging you for weeks to get your hair cut,' she whispered to Andrew, the half-smile on her face showing amused annoyance.

Andrew, whose eyes had been closed as he attempted to block out Margaret and Aziza's heart-breaking sobs, snapped them open abruptly to reveal piercing green eyes, under whose gaze many a suspect had crumbled and confessed, which showed amusement (just as Margaret's did). 'More like months,' he corrected her under his breath.

He listened as Margaret walked away and she began talking to Aziza and Ray in hushed tones. He wanted to scream; he could hear them, he knew they were right there, but he couldn't move or speak or even open his eyes. Instead he was stuck in what must be a dream, he mused as he surveyed his familiar living room, and he couldn't even let them know that he could hear them and that he was fine. Frustrated, he heaved a deep sigh and attempted, for what must have been the hundredth time that day, to wiggle his fingers but he failed and gave up with a furious sigh. His annoyance turned to anguish as he listened to Margaret's voice, dominating the conversation as usual, and then to anger as he spotted those *shoes* – he practically spat the last word – out of the corner of his eye and, for what must have been the thousandth time today, he wondered why he was wearing a pair of brown leather shoes.

3

Genesis

Caley was sitting in her chair, leaning back with her feet resting on top of a stack of papers with the tips of her boots touching the underside of her desk. She was watching William with her elbows on the desk and her fingers interlocked and therefore, creating a shelf for her chin to rest on.

'So, you mean to tell me that the word Andrew had written on his hand relates to–'

'Could relate to,' Caley interrupted.

William nodded. 'Could relate to,' he corrected. 'Although you've got to admit that it's a bit of a coincidence if it doesn't; I mean, what else could it mean?'

Caley shrugged. 'He could just be reminding himself to read the Bible or learn Hebrew,' she suggested, the ghost of a smile evident on her lips. 'All I'm saying is not to rule out any options; it probably does mean this, but we don't know for sure.'

William shook his head exasperatedly and smiled. 'Fair enough. I did remember Andrew telling me once that he fancied learning a new language.' He laughed as he tried to dodge a well-aimed kick from Caley but failed due to the fact that there was nowhere to dodge to. He held up his arms in mock surrender and Caley, laughing, gestured for him to continue.

'The case "Genesis"' – Again, William made quotation marks

27

around the word 'Genesis' while Caley rolled her eyes in response – 'consists of a twenty-seven-year-old man called Dominic Smith found stabbed to death in a back alley near his house at six in the morning. He lived in a terraced house with his two brothers and their mother on a – would it be politically correct to say *rough*? – council estate where practically his whole family lived in Markston. He was found about ten minutes away from his house and it was concluded, by the investigating officer, Chief Inspector Dave Baxter, that he was killed by a member of a "rival" family' – again with the use of quotation marks – 'who also lived about ten minutes away from where Dominic was found, called Daniel Jones. The knife used to kill Dominic was found in Daniel's room when the police searched it.'

'Exactly,' Caley agreed. 'That wasn't the end of it, though.'

William nodded. 'Give me chance,' he complained, his tone and expression making it clear that he was joking. 'Daniel was a suspect from the start being from the "rival" family' – this time Caley was expecting the quotation marks and refrained from rolling her eyes – 'and being around the same age as Dominic. When Baxter went round to arrest him, however, after finding the knife, Daniel was gone!' William raised his hand to his head in a mock dramatic pose but, after a painful kick to the shin, lowered his hand somewhat hastily and continued speaking. 'The next day Baxter's body was found in our very own Domsville Park. Chief Superintendent Richard Taggart took over the case and traced Daniel to a bedsit he was renting under a fairly unimaginative alias. When the police arrived they found Daniel's body hanging from the ceiling. Taggart concluded, fairly, that Daniel had killed Baxter and then committed suicide possibly out of guilt, but probably because he could see no other way out.'

'Precisely and when questioned, the two families confessed to a feud that had been going on for several years with injuries sustained on both sides and rather like any feud of this kind which had lasted for several years, no one could really remember the cause of their disagreement. Dominic and Daniel obviously

28

took matters into their own hands and were both described as being rather hot-headed,' Caley concluded.

Silence filled the room as they both pondered what had been said until William broke the silence in a rather tentative voice. 'There's something that we're forgetting.'

Caley nodded silently and then waited a moment before speaking as though weighing up her words beforehand. 'Our involvement – mine and Dad's.'

'You two were out for your customary morning run when you found Baxter's body.'

'It seems too much of a coincidence doesn't it,' Caley agreed.

'So, what happened?' William asked. 'I mean, I have the official version here.' He gestured to Caley's battered computer – quite literally, as it bore the imprints of Caley's fist and boot in several places. 'But there's no point pretending that the official version is the accurate version.'

Caley smiled, took a deep breath and began. 'Dad and I met at the park gates as usual at half past six. It was just like any other day when we go for our run together and we were jogging round the park, chatting about the usual trivial topics, such as work and Mum's birthday, when we approached the centre of the park where the fountain is. That was when we saw Baxter's body. We ran over and Dad automatically recognised him. You could tell by his face, but we both went into autopilot. He had been badly beaten and I checked for a pulse while Dad called for an ambulance . . . but he was already dead.' Caley shook her head softly. 'There was nothing we could do.' She looked towards William and waited a few minutes before speaking again. 'Penny for them?'

William looked at her questioningly, his head tilted slightly to one side.

'Your thoughts, a penny for your thoughts,' she elaborated. 'It's quite a common saying. I know you've thought of something; I can practically hear the cogs turning.'

William grinned. 'Squeaking more like from ill-use. I was

just wondering,' he added after a moment's hesitation, 'why Andrew had "Genesis" written on his hand. How close were he and Baxter?'

Caley pursed her lips in concentration. 'Dad always said how they've known each other forever.' Caley smiled reminiscently, exaggerating the word 'forever'. 'But I think they met at work.' She paused while she tried to remember. 'Dad was a sergeant when Baxter first joined as a constable I think, and they were in the same department–'

'Homicide?' William interrupted.

'Yes, Dad loved it so he just stayed there, even after he got promoted. They worked together on a case and just got on really well.'

'Did they just stay friends?' William asked.

'Pretty much,' Caley confirmed. 'When Baxter was murdered last year he was chief inspector and Dad was superintendent still, like he is now. Dad just stayed one rank ahead of him throughout their careers.'

There was another pause and William's train of thought began to become apparent to Caley.

'Are you asking because you think that Dad was going over what happened – that was why he had "Genesis" written on his hand?'

'It was just an idea. I'm not sure yet,' William replied. 'I'm still thinking things through.'

Caley nodded. 'What we could do with is getting into Da ... Andrew's office and having a look through his files and notes to see what he was working on.'

'I agree. That should be interesting,' William smiled humourlessly.

Caley returned the reluctant smile. 'What time is it?' she asked, glancing at her wrist only to realise that she had left her watch at home in her haste to change out of her running clothes that morning, after Andrew had been admitted to hospital.

William lightly pulled up his shirt sleeve to uncover his watch. 'Three o'clock.'

Caley nodded and sighed, 'Do you want to grab a bite to eat?'

'I thought you'd never ask.'

Caley smiled fondly as William gingerly swung his legs over to the other side of her desk and then moved to one side as she vaulted gracefully over it. Between them, and with great difficulty, they then managed to manoeuvre themselves around the whiteboard and out of the door, with Caley locking it behind them.

'I'm sick of all of the sympathetic looks,' Caley growled as a young woman walked past them and smiled patronisingly at her while informing her, in a sickly sweet voice, how sorry she was for what had happened.

William laughed and climbed into the front seat, literally, as Caley's battered 4x4 was about 2 feet off the ground. 'They're just trying to be supportive and friendly.'

'I don't even know who half of them are,' Caley muttered as she fastened her seatbelt and started the engine. The car spluttered to life and Caley shot out of the underground garage like a bullet out of a gun. William, who was used to Caley's driving, congratulated himself on concealing his wince as she narrowly missed being flattened by a double-decker bus.

'You really need to get a new car,' William commented as the engine complained when Caley went into fifth gear.

Caley barked out a laugh as she weaved in and out of a line of traffic.

'You do realise you're not a motorbike, right?' William asked sarcastically, his knuckles white as he clutched the sides of his seat.

Caley laughed once more, but this time joined the queue of traffic. 'Relax, it's fine!'

William shook his head in exasperation, but loosened his vice-like grip on the seat.

'Do you want to give Aziza a call and ask if they want us to get any food for them?' Caley asked, reaching into her jacket pocket to retrieve her mobile phone.

'Sure,' William replied, taking the phone out of her hand.

Fifteen minutes later, William and Caley were back in the car with various bags filled with Chinese takeaway and pizzas on the backseat, sliding precariously as Caley raced through the town centre.

'Tomorrow, do you want to meet me at Mum and Dad's house and we can have a quick search through Dad's office? That way, we can find out if he was working on anything interesting and see if his mobile phone's home too.'

William nodded and hastily swallowed his coffee. 'That's hot,' he complained.

Caley rolled her eyes. 'Is seven o'clock okay?'

'Sure, I'm used to being overworked; my boss is such a slave driver.'

'You'll be wearing that coffee in a minute,' Caley threatened. 'Is eight o'clock better?'

'Much better thanks,' William grinned.

'After that are we going to see about searching Andrew's office at work, get it all over at once and then we can go back to your cupboard, sorry, office,' William sarcastically corrected, 'and review what we've found.'

Caley nodded slowly. 'I'll sort it tonight. Now that we've found out what Genesis is, we need to find out how it relates to Dad and the best way to do that is to see what he worked on last.'

As Caley swung into a space at the hospital, William asked, 'I'm guessing that we're keeping this investigation under wraps for now?'

Caley nodded. 'And Genesis under even thicker wraps.'

William looked questioningly at Caley. 'I thought it was written on his hand?'

'It *was*,' replied Caley simply.

4

Memories

Hearing voices wasn't a good sign. Andrew sighed deeply and tried to rearrange his position so that he was more comfortable. He had been sitting in the armchair for far too long and there was nothing he could do about it; he still couldn't even move so much as his little finger. He let out another frustrated sigh as he tried to determine the source of the voices he could hear. It sounded like there was a radio somewhere nearby, but it wasn't quite in tune so the voices sounded distant and slightly crackly. If he concentrated, Andrew could make out occasional words and maybe even the odd phrase, and he was sure that he recognised the voices: it sounded like two women talking, but he couldn't work out who the voices belonged to, where they were coming from – because Andrew couldn't see a radio anywhere or anything else which would explain the voices that he was sure he could hear – or even what they were actually talking about. The infrequent words and phrases which he picked up didn't seem to make sense when Andrew tried to connect them. He strained his ears, his eyes immersed in his eyebrows as he furrowed his brow so much that his forehead seemed to double in length, and managed to make out the word 'rugby' followed by 'looks asleep', and then what sounded like 'Hawaiian pizza'. Andrew relaxed his body and shook his head;

it was no use. Suddenly a door slammed shut, Andrew jolted in the chair and made to get up before he remembered that he couldn't. He waited, his eyes darting around the room, not daring to make a sound, and listened. Then he sighed, partially in relief and partially in frustration. The former was because it wasn't their front door – or any door in their house for that matter – and the latter because it was coming from the same place as the voices, which was probably his own imagination. Andrew laid his head onto the back of the armchair and closed his eyes. Part of him had hoped that the door was their front door and that Margaret was home.

What was happening to him? It felt like he was in a dream, because so many things didn't make sense, such as the fact that he couldn't move out of his armchair, the voices that he could hear in his head and those stupid brown leather shoes, Andrew added as an afterthought, as he opened his eyes to frown down on the monstrosities that were currently surrounding his feet. He was sure, however, that it wasn't a dream because he couldn't wake up. He shut his eyes tightly and forced them open abruptly once more, trying to wake himself up. After several attempts he gave up. Instead, he sat in silence, the voices murmuring in the background accompanied by an irritating, incessant, high-pitched beeping noise which seemed to be originating from the same place as the voices, but which he had been able to hear ever since he had found himself in his armchair and in this predicament. The voices had started later and worried Andrew even more than the beeping noise; maybe he was losing his mind; maybe he would start seeing people next. He shuddered involuntarily and with no other choice presenting itself, sat still for a few moments, ignoring the voices and the beeping, ignoring everything (including the brown leather shoes) and simply sat staring at the wall opposite him. He felt tired and for the first time in his life, he felt old. He had always said that you were only as old as you felt which, Margaret had informed him, made him about twenty-three years old. However, at the moment, he felt every one of his fifty three years, if not more. Andrew closed his eyes and inhaled and exhaled slowly. The beeping slowed down and seemed to grow less frequent and less irritating. Its previous shrill pitch had been replaced by a rather soothing sound, with each beep sounding further away from the next beep as the previous one had. Andrew relaxed his whole body and let all of his tension and worries slip away.

It was only as Andrew relaxed and sat in the silence that he began to hear the voices more clearly. He definitely heard the words, 'His heartbeat has slowed right down,' and then a door slam again as someone shouted, 'Get a doctor.' Andrew smiled and the voices began to fade away; he was tired and he just wanted to sleep. The more he relaxed the more the voices and the beeping subsided into a soft lull. It was then that he heard Margaret's voice shout his name. She sounded upset. The voices grew slightly louder and slightly stronger and Margaret repeated his name. 'Andrew! Don't you dare leave me!' she said. He could hear the emotion in her voice and wanted to be with her. She said that she didn't want him to leave her, but he wasn't leaving her. He didn't want to leave her. It was then that he realised that the more he relaxed, the quieter Margaret's voice grew. He *was* leaving her. Andrew shook his head. He wasn't going to give up, he wasn't going to leave her, but he began to struggle to keep awake. His eyes didn't want to open but he could hear Margaret's voice pleading with him to stay with her and he was determined not to leave her. He wouldn't give up, he was a fighter, and he refused to go to sleep, he refused to leave Margaret. Slowly, he managed to force his eyes open and as he sat in his armchair with the voices and the beeping as loud and incessant as ever, he realised that tears were rolling down his cheeks. He didn't know what was going on, but he was definitely going to find out and he vowed to find a way to wake up properly and be at Margaret's side where he belonged. He blinked back tears, slightly embarrassed at his show of emotion, which he had always considered to be a sign of weakness, and struggled to recall when he first found himself in this predicament. How long had he been here? Perhaps he had been here for a day, maybe two? He wasn't sure, and he looked out of the window to see if the time of day was evident, but the sky was a thundery grey and the rain was relentless. It could have been day or night; the weather outside gave him no clue.

Where to start? The answer, of course, was clear: at the beginning. So what was the last thing that he remembered before . . . ? Well, Andrew wasn't really sure what it was before, but it was before something and it was that something that left him in this . . . Predicament was probably the best word to describe his current situation. Andrew wasn't really sure what was happening or why. He sighed deeply. This was going to be more difficult than he thought.

He closed his eyes as he racked his memory. What was the last thing that he remembered? He remembered getting up in the morning; he was always a naturally early riser, and leaving the house. Where had he gone? Andrew's eyes suddenly opened and he looked down at his clothes. He was in his running clothes and if he remembered correctly he had been yesterday morning, or was it the day before? He didn't think it was that morning; it seemed further away than that, but then again all of his memories seemed further away at the minute. His memories all seemed to be distorted and blurred, and what worried him was that he was sure he had been in this dilemma before, when he first found himself in his armchair. Andrew furrowed his brow, an unconscious display of frustration or concentration, and struggled to recall his memories, even from (what he thought was) yesterday. He remembered that yesterday (if it truly was yesterday) he found himself in his armchair and he was puzzled over his attire: his running clothes. He figured out why he was wearing these clothes then, so why couldn't he now?

He was itching to pace up and down the room. He hated staying still at the best of times. Margaret was always nagging at him to stop fidgeting, but he found it especially difficult when he was annoyed or trying to figure something out. He glanced around the room and saw a watercolour painting on the wall. It was a beautiful painting and Andrew was sure that he recognised what the painting was of. He gritted his teeth and hissed out a frustrated burst of air. That was when he remembered. The painting was of a beautiful set of ornate iron gates. They were the gates for a park; Domsville Park, Andrew was sure it was called, which was his local park . . . where he goes running. He goes for a morning run, which was where he went yesterday morning and why he was wearing his running clothes.

He smiled contentedly; he may have only solved one tiny piece of an immense puzzle, but it was a start. His smile turned into a frown, however, when he realised that this explanation didn't account for the brown leather shoes. He surveyed the rest of the room, which was so familiar to him because it appeared to be his living room, but it seemed strange to him because so many parts of it were different. The picture, for example, of the gates of Domsville Park (it was definitely Domsville, because that was where Margaret and he lived; Andrew remembered because they had moved here because they appreciated the irony of the name: 'Dom' is Latin for home) seemed familiar to him but he wasn't sure where it was from, for Andrew was sure that it didn't belong in his living room.

He continued to scan the room until his eyes hit upon a photograph on a small table nearby. The photo was of four people: he was in it and, he realised with some excitement, so was Margaret. He grinned broadly at the sight of Margaret and felt a pang in his heart. The distant beeping quickened slightly and then slowed down again after a short while. Andrew studied the photo; Margaret and he were there, but he wasn't sure who the other two people were. They were two young

38

women; the first must have been almost 6-foot tall, with piercing green eyes, dark-brown hair worn in a no-nonsense bob, which was actually quite flattering on her, and was wearing faded jeans, a simple white V-neck T-shirt, scarred leather boots and an equally scarred leather jacket, which reached down to her knees. Andrew chuckled at how similar her appearance was to his own: from her muscular and tanned body, sparkling emerald green eyes, which looked like they never missed a detail, and height, to her apathetic view to fashion, evident from her simple and practical outfit, which looked like it had been thrown on, which it probably had. The eyes were identical to his own; his figure was also broad but toned with muscular arms and legs and tanned skin, which was now slightly lined, but it seemed to show his authority rather than his age. He too, haphazardly, threw on his clothes, much to Margaret's dismay. There was no doubt that this was Caley, just as there was no doubt that the other woman, who looked as much like Margaret, with her blonde wavy hair, which reached down to her shoulder blades, slim and slender build, pale skin, dazzling light-blue eyes, carefully matched outfit – even down to the peach nail varnish on her fingertips – was Aziza: Margaret's and his eldest daughter.

Andrew laughed and his round, boulder-like shoulders, rose and fell as he did: a deep, resounding chuckle.

'Did you see that?' Margaret asked, standing up slightly in her seat and she gazed at Andrew in amazement.

Aziza laughed, a soft laugh that sounded like pealing bells, and nodded her head. 'I certainly did, obviously something is amusing!'

Margaret joined her laughter. 'Obviously. He always did have a distinctive laugh.'

'Chuckle,' Aziza corrected.

'Chuckle,' Margaret agreed. 'I wonder what's so funny?'

Maybe it was just seeing the photo of his family, but Andrew was sure that he could hear their voices again. His eyes returned to the photo of Margaret, Aziza, Caley and him, when a photo beside it caught his eye. The latter photo looked like it had been taken at some sort of formal event, maybe even a wedding. Andrew was in the photo and was wearing a tuxedo with a flower in his lapel, and was standing next to another man wearing a similar tuxedo with the same type of flower, but in a slightly bolder colour scheme. Andrew wasn't sure *what* type of flower it was, though; he wasn't very good with things like that. Margaret, on the other hand, not only knew all about flowers and what they were called, what they looked like, where they grew, what they 'went' with, but also their Latin names, which Andrew thought was a bit excessive. Andrew recognised the man, but couldn't quite match a name to the familiar face. They must be good friends, because if it was a wedding, which it appeared to be, then it seemed that Andrew was the best man. There was also another thing annoying Andrew about the photo, and that was that the man whom Andrew was stood beside, 'the groom', brought emotions of sadness with him; Andrew connected him to a sad and quite painful event, but he couldn't for the life of him remember what.

Andrew also knew that this photo, in particular 'the groom', was important and he wasn't sure how. He glanced down at his feet in frustration, as he knew that those ridiculous brown leather shoes were also important somehow. Then he suddenly had a memory flash into his mind, rather like when you have a dream and something suddenly reminds you of it later in the day and it returns to you. He remembered writing something on his hand, but he wasn't sure what; the memory suddenly appeared in his mind and then, just as quickly, disappeared again. He mentally kicked himself for not checking before; he always wrote things on his hands to remind himself of things he had to do: jobs around the house, people he had to call, reports he had to file, the list was endless. Andrew glanced down at his hand, full of sudden hope and saw with disdain that his hand was facing downwards so that his palm was touching the arm of the chair. The weathered and scarred back of his hand stared up at him, taunting him, because he knew that on the other side something was written, something important.

Andrew closed his eyes and tried to empty his mind of everything, something that he never had been very good at; there were always things he had to do or remember, cases he was mulling over and people he was worrying about, and to concentrate on one thing and one thing alone was quite a challenge: in this case, turning his hand over so that he could see what was written on his palm. He attempted to do just that for about ten minutes, with each minute seeing him more and more frustrated, but it was in vain. His hand remained firmly in its position: his palm facing downwards and his fingers curled over the edge of the arms of his chair. Andrew sighed deeply and allowed all of his previous thoughts, worries and various other distractions to return to him in a sudden flood of thoughts and memories. It was useless; he could move his head slightly, he could speak, blink, breathe and furrow his brow, but that was about all. He definitely could not move his hands, just as he definitely could *not* remove the ugly brown leather shoes.

5

The Last Case

William strode down the wide pathway, the gravel crunching beneath his feet, admiring the Arling family home. Despite how often he had visited the impressive house it still ... well, impressed him.

The house where Caley and Aziza had grown up, and where Margaret and Andrew still lived, was a large detached house in the centre of Domsville, set slightly back from the rest of town somehow. This gave it the appearance of being completely isolated. William stopped walking and took a moment to admire just how isolated and peaceful their home was. The only sound was the water from the water fountain, which stood in the centre of the winding driveway. William continued forward until he reached the fountain, which was made entirely of marble and was beautifully ornate and inscribed with hundreds of symbols, which William was sure that Margaret and Andrew understood but he, however, was at a complete loss.

William stared up at the magnificent house, with its large bay windows and towering pillars either side of the doorway, which were entwined with blood-red roses and added to the beauty of the house. The house itself seemed to belong in a different time, a feeling which was enhanced upon entering it. This was largely because Margaret had, naturally, decorated and furnished the entire house herself in her own style.

Margaret owned a shop in Domsville's bustling town centre called Pearls of Wisdom, whose tagline was 'The Pearl is the Queen of Gems and the Gem of Queens'. It was appropriately named as Margaret is Latin for 'a pearl'. William had been inside this shop and it was like stepping into Aladdin's cave; it was filled with antiques, from vintage jewellery (Margaret had actually started out just selling antique jewellery, but then expanded), to Persian rugs. Naturally, therefore, their home was full of exquisite antiques.

William glanced behind him and saw that there was still no sign of Caley. He pushed back the sleeve of his suit jacket slightly so that he could see his watch; it was only just eight o'clock and Caley was always late. He slipped his hand into the inside pocket of his jacket and retrieved a packet of cigarettes and his lighter. As he lit the cigarette he studied the fountain once more and noticed something that he had never noticed before: Caley's name engraved in the marble fountain and slightly above it, Aziza's name too. William grinned to himself and leaned closer, trying to ensure that he didn't get any ash in the fountain. Caley's name was surrounded by various other engravings, as was Aziza's, none of which William understood. They were all foreign words and unusual symbols, which were all foreign to William and presumably related to their names, which Margaret and Andrew had chosen for their etymology.

Aziza, William knew, is Egyptian for 'precious', which Andrew and Margaret had aptly named her because she was their first child: the child the doctors had insisted Margaret wouldn't be able to carry full-term. Margaret, however, proved them wrong (naturally) and went on to give birth to Caley. Caley was premature and fought for her life in hospital but went against the odds and, naturally (once more), survived and influenced her name, Caley, which is Celtic/Gaelic for 'brave warrior'.

The sound of crunching gravel alerted William that Caley had arrived. William, who was familiar with Caley's driving, darted out of the way and stood instead in the entrance of the house, leaning against a rose-entwined pillar, and sarcastically tapping his watch.

Caley turned off the engine and climbed out of her car, slamming her door behind her, and headed over to William.

'What time do you call this?' he asked, smirking as he did so.

Caley looked down at her own watch and replied in an aloof manner, 'Quarter past eight'. She smirked at William's slight shake of the head and reached into her bag to retrieve her set of keys for her parents' house.

'Put the cigarette out before you come in,' Caley called behind her as she entered the hallway and tapped in the intricate alarm code that her security-conscious father had bought and installed himself, despite being useless with electrics. Caley, however, would be hypocritical to comment as she had followed in Andrew's footsteps when she joined the police force, just as Aziza had followed in Margaret's when she bought her own business: Elegance, which was a shop selling clothes and matching accessories for weddings and special occasions.

William entered the house slightly behind Caley, having found a suitable place to stub out his cigarette, and shut the heavy wooden door, which wouldn't have seemed out of place in a medieval castle, William mused.

'What's the plan of action?' he asked, following Caley down the hallway.

'I thought we would go through Da . . . Andrew's study and then, if need be, have a brief scan of the house?' Caley replied, heading up the impressive marble staircase.

William nodded his approval and as they reached the top of the stairs, added, 'Does Margaret know we're here?'

'Yes, but I didn't go into details.' Caley placed her hand on the brass doorknob and paused. 'This doesn't feel right; Dad's study was always off-limits. It was just an unspoken rule. He and Mum never entered each other's studies and we never entered theirs. If we wanted Dad when he was working we would knock and wait for him to come out. I remember the only time I've ever actually been inside here was when I applied to join the police force and Dad and I had a "chat".' Caley used her fingers to make quotation marks in the air. 'It was all Mum's idea, obviously, although Dad naturally denied it,' Caley laughed.

'I know what you mean,' William replied softly. 'It always feels wrong to go through someone's property when we investigate cases, whether they are dead or alive, like we're somehow betraying their privacy, and it must feel even worse because Andrew is your dad.' William paused and Caley still stood outside the study door, gently nodding her head and running her fingers around the doorknob. 'It's what he'd want, you know that; it will help us to find whoever did this to him and that is what he'd want. He'd understand,' William stated, his voice barely louder than a whisper.

Caley nodded. 'Thanks,' she smiled weakly at William and then turned to face the door. She inhaled deeply, as if preparing to submerge herself in water and then turned the doorknob. The study door clicked open and Caley gently nudged it towards the wall so that there was a gap large enough for her to fit through.

Caley entered first, treading softly on the thick cream carpet, and headed over to Andrew's desk. William followed her and clicked the door softly behind him. The silence was tangible and it made him uncomfortable. After a few minutes, he gestured towards the Persian rugs which were thrown haphazardly on the floor around the room, with their patterns and colours clashing terribly with one another and the rest of the room.

'What's with all of the rugs?' he asked Caley.

Caley turned towards William and grinned. 'It's no wonder that Dad doesn't let Mum in here,' she laughed. 'Mum always told him off for pacing, telling him that he would wear the carpets thin, so she started laying Persian rugs around the house.

She obviously gave some to Dad to put in here and he just threw them around the room, not really sure what else to do with them, and because Mum doesn't come in here she doesn't know the colour schemes. She probably told him to pick some matching ones.'

William laughed softly and headed over to where Caley was standing beside Andrew's mahogany desk. William's laughter stopped abruptly, however, when he saw the mountains of paperwork and Post-it notes covering Andrew's desk; the only way you could tell it was a mahogany desk was by looking at its legs.

'I can see where you got your organisational skills from,' William muttered.

Caley raised her eyebrows and grabbed a wall stapler off Andrew's desk. 'Beware, I'm armed,' she warned, aiming it at him.

'And dangerous,' William added, ducking as Caley threw the stapler at him.

'This is going to take us all day,' William moaned as he bent down to retrieve the stapler.

'Good thing we're here to help then isn't it?' a voice from behind Caley and William replied.

Caley and William spun around to face the doorway, which is where the voice had originated. Margaret and Aziza were standing in the doorway, just outside the study itself, their expressions ones of sheer determination.

Caley smiled weakly. 'You two look as stubborn as each other. I thought Dad and I were the stubborn ones in this family.'

Margaret returned the weak smile and clasped her hands together firmly, her fingers lingering over her wedding ring for a moment too long.

'We thought you might need the help,' Aziza smiled, stepping past the door and into the study. 'Ray offered to help, bless him, but I thought it was best if he went to work; he would

46

be more of a hindrance than a help. He has to be the clumsiest athlete that I know,' she laughed affectionately.

'Thanks,' Caley replied. 'From the looks of Dad's paperwork system we'll certainly need the help,' she grinned. Her smile faded slightly as she noticed that Margaret was still standing in the hallway. Caley stepped towards her mum and held out her hand. 'Are you coming in?' she asked. 'I don't think we can do it without you.'

Margaret nodded determinedly and taking a deep breath, placed one foot over the invisible barrier between the landing and Andrew's study, and then another. She exhaled deeply and shutting the door behind her, took Caley's hand in her own.

'It just feels . . .' Margaret trailed off, her voice wavering slightly.

Caley nodded in understanding, 'I know; it has always been Dad's space.'

Margaret nodded softly, although she still looked slightly unsure of herself.

'It will help, though, Mum,' Aziza added. Her voice, with its soft, smooth tones, was naturally reassuring. 'It will help to find who did this to Dad.'

Margaret slid her hand out of Caley's and pinched her nose lightly. When she returned her hand to her side, her chin was high and her face had regained its normal colouring.

'You know,' Margaret began, 'when your dad does wake up, which he will,' she added confidently, 'I'm going to flipping kill him! Have you seen this place?'

They were all grateful for the moment of humour until Caley said a sharp, 'So,' bringing an abrupt end to the laughter. 'Where do we begin?'

'If I say at the beginning will you hit me again?' William teased.

'If I said yes would you say it anyway?' Caley replied lightly.

William grinned and hopped off the end of the desk. 'What if we take everything off the desk and begin sorting it into piles?' he suggested.

'Sounds good,' Margaret agreed. 'We can have a pile over

here for documents which are irrelevant for our investigation.'

Caley raised her eyebrows at William and smirked. '*Our* investigation?'

'And documents over there which are relevant,' Margaret continued. 'If you're not sure about anything put it into the middle, then we can leave this side alone.' She gestured to the corner in which the irrelevant documents were designated. 'But split the ones which we know are relevant and aren't sure about into appropriate files, depending on their content.'

'How come you never let me take charge like this?' William asked jokingly. 'What happened to being in control?' he teased, stressing the last three words.

Caley playfully punched him on the arm and William naturally pretended to be in agony.

'She doesn't mean to take over; it's just her natural instinct, which is why she is best working for herself,' Caley added in an undertone. 'And besides, look how much more confident she is now that she is taking charge.'

'Someone should also do something with the computer,' Margaret added as an afterthought, waving her perfectly manicured hand towards the computer sitting beneath the sea of papers and Post-it notes.

William raised his hand in the air slightly. 'I'll do that,' he volunteered.

'Excellent! Let's get cracking!' Margaret beamed, clapping her hands together.

William and Caley simultaneously turned their heads to smirk at one another.

'Let's get cracking?' Caley repeated in a disbelieving voice.

William chuckled. 'Do you think she should switch to decaffeinated drinks for the rest of the day?' he asked in mock seriousness.

Two hours later, Aziza and Margaret were sitting downstairs in the living room, a pot of Earl Grey tea sitting between them, discussing what they would do for lunch. Meanwhile, Caley and William were sitting in the centre of Andrew's study completely surrounded by paperwork, which was scattered around them in a form of organised chaos, from formal police documents (Caley did not want to question how Andrew had obtained these) to Post-it notes in various neon colours and obliterated by Andrew's scrawling handwriting, which Aziza had deemed undecipherable.

William heaved a sigh of relief. 'After spending two hours with Margaret,' he began before glancing behind him towards the door, 'I have newfound respect for Andrew,' he concluded in a whisper, despite having only just confirmed that Margaret was out of earshot.

Caley laughed. 'I agree, but you do have to admit that we would have taken twice the time without her and Aziza's help.'

'Touché,' William agreed.

Caley heaved a pile of paperwork onto her lap and began sifting through it, tossing occasional pieces of paper to her left, some to her right and some directly at William, the first unannounced piece of which caused him to topple backwards in shock. When she had finished this 'filing', she looked directly at William in an expectant way. William was completely nonplussed and after darting his eyes from Caley to the pile of papers in his hands to a random point in the room and back again several times, he decided to articulate his thoughts.

'Are you waiting for a round of applause or something?'

Caley rolled her eyes. 'I'm done.'

William looked around the room, as if for clues as to what Caley was talking about, before asking, 'Done what exactly? I mean, apart from making more piles of paper for us to sort out?'

Caley shook her head and impatiently seized the papers she had thrust at William during her 'filing' bout. 'These papers' – she waved them dangerously in the air to demonstrate her point – 'are all official police documents about the last case –'

'That sounds like an episode from a detective series,' William interrupted.

' . . . that Andrew was working on before. Those papers' – Caley gestured to the pile to her right – 'are Andrew's notes and those are other . . .' She waved her arms around at this point, trying to think of an appropriate word and in the end settled for, '*things* pertaining to the case that Andrew was working on last'. Caley looked at William expectantly once more.

'Am I supposed to leap for joy?' he suggested dryly.

Caley sighed impatiently. 'This will help us to understand the case that Andrew was working on last, which we agreed is probably important in finding out a motive and therefore, a suspect in Andrew's attack.'

'I agree, now I know what you're talking about,' William added in an undertone. 'I think that there are lots of possible motives and therefore, suspects in Andrew's attack and I think it's safe to presume attempted murder. There's definitely opportunity, but what is vital is the timing. Why now?'

'Definitely,' Caley agreed.

'The first step is determining what Andrew was working on last, whether it was an old case or a new one, and if that could be the motive we're looking for.'

'What if it's a dead end?' Margaret's voice sounded from behind them.

'You've really got to stop doing that; between you creeping up on us and Caley throwing things, ranging from staplers to piles of paper, my heart won't stand out much longer,' William teased.

'Maybe your heart would stand a better chance if you stopped smoking?' Margaret suggested dryly.

'Touché,' William muttered. 'Speaking of which, actually,' he added. 'I won't be long,' he called behind him as he walked out of the study, rummaging in his pocket for his cigarettes and lighter.

Margaret shook her head disdainfully. 'Why don't you make him stop that *filthy habit*?' she demanded, practically spitting her final two words and turning to face Caley as she spoke.

Caley rolled her eyes skyward. 'I'm not in control of his life.'

Margaret began to speak once more and Caley, sensing a lecture, jumped to her feet. 'Why don't I get you two a chair to sit on?' she suggested, all but sprinting from the room.

Caley and William returned five minutes later carrying two chairs each, with William looking more relaxed and smelling distinctly of tobacco.

'Here you go,' Caley smiled, placing a chair behind Margaret.

William did the same for Aziza then placed the other chair he was carrying beside Caley's so that they were all sitting in a circle with the paperwork pertaining to Andrew's last case in the centre.

'Why don't we sort the papers into piles according to their content, their topics?' Aziza suggested.

Margaret nodded, collecting the papers in her arms as she did so. 'That's a good idea; it will help us to understand the case better.'

Margaret handed the police reports to Caley, the notes to William and the final pile, which basically consisted of anything else related to the case, to Aziza.

'Now, Caley, what is this case actually about?' Margaret asked. 'I mean, I presume you two determined that after we all sorted out the papers and Aziza and I popped downstairs for our Earl Grey break?'

William bit back a grin and could see Caley struggling to do the same. 'Yes we did,' she confirmed. She paused for a moment as she realised that both Margaret and Aziza were completely unaware of police terms and procedures.

As if reading her sister's mind, Aziza leant forward slightly and began speaking in her soft soothing voice. 'I know that we aren't educated in police routines and procedures, but I am sure that you have had to discuss similar things with *civilians* before,'

Aziza smiled wryly, 'and that you can portray it in a way that we' – she gestured to herself and Margaret as she spoke, using dainty hand gestures which were a contrast to Caley's usual dangerous arm-waving – 'will understand. After all,' she added, 'we are fast learners.'

Aziza leant back in her chair and smiled softly at Caley.

Caley nodded, took a deep breath and began to talk. 'Each department has informants that aren't in the police force or related to the police in any way other than being informants. They are often either criminals or reformed criminals, or at least hang around with criminals, both reformed and not, and they sometimes become an informant voluntarily or they may be head-hunted by a police officer, but usually they have been arrested and to lessen their sentence or abolish it completely they become an informant. They aren't the most trustworthy of people shall we say,' Caley smirked, 'but they are pretty much vital to the running of police departments because they are out there on the streets and they see what is going on, and even if they don't see it themselves they at least hear the rumours.' Caley paused to check that Aziza and Margaret were following so far.

William took advantage of Caley's hesitation to add, 'You see, we – that is the police in general – tend to stick out; we're noticeable and people, especially criminals, can often spot a police officer a mile off, even in plain clothes,' he added with a grin, 'but weasel-informants don't have that problem; they blend in.'

Caley nodded. 'Exactly, they're useful basically and almost every department has them; they may not be official but they're there, even if it's a friend of a friend who passes on information every now and again when we go to them to keep up with the gossip. As you presumably know, Dad worked in the Homicide department originally and even though he is now a superintendent, he is still heavily involved and particularly in the Homicide department. This case was when an informant was killed,' she paused momentarily and then continued once more when both Margaret and Aziza signalled that they were following so far. 'And it was suspected that he had found something out and because of what he knew–'

'And particularly because he was an informant and whoever killed him obviously knew this, just as they knew that he was likely to report his discovery to the police,' William interrupted.

'. . . he was killed. Anyway, the case was solved and the murderer was a small-time drug dealer who had recently expanded and was using a business as a cover for dealing drugs. He is now in prison.'

'This was the last case that Andrew worked on?' Margaret confirmed.

Caley nodded. 'According to what we found on his desk in his filing cabinet and on his computer, yes.'

Aziza nodded slowly. 'Without meaning to sound slow, what exactly does this tell you?'

William and Caley exchanged a brief glance. Caley knew that the fact that this last case was drug-related was unlikely to be a coincidence, because Andrew had 'Genesis' written on his hand when he was attacked and she also knew that William had come to the same conclusion. Their question, however, was whether or not to tell Margaret and Aziza about Genesis.

'What are you not telling us?' Aziza asked gently, acknowledging the secretive glance between the two colleagues.

Caley hesitated and looked to William once more.

'I think we should tell them,' he mouthed to Caley, who nodded in response.

'As long as they keep it a secret,' William added in an undertone. 'What do we have to lose? Maybe they could even help?' he suggested.

Caley nodded once more and turned to face Margaret and Aziza. Margaret's eyes were wide and her lips were pursed. Caley knew that her mum didn't like to relinquish control and she was aware that Margaret wanted to demand to know every little detail, but also that it wasn't her decision to make. She knew that this was Caley's job and Caley's investigation. Caley appreciated that Margaret wasn't interfering (for a change) or making demands, that she respected and trusted Caley.

'When I went to visit Dad in the hospital after he had first been admitted, I noticed that he had writing on his hand.' Caley noticed that Margaret was about to say something, so she hastily added, 'I wiped it off.'

'You asked me for a wet wipe,' Aziza recalled.

Caley nodded. 'I'm not sure why I removed it; I just followed my instincts,' Caley shrugged.

'Good,' Margaret stated brusquely. In response to Caley's questioning gaze she added, 'That's what Andrew always told you to do.'

Caley smiled softly and then reached into the pocket of her jeans and retrieved her mobile phone. She then found the picture she had taken and showed it to Margaret and Aziza in turn.

This, as Caley had expected, prompted the question: 'What is Genesis?'

Caley explained the basics of the case, aptly named with the Hebrew for 'the beginning', for it seemed that Dominic's murder set off a chain of events which resulted in the deaths of Chief Inspector Baxter and Daniel. There was then a moment's silence while Margaret and Aziza digested the information they had just been given.

'So can we presume that you two are linking these two cases?' Aziza asked.

'If you mean the case that Andrew last worked on and Genesis, then yes,' William replied.

'How are these two cases related?' Margaret asked. 'Theoretically,' she added, 'how do you imagine they are connected?'

'There's the obvious connection of drugs; Genesis involves three separate deaths, yet it all stems from drugs,' William began.

'And then there's the last case that Dad worked on, which consisted of the murder of an informant. Again drug-related,' Caley finished.

'Other than that, I'm not sure,' Caley admitted.

'We thought that Andrew's last case might shed some light on his attack and it seems too much of a coincidence that it was drug-related, as was Genesis – which his attack is obviously related to because it was written on his hand when Caley found him,' William mused.

Caley nodded and then, shifting slightly in her seat to face William, she asked, 'What would you do next?'

William barely hesitated; as usual he spoke before he thought. He often had a tendency to leap before looking. 'We have all of the details of the last case that Andrew worked on . . . but we can't see a clear connection yet . . . so I would . . . interview the person convicted of murdering the informant in The Last Case.'

Caley raised her eyebrows at the name which William had just christened the last case that Andrew had worked on.

William shrugged in response. 'It seemed like a sensible name . . . plus,' he added with a grin, as a new thought formed in his mind, 'we could call it TLC when we don't want to be overheard!' His voice dramatically hushed so that his last seven words were whispered and then, to further emphasise his point, he pressed his index finger to his lips and winked in an obvious manner at Caley, in a way that caused his head and shoulders to move too.

Caley laughed and shook her head then said, 'I agree.'

'With the plan to interview' – he paused while he consulted the case file – 'Malcolm Wood in prison to see what he has to say for himself?'

Caley nodded. 'It certainly sounds like a plan.'

'Is there anything we can do?' Aziza asked tentatively.

Caley glanced sideways at William who merely shrugged in a way that clearly said, 'I'm not getting involved.'

Caley thought for a few moments, her brow furrowed slightly in concentration, and then slowly nodded. 'There's something, actually, that we're not very good at but that I think you two would be.'

Aziza leant forward in curiosity.

'Organisation,' Margaret stated in her usual brusque manner. 'Research of some sort, or filing?' she guessed.

'I'm good at that,' William frowned.

'So why do you never do it?' Caley demanded, her lips curving as she spoke.

William grinned and shrugged. 'I get bored,' he replied simply.

Caley grinned and shook her head and then, turning back to face Margaret and Aziza, her smile faded slightly into a more bashful expression. 'Would you mind?'

'Definitely not,' Margaret replied wholeheartedly.

Caley looked to Aziza for her opinion. Aziza nodded softly. 'If it will help . . . it might actually help us too; we're going stir crazy in there. We just sit around Dad's hospital bed waiting for him to wake up, reminiscing and suffering lots of visits from people who wear sympathetic faces, inform us that they are "sorry for our loss", and speak about Dad in the past tense.' She exhaled angrily and Caley watched, slightly amused.

It was the angriest that she had ever seen her sister, who was usually the height of calmness while Margaret would purse her lips and try to regain control of a situation and she and Andrew were more likely to pace around the room, yelling at sporadic intervals and occasionally kicking a piece of nearby furniture.

Aziza inhaled and exhaled slowly and then returned her focus to Caley. 'I'm sorry,' she apologised, her voice back to its usual dulcet tone. 'It's just hard.' She managed a weak smile. 'What is it you want us to do?'

'Well, Genesis is beginning to irritate me, so it would be helpful if one of you could research other possible meanings of the word and make a note of any possible connections, and the other one would go through the Genesis case file and just see if anything stands out to you,' Caley replied.

'Not a problem,' Margaret stated.

Aziza nodded briefly to Caley and then turned slightly in her chair to face Margaret. 'Shall I research other possible meanings of Genesis?' she asked.

Margaret nodded decisively. 'That's what I was about to suggest.'

William slapped his hands on his thighs. 'Right then,' he announced, 'I'm going for a cigarette.' He then got to his feet and left the room, acknowledging Caley with a sharp nod of the head, offering a brief smile to Aziza and carefully avoiding Margaret's disproving gaze altogether.

'Is there anything else you need?' Caley asked, handing the bulging file to Margaret with 'Genesis' scrawled on its cover in permanent marker.

'I don't think so. Aziza has a laptop she can use.' Margaret glanced at Aziza to confirm this and when Aziza nodded in reply, added, 'Thanks, though.'

Caley nodded. 'Good. We'd better get tidied away and then we can get started,' she replied, standing as she spoke.

Margaret began flicking through the file on her lap. 'Where did you get this?' she asked suspiciously.

Caley raised an eyebrow in response. 'Officially or unofficially?'

Margaret shook her head, shut the file and fixed her unfaltering gaze on Caley.

Caley grinned and leant against her chair. 'If you want to check out a file you have to go through official channels and our investigation is ... shall we say, low key? This was just simpler. Plus, you can write all over it as much as you want.'

Margaret sighed deeply. 'What am I going to do with you?' she asked in mock exasperation, slowly getting to her feet, the file still clutched between her hands.

Caley began to pick up the chair in front of her and then

suddenly stopped. She stood in silence, her hands slightly above the top of the chair, her brow furrowed, for several seconds.

Aziza and Margaret watched her questioningly.

'I was just thinking,' Caley began slowly. 'What did I say to you before?' she asked, directing her question at Margaret.

'You said that your investigation was low key?'

'No,' Caley shook her head so slowly that you could practically hear her brain whirring like an overloaded computer, desperately working overtime. 'Before that.'

'That to check out a file you would have to go through official channels.'

Caley nodded. 'That's it. To check out a file you have to go through official channels,' she repeated. Slowly, Caley moved from the position she had previously frozen in, and nodded to herself. 'If Dad was looking into Genesis, I bet he would have checked out the file, and official channels mean records. Plus, if anyone else had checked it out there will be a record of them, too.' She scribbled a note to herself on the palm of her hand. 'Well, I guess that's another thing to do,' she added sardonically.

'Glad I could be of assistance,' Margaret teased, taking the chair that Caley had still not picked up out of her outstretched hands.

'Was there anything else you wanted, while you're here?' Margaret asked as she headed for the door, the chair in her hands.

Caley thought for a moment and was about to shake her head when she suddenly remembered something else from her and William's extensive to-do list. 'Do you remember that I asked you if you could have a quick search for Dad's phone?'

Margaret placed the chair on the floor while she replied to Caley. 'Yes, I had a look but couldn't see it anywhere. I even tried calling it a few times.'

Caley nodded. 'I thought that would be the case. Thanks anyway. I'll have a quick check in here but I expect it won't be here.'

Margaret nodded and lifted the chair up once more, leaving Caley to her thoughts.

'Thanks,' Caley called behind her as they left to return the chairs to where they belonged.

William returned to the room five minutes later and looked around in surprise. 'Where is everyone?' he asked.

Caley looked up from the desk where she was trying to return everything to its original place. 'They put the chairs away and then they went downstairs for a drink and lunch I think.'

'I can tell you were listening,' William grinned and then reached out and swiftly caught the pencil that Caley hurled towards him. He then leisurely strolled across the room and round the desk to where Caley was standing. He placed the pencil on the desk and then hesitated as something caught his eye. Next to where he had put the pencil stood a photograph in a simple wooden frame. He picked it up and held it close to him so that he could see it better. The photo was tattered around the edges as if it had been taken out of the frame repeatedly and looked at. William studied the people in the photograph: there were two men standing next to one another. They were both dressed smartly, in tuxedoes, and it looked like a wedding, mainly because of the flowers in the lapels of both men. They were dressed similarly, but one man was wearing a bow tie and flower in a slightly bolder colour scheme than the man at his side. This, William presumed, was the groom, which would make the other man the best man. The best man was undoubtedly Andrew, but William wasn't sure who was with him. He did know, however, that he recognised his face from somewhere.

Glancing to his right, William saw that Caley was engrossed in a notepad covered in her father's distinctive handwriting – if it could be called that – and carefully placed the photo frame face-down on the desk. He then undid the clasps on the back of the frame and gingerly removed the photograph. As well as the photo, there were some other fragments of paper in the frame. He tipped them out onto the desk and examined them more closely. There was the wedding photo and what appeared to be a graduation photograph. Holding the latter photograph close to his face, William noticed Andrew in the crowd of people as well as the man from the wedding photograph. There were also several newspaper clippings: one announcing the wedding of a man whose name William didn't recognise, but he presumed referred to the man in the photographs, and the rest of the articles were clipped together with a small metal paperclip in the corner. William gently tugged the articles free of the paperclip, so as to not rip them, and read the first article to himself. He only had to read the headline to realise where he recognised the other man's face from and why these clippings were here.

'Caley,' he called softly, 'I know you said that Andrew and Baxter were close, but I didn't realise how close.' Without waiting for Caley to respond, William began reading the article aloud. 'Chief Inspector Murdered. A second body has been found in connection with the murder of Dominic Smith as reported last week. This second victim was none other than Chief Inspector Dave Baxter, the investigating officer in Dominic's death. The media have called these murders "Genesis" as Dominic's death seemed to be the beginning of something, though nobody, including the police, seem sure as to what it is the beginning of. Chief Inspector Baxter's body was found in Domsville Park in the centre of town by his close friend and colleague–'

'Superintendent Andrew Arling,' Caley whispered.

William replaced the articles in the photo frame and passed it to Caley.

'The front photo is of Andrew and Baxter at Baxter's wedding. As you can see, Andrew was best man.'

'What about the other photograph and these clippings?' Caley asked.

'They were behind the wedding photograph. One newspaper clipping is an announcement of Baxter's wedding, the other photo is of Andrew and Baxter's graduation, and the rest of the clippings are about Baxter's murder ... he kept them all this time,' William explained as Caley thumbed through them.

Silence crept into the room and began to slowly seep into all four corners. William abruptly barred its way as he coughed loudly and violently.

'You really should give up,' Caley commented exasperatedly, with the air of a woman who had repeated herself many times before and whose advice had fallen on deaf ears.

'I know,' William replied. 'I will ... tomorrow.'

Caley rolled her eyes and muttered under her breath, 'Tomorrow never comes.'

William grinned and glanced at his watch. 'It's just gone two o'clock. Why don't we get sorted out and take what we need over to your cave – sorry, office,' he smirked, 'and then we can grab some lunch?'

'Good idea. I'm quite hungry. I never did get around to breakfast,' Caley agreed. She shuffled some papers around and piled them into a box which Margaret had intentionally left beside Andrew's desk. She then gently placed the photograph, with the newspaper clippings resting on it, on top of the contents of the cardboard box.

'By the way,' she added, as she pushed Andrew's chair back underneath his desk, 'it is *not* a cave,' she smirked.

William laughed, reached over and snatched the box out of Caley's hands before she had time to lift it off the desk. He then scuttled out of the room before Caley had a chance to protest.

6

A Drop in the Ocean

'I hate this place,' William shuddered.

'Excuse him, he's only in a bad mood because the receptionist he just hit on was completely unimpressed,' Caley smirked.

The man whom Caley was addressing frowned slightly and nudged the piece of metal joining the two lenses of his glasses gently with his index finger, causing them to edge slightly higher up his face. William concealed a grin and stepped forward to hold the door open for John, the record keeper, and Caley.

'Thanks,' Caley called behind her as she strode through the open door and hurried to keep up with John's fast pace. He walked purposefully through what was known as the Labyrinth of the police station, confidently following the twists and turns of the subterranean passageways. William strolled casually behind them, confidently taking several wrong turns and apathetically correcting himself, his hands jammed in the front pockets of his crisp navy blue suit trousers.

After what could have been no more than ten minutes, John abruptly came to a stop in front of a thick metal door, which seemed to Caley to be identical to all of the other doors. He jerked the long, protruding handle upwards and opened it in an effortless motion. As if unaware of Caley and William's presence, he strode into the vast cavern that lay behind it, leaving the heavy metal door to slam shut behind him.

Caley paused with her right hand resting on the door handle, which reminded her of the submarine door handles that she had seen in the action, spy and thriller films she favoured, and turned to face William, who was happily ambling up the corridor as if he didn't have a care in the world.

Caley rolled her eyes. 'Can you believe this guy?' she asked in disbelief.

William laughed. 'If you think he's bad you should see our IT support staff!'

Caley grinned and heaved the door open.

She, unlike John, held the door open for William and stepped into what she could only presume was John's office. The walls consisted of the same grey stone as the rest of the Labyrinth and they bore no decoration or ornamentation. They were bare and the ceiling was studded with spotlights. In the centre of the room was a wide glass desk in the shape of a horseshoe, and its surface was covered in various electrical devices, none of which Caley could make head nor tail of.

'This is quite an impressive setup you have here,' Caley commented, visibly impressed and also surprised at the masses of technology that filled the room. 'I've got to admit, I half-expected a room filled with moth-eaten books and dusty files,' she whispered to William.

John turned to acknowledge them with a slightly surprised expression on his face, as if he had forgotten that they were there.

'This equipment must have cost quite a bit,' William mused, wandering around the room and eying certain pieces of technology admiringly. 'How come you don't have more security?' he asked curiously.

'Would *you* be able to find your way back out of here?' he replied simply. 'Now,' he continued. 'I have all of the archives on the computer.' He waved his hand absently towards the monstrous machine on the floor underneath his desk, which did not, in any shape or form, resemble the old-fashioned box in Caley's office, 'but I also have paper copies of a lot of files,' he added, this time gesturing towards a door behind him. 'So what is it I can do for you?'

Caley glanced briefly at William in an acknowledging way which clearly said, 'I'll take the lead, but feel free to jump in,' and then turned back to face John. 'A few things if it's possible,' she began, scanning the room in search of a second chair but, upon finding none, she settled for leaning against the table behind her. 'Firstly, I'd like access to a file, just to view and if necessary to make a few copies; secondly, to run a quick search through the archives and again maybe request a few copies of documents if necessary; and finally, to see who else has checked out the file in question. Would that be possible?'

'I don't see why not,' he replied, rising from his seat.

John meticulously pushed his chair back underneath his desk then quickly and automatically entered a few commands to password-protect his computer while he was away. He then conscientiously tidied a stack of papers in his in-tray, which appeared to be already perfectly neat to Caley and William, by ensuring that all of the edges were exactly in-line with one another. Once he had perfected his surroundings, John headed over to one of the submarine-style doors, identical to all of the doors in the Labyrinth, which he had gestured towards previously when referring to the paper archives.

'You will probably be better off searching in here.' He tapped the metal door behind him, the noise resounding around the cave-like room. 'Because you can easily access the file you need and make any necessary copies from in here.'

'Thanks,' Caley replied gratefully.

'What about the archive search and the list of people who have checked out the file?' William asked, strolling over from where he had been admiring an impressive gadget towards where Caley and John were gathered around the door. He looked at John expectantly.

'I can run them for you in here; it will be quicker that way and more beneficial for everyone.'

William nodded his agreement and John removed a thick metal ring from his belt, which was completely filled with keys of various sizes and colours. He selected an old-fashioned gold key and inserted it into a concealed lock below the door handle. He twisted the key anti-clockwise and the door opened with a loud click, which echoed through the room. He then stepped back to let Caley and William through.

'Thanks,' Caley repeated as William stepped into the room. 'The search is–' she began, but she was stopped by John. He raised a large saucer-like hand in the air and headed over to his desk. When he returned to a somewhat puzzled Caley, he had a scrap of paper and a pen in his hand. He pushed the pen and paper towards Caley.

'Write down what you want me to search for. That way I don't pay attention to what you want to look for and that way I remember what you want me to do.'

'Fair enough,' William commented as Caley scribbled something onto the piece of paper. William stuck his head, not too subtly, over her shoulder to see what she had written. Scrawled in her child-like handwriting, the note read: *General search for Superintendent Andrew Arling.* Directly underneath it, in equally messy handwriting, she wrote: *Who has checked out Genesis case file in the last year?* She finished writing and handed the paper and pen back to John, who was staring at the ceiling, mouth slightly open, in a dazed manner. William sniggered and the noise seemed to snap John back into consciousness. He blinked and turned to face Caley, a slightly confused look evident on his face at first as he tried to remember who she was and what she was doing in his office. He then took the pen and paper from her outstretched hand.

'Thanks.'

He strode towards his desk once more and then suddenly turned towards the door where William and Caley were standing. 'If you, er, need anything then you can just, er, ask, I guess,' he called to them somewhat awkwardly. He then turned back around, pulled out the chair from underneath his desk, sat down and once he had unlocked his computer and straightened the stack of papers in his in-tray once more, began working again, seeming to immediately forget about William and Caley's presence.

William let the door slam shut behind Caley with a smirk evident on his face. 'I guess we'd better get started,' he suggested.

Caley nodded and surveying the room around her (for it was circular in shape), sighed deeply. 'I guess we had,' she agreed.

The walls of the room were completely covered in shelves, from carpet to ceiling, all of which were filled with files.

'Luckily for us John is extremely organised,' William commented, pointing to the labels underneath each file. He began to circle the room and had only gone a few paces when he turned to Caley with a grin. 'They're even in alphabetical order!'

'Of course they are,' Caley replied, half to herself.

William began muttering as he continued to circle the room, studying each label as he passed it and Caley distinctly heard him sing the alphabet song to himself under his breath.

'G,' he muttered and began running a finger along the shelves, and then a few seconds later: 'Got it,' he called out, lifting a file down from one of the shelves.

There was a round and extremely chipped, wooden table in the centre of the room with several mismatched stools and chairs surrounding it. William dived into the only armchair and Caley, with a disbelieving shake of her head, sat down next to him on what appeared to be a kitchen stool.

'No change,' Margaret muttered. 'No change,' she repeated twice more, her voice peaking each time as she threw herself into a chair beside Andrew's bed.

Aziza watched helplessly as Margaret buried her head in her hands and struggled to regain her composure. While she watched, her eyes were drawn to her father and she began to feel her own hope fading. She sat in silence and listened to the heart-wrenching incessant beeping that represented his steady heartbeat and she wondered how much longer it would continue to beep.

Caley dropped her head into her arms, which were resting on the table in front of her, and let out an exasperated sigh. William paced around her, his teeth gritted and his fists clenched in his pockets.

'We're getting nowhere,' Caley sighed, her frustration evident. She lifted her head off the desk and raked a hand through her already rumpled hair. 'What's the matter with you anyway?'

'I'd kill for a cigarette.'

Caley dragged her fingers through her hair once more, this time on the opposite side so at least it was equal even if it was equally messy.

'Come on, let's get out of here,' Caley sighed.

'Thank you,' William all but cried. 'I thought I was going to have to send out change of address cards.'

Caley smiled exasperatedly and replaced the Genesis file.

'Make sure you put that back on the right shelf, or you'll have John to answer to,' William commented sardonically, jerking his head towards the door behind which John sat working, probably having completely forgotten about Caley and William.

They returned to the cave-like space that acted as the record keeper's office and approached a totally oblivious John, who appeared to be deep in concentration. As Caley got closer, she saw the strange symbols which filled his multiple computer screens. She was about to subtly cough, because John still seemed unaware of their presence, when William abruptly banged his fist on his desk. Caley rolled her eyes and moved slightly to her right so that she was standing beside William.

'Sorry to disturb you,' she began, 'especially since you seem so busy–'

John, appearing to have finally worked out who they were and what they were doing in his office, interrupted her and explained exactly what it was he was working on, or at least Caley presumed that was what he did as she had absolutely no idea what he was talking about. He seemed to use lots of technical jargon and gestured repeatedly towards his computer screen, seemingly unaware that the odd-looking symbols that covered it may well have been Swahili as far as Caley was concerned.

While John talked, William resumed his pacing, his teeth gritted together tightly and his clenched fists protruding through the pockets of his suit trousers.

'Right,' Caley commented when John had finished explaining what he was currently working on. 'We've finished with the records,' she explained. 'Thanks. I was just wondering if you had done those searches I asked for?'

'Oh right,' he replied, seeming to suddenly remember the searches Caley had requested, and began rummaging through the various drawers, which seemed to be randomly scattered underneath his desk.

William sighed loudly. 'You've sorted through hundreds of paper archives and alphabetically ordered them, as well as having inputted them into a computer database, and you probably have them all backed up in several different places around the globe, but you can't find–' he began, muttering under his breath at first but slowly increasing in volume as he spoke until Caley interrupted him.

'William, why don't you wait for me outside?' she suggested.

William began to protest, but Caley raised her eyebrows threateningly.

'I won't be able to find my way back.'

'I can get someone to show you the way out if you want,'

John interjected. 'There will be some technicians around here somewhere,' he muttered absently, waving his hand around the room vaguely.

'That would be great, thanks,' William replied in a forced-polite voice.

John nodded and typed something on his keyboard. Almost immediately, one of the submarine-style doors opened. John continued to search through the drawers of his desk while a man appeared and approached William. He had pale skin and eyes that darted nervously around the room. He was wearing large, owl-like glasses that constantly slipped down his nose and a blue, checked, short-sleeved shirt with a tie decorated to make it look like a circuit board. When William nodded to him by way of salutation the man seemed slightly startled as if unsure how to deal with people. He smiled hesitantly and, eyes still darting around the room, glanced towards John nervously. He then made a noise which sounded, to Caley and William, like a grunt. John reciprocated and then, keeping his eyes on William, the technician jerked his head towards the door straight in front of them. He then started towards it, checking behind him briefly to ensure that William was following him, which he was, and then swung it open and strode through it, William close behind him.

Just before the door shut, Caley heard William say to his guide, 'It's cold down here. How come you're not wearing a jacket? Aren't you cold?'

She also saw the technician's response, which was to turn to look at William and then look down at his bare arms, as if to say, 'I never thought of it', and then simply continue walking down the corridor.

'Right,' John began, after discovering the fragment of paper that Caley had written on earlier in his shirt pocket, presumably for safe-keeping. 'These are the results of my first search,' he began, pointing to a monitor to his right that showed a list of files and folders. 'There's nothing really out of the ordinary and I'm sure you are already aware as to the content of most of it anyway,' he commented in a bored voice.

Caley nodded pessimistically, as if that was what she had been expecting, and briefly scanned the list on the monitor in front of her.

'What about the second search?' she asked once she had a hard copy of the first search results in her hand. 'Do you have a list for me?'

John sighed apologetically. 'Well . . .' he began hesitantly.

'Can you not do it?' Caley asked.

John looked deeply offended, so Caley hastily added, 'Obviously I'm confident in your abilities; I'm just not really sure what this sort of thing entails. I just presumed that, that was the reason for your hesitance,' she stuttered apologetically. 'Sorry,' she added in a whisper.

'That's fine,' John replied, waving his hand absentmindedly in what Caley presumed was a gesture for 'Forget it', and muttering something to himself that Caley guessed was something to do with her lack of knowledge in his specialised field.

'No, the problem is when I ran the search it bounced back. It's nothing to worry about of course; just an amber flag.'

Caley's nonplussed expression urged John to explain.

'That is to say, the search is sensitive of sorts.' Again he vaguely waved his hand, which appeared to be the approximate size of a plate, and Caley wondered absently how he managed to use a keyboard so efficiently with such large hands. 'Basically, the search has to be approved before the results are sent back. Sorry.'

Caley sighed. 'No problem.'

John nodded and muttered, 'Politics,' under his breath.

Caley bit back a grin and stepped away from the desk.

'Thanks for this.' She held the thin stack of paper containing the results from the first search briefly in the air. 'And for requesting that list. I'll come back for the results.'

John nodded once more and already halfway round to facing his computer screens (multiple) once more, added, 'It shouldn't take long; no more than a few days.'

Caley nodded and headed towards the door. 'Thanks again, and if someone was able to show me back that would be great,' she hinted.

The second she had finished speaking, the submarine-style door to her right opened and the same mousey-haired technician appeared. Caley gazed at him for a few seconds in wonderment, as she had not seen him return into the main office area from guiding William out, and then simply shook her head and stepped towards him.

'Whenever you're ready,' she smiled, gesturing for the technician to lead the way.

The man grunted and headed for the main door with Caley close behind. With one final word of thanks, she stepped through the submarine-style door and left John behind, heading for the surface and hopefully a much more cheerful William. As she followed the technician out of the Labyrinth, through the subterranean passageways and identical, heavy, submarine-style doors, she sighed deeply and muttered to herself, 'Today is *not* my day.'

Two hours and a long and refreshing lunch later, William and Caley were sat in Caley's faithful 4x4 on the way to the prison where Malcolm Wood was currently serving a life sentence.

'Why doesn't your radio ever work?' William asked, desperately trying to tune into a radio station, any radio station. Eventually he gave up, slamming a fist into the dashboard where the radio resided, and leant back in his chair.

'Leave my car alone,' Caley protectively demanded. 'If you want a radio that works, drive your own car,' she grumbled, possessively caressing the steering wheel as she drove.

'I hate these places,' Caley complained as she struggled to get comfortable on a metal chair, which she was sure was designed by someone who hated people.

'At least the décor matches,' William commented sarcastically.

'I mean, I really think we should take a moment to admire the way these stainless steel chairs complement this stainless steel table.'

Caley rolled her eyes and settled in a spot on the chair, which she decided was the comfiest position she would find.

When Malcolm Wood was led in by two prison guards, William was preoccupied, admiring his reflection in the two-way mirror, so it was Caley that explained who they were and what they were doing there. Malcolm nodded apathetically as Caley introduced herself and William, and as the prison guards left the room. William eventually joined Caley and Malcolm at the table in the centre of the room, sitting beside Caley and diagonally opposite from Malcolm, but only once he had perfected his hairstyle.

'This interview isn't a formal interview so it's not being recorded, but we're just going to ask some questions that relate to the case we are currently investigating, and which we believe may concern you.'

Malcolm seemed completely unmoved by Caley's introduction and simply sat examining the edge of the table.

'I wouldn't bother trying to use this filthy surface as a mirror,' William commented sardonically, rapping his knuckles on the solid metal surface. 'That mirror is much better,' he added, jerking his head towards the two-way mirror to his left.

Malcolm reluctantly raised his head to meet William's eyes. William stared coolly back, his piercing blue eyes unyielding, until Caley's question gained Malcolm's attention instead.

'Why don't we start by you telling me why you're in here?' Caley suggested.

Malcolm simply shrugged in an arrogant manner.

Caley took a deep breath and asked in a very final tone which demanded an answer, 'Who is Simon Chester?' She emphasised each word separately and left a slight pause between each word to allow them to sink in.

William didn't bother to hide his smirk at Caley's intimidating tone and her even more intimidating glare. Malcolm glanced sideways, nervously, to catch William's gaze, who simply stared coolly at Malcolm once more.

He then turned back to face Caley defiantly. 'Ask my lawyer,' he shrugged.

'I'm asking you. This might not be a formal interview, but we can soon make it one.'

Malcolm seemed to lose some of his earlier defiance, and glanced nervously at William once more, and back again, but didn't add anything more.

'This case we're currently investigating . . . it involves an attack on a Superintendent.'

Malcolm's eyes widened. 'I didn't do that, I didn't attack a policeman, that guy, they said he was a weasel, no-one said he was a policeman.'

'I didn't say you attacked him; you were in here when it happened. I said that our case *concerned* you,' Caley replied calmly. 'But now we're on the subject, what can you tell me about this "weasel": Simon Chester.'

Malcolm's eyes darted nervously between Caley and William once more, until he finally cracked.

'All right! All right!' Malcolm replied, a slight shake to his voice. 'Look, I don't know what you want with me, dragging all of this up again.'

Caley and William simply sat still, never breaking their gaze, waiting. Malcolm took a deep breath and began speaking.

'I was never into anything serious, you know.'

At this, Caley and William exchanged a sarcastic glance, but subtly enough not to deter Malcolm from answering. They had plenty of experience in subtle sarcasm, having had to control their sardonic comments often during work-related meetings.

'I was into the odd bit of drug-dealing, you know,' Malcolm continued, 'nothing major of course.'

'Malcolm, you've already been arrested and we're not here to add to that list of charges,' William interrupted. 'We've just come to ask you a few questions about an unrelated incident that we think you may be able to shed some light on. So please stop trying to understate the crimes you're in here for; you're only wasting our time and your own.'

'Right,' Malcolm replied. 'In that case, I had been involved in drugs for quite a while before I was arrested. I had been arrested a few times before for minor drug-related crimes, such as taking drugs and occasionally possession of drugs, but never so much as possession with intent before, never mind dealing. I then began getting into the odd bit of drug-dealing, again nothing serious really, but it began to escalate and eventually I got lucky and managed to end up with a small drug-dealing, er, business in one of the rougher ends of the town where I was living.'

'This would be Markston?' Caley confirmed, referring to one of the poorer towns on the outskirts of Alexia, Domsville's nearest city.

'That's right. Anyway, I ended up with this, er, business dealing drugs, only small-time you understand. Although, it would probably have expanded over time.'

William coughed as if to say, 'Get on with it.'

Malcolm picked up on the not-so-subtle hint and stuttered back into his story. 'Right, er, I, er, well, this man turned up pretending to be interested in what we, er, I . . .' He hesitated, seeing if Caley and William were going to question him on his sudden slip which revealed that he had been covering for someone in his official statement, although it was presumed that he hadn't worked completely alone. When they didn't, he continued. 'In what *I* was selling. I was talking shop, though, and trying to figure out what wasn't right, because something was off, you know. I mean, you're in the business for so long and you sort of develop a nose for these things.' He paused, tapping his own nose and when he realised that both William and Caley were completely unimpressed, he resumed talking. 'Anyway, while he was still hovering around, I heard about this weasel, you know, who had snitched on another operation recently. It wasn't this guy, but all the same it made me think, you know . . .'

William and Caley exchanged a quick glance as if to say, 'You mean you're capable of thinking?'

'And I went over to this guy and asked him a few questions, you know, and he admitted to being a weasel for you lot.'

'So you killed him,' she stated.

Malcolm gulped. 'Well, you know, he was going to run to you lot anyway, so I just . . . silenced him.'

Caley practically bored holes into Malcolm's skull, until Malcolm eventually looked away, choosing instead to gaze intently at the table in front of him. Caley waited for a few minutes before asking, 'You were born in Markston. Is that correct?'

Malcolm nodded, a bored expression on his face. 'Yes.'

'How old were you when you moved away?'

'Sixteen.'

Caley nodded. 'And when you moved back?'

'Twenty.'

'So you didn't stay away for very long then. Why was that?'

Malcolm sighed deeply, as if he was tired of repeating his answers and reciting his life story to various police officers.

'No, I didn't. I moved away when I was young because I know that will be your next question, because I was bored of Markston. It was all I had ever known and as they say, the grass is always greener on the other side.'

'Ovid,' William muttered.

Caley, who had grown accustomed to her colleague's unusual passion for poetry, simply ignored William's mutterings, identifying the origin of the proverb that Wood had just quoted.

'Anyway, I soon grew tired of where I was living, I ran out of money quickly and realised that the grass isn't actually any greener on the other side, and so I returned home.'

Caley glanced sideways towards William, who asked Malcolm,

'What about your family? What can you tell us about them?'

Malcolm sighed heavily once more. 'Look, what is this all about? You could just find all this out by looking in my file,' he complained.

'Just answer the question,' William replied in a bored voice.

'Fine. I never knew my Dad; he left when I was young. I have two older brothers and a younger sister, and we all lived together with my mum in our house in Markston.'

William nodded. 'What about your siblings?'

'What about them?' Malcolm moaned.

'What was your relationship like with them? Where are they now? When did you last hear from them? I'm sure you get the drift,' he added, purposefully forgetting to ask about Malcolm's mother because William was aware, from the research he and Caley had done on Malcolm, that she had died several years ago of alcohol poisoning.

'My two brothers are in jail, or were when I last checked. My eldest brother was always in and out of fights and the last I heard he was arrested for assault, and my younger brother was just in for shoplifting I think.'

'What about your sister?'

'I'm not sure. I lost touch with her first because she moved away. The last I heard was that she was engaged to some guy.' Malcolm shrugged apathetically. 'Is that all?'

William glanced at Caley and nodded his head so briefly that Malcolm didn't actually notice their swift communication.

'Almost,' Caley replied.

Malcolm tilted his head uninterestedly towards Caley.

'Were there any arguments or fallings out that you remember when you were younger and living in Markston? For example, maybe a family argument of some sort, or perhaps between yourself and someone else, or maybe just someone else in the estate you lived on?'

Malcolm thought for a few moments and then shook his head. 'No, I don't think so. Nothing of any consequence anyway.

You know, there was the odd argument here and there, as to be expected, but nothing that I think would interest you.'

Caley waited for a few seconds, evidently deep in thought and then suddenly stood up. 'I think we're done here.'

William nodded and pressed his hands against the metal table to push himself to his feet.

'Thanks,' Caley called behind her as she left the room, holding the door open behind her for William who was distracted by his own reflection in the two-way mirror as he passed it, and ran a reassuring hand through his thick, carefully styled hair.

William and Caley were back in Caley's 4x4 and on the road on the way home. Only, this time, William was driving instead of Caley. William's style of driving was completely different to Caley's and although he was much more laid back and much less frightening when he drove than Caley, he was equally fast. Caley tended to weave in and out of traffic when she drove, her speed always far too fast and her driving erratic, whereas William drove with one elbow out of the window, the music preferably on and turned up as high as was possible for his eardrums to stand and his foot flat down on the accelerator.

'I hate driving this truck,' he complained.

Caley punched him lightly on the arm and William mockingly grabbed his arm and cried out in pain. This time Caley punched him harder.

'Stop insulting my car. If you don't like driving it then don't.'

William laughed. 'Fine. I just miss my car. Why do we always go out in your car and not mine?'

'I'm not being seen, especially on official police investigations, driving round in that thing.'

'That *thing*, as you refer to her, is a beautiful red Ferrari F430.'

Caley laughed alone until the energy faded away and they were left sitting in comfortable silence. 'What did you make of Wood?' she asked after a few minutes.

William drummed his fingers against the steering wheel as he pondered the question. 'I want to say, it was him. He was part of Genesis and it was his arrest that led Andrew to rake over the Genesis case.'

'So why don't you?'

'Because I would be lying,' he replied simply.

William pulled into the hospital car park three quarters of an hour later. 'I'm starving,' he complained as he slammed the car door shut behind him.

Caley rolled her eyes, a response she found William elicited, and followed William down the familiar hospital corridor towards Intensive Care. 'You're always hungry.'

William, however, was too busy admiring a passing nurse to reply.

Caley only had to walk into the room to realise that Margaret and Aziza had experienced as much luck as she and William had. She wandered over to her father and stood by his bed for a few moments, silence engulfing the room. Her hand was lightly touching his as she looked hopelessly at his closed eyes, still body and slow but steady heartbeat. There was so much she wanted to say to him, wanted to ask him, but the one word she said communicated it all.

'Dad,' she whispered. She sighed deeply and with a faint squeeze of his hand, returned to where Margaret and Aziza were sitting. She threw herself into the nearest chair with a heavy sigh and turned away slightly so that her back was to them, struggling to blink back tears that were threatening to fall. When she turned back to face Margaret and Aziza, her face was completely void of any emotion. It was at that moment that William waltzed into the room, hastily stuffing a scrap of paper, which no doubt contained the passing nurse's phone number, into the pocket of his leather bomber jacket. He took one look at Margaret, Aziza and Caley's similar expressions of exasperation and frustration, and collapsed into a chair beside Caley.

'I guess it's been one of those days,' he sighed.

Caley sat up slightly straighter in her chair. 'You haven't found anything interesting?'

'Sorry,' Aziza replied, with a delicate shake of her head.

'I haven't found anything new or particularly useful either,' Margaret added. 'I'm guessing that you didn't have much luck going through the records at the station.'

Caley shook her head and slumped back down in her chair.

Aziza leant her head back so that it was against the top of the chair and she was facing the ceiling, and Margaret simply buried her head in her hands.

'Do you think we're almost there?' Aziza asked.

Caley barked out a humourless laugh and William, who was so far down in his chair he was practically sat on the floor, replied. 'I'm afraid this was just a drop in the ocean.'

7

The Ever-Growing Puzzle

Andrew might not have been able to hear and understand everything that was being said around him, but he certainly picked up on the atmosphere. He sensed hopelessness, which frustrated him because he knew that he had the answers. The trouble was that he couldn't remember the question.

He had just woken up, but he wasn't feeling particularly refreshed as his sleep had been troubled and disturbed. Everything about his predicament annoyed him, from his inability to move, his confusion over where he was and what he was doing there, the way that he could hear his family but couldn't even let them know that he *could* hear them and that he was fine, to the ugly brown leather shoes he was wearing and was incapable of taking off.

Although he had just decided that he was fine and that he was annoyed that he couldn't inform his family of this fact, he found himself feeling doubtful. What worried him and therefore caused this doubt, was that the incessant beeping that he could hear had slowed down considerably from when he had first woken up in his armchair; it was only a subtle change, but the beeping had been gradually slowing down every day that he had woken up in this room in this dream-like state. He wasn't sure what the beeping represented, but he was sure that its *ritardando* could only be a bad thing. He also knew that each morning he awoke in his armchair, each morning when the beeping was that bit slower by such a modest amount that it was barely noticeable, he felt weaker, more tired and he had to admit, older.

He sighed deeply and contemplated this, amongst other things, for Andrew felt that he had a lot to think about. Last night, while he had slept, in the little sleep that he had managed to grasp in between strange dreams and stranger nightmares, he had decided to use this ample time he suddenly had to his advantage. Instead of being frustrated with all of the things that he couldn't do, Andrew had decided to be glad about all of the things that he could do. For example, all of this sitting around meant that he had more time to think and therefore more time to figure out this mystery, for that was how Andrew thought of it.

He began his morning exercises, which involved exercising what little of his body he could move. He had never been one for meditation, but instead started and ended every day with a little bit of exercise (or sometimes a lot of exercise, depending on what mood he was in). As he stretched his neck muscles, by gently rolling his head around and tilting it from side to side, he glanced out of the window. Usually dark nights and heavy rain soothed him, but the continuous darkness, swirling fog and incessant pouring rain seemed to encircle the house, trapping him and taunting him. There had been no change in weather since he had first woken up in his armchair and the unchanging weather gave him no clue as to the time of day, which meant that he had no idea how long he had been sitting in his armchair – and how much longer he would remain there.

Once he had finished his morning routine of exercises, which were so mild that he actually found them frustrating, he sat quietly hoping to hear Margaret and Aziza, and maybe even Caley and William whom he heard frequently, although not as often as he heard Margaret and Aziza. He had even heard Margaret last night while he slept and her familiar voice and constant presence soothed him; she never seemed to leave him, for which he was extremely grateful.

As he waited, he seemed to tune into his surroundings. The silence of his 'living room' (for Andrew knew it wasn't *actually* his living room) was pushed away and held there by the incessant beeping and the murmured voices. The voices weren't completely clear; he heard them as if he was underwater and they were on the surface, above the water and their voices were slightly muffled, but they were there all the same.

Andrew strained his ears and heard the familiar voices of Margaret and Aziza, followed by the abrupt slamming of a door and then the voices of Caley and William. He also thought that he could hear Ray's voice, and the voices of his family, including William and Ray whom he thought of as family (as Ray was soon about to become), raised his spirits. Suddenly, amidst the inane chatter and vacuous gossip, Andrew heard the word 'Genesis'.

Caley stopped talking.

'What just happened?'

Margaret stood up and walked over to the heart monitor beside Andrew. She studied the steady peaks for a few moments before replying, 'I'm not sure; it seems fine now, perfectly steady.'

'Maybe we should get a doctor, just to be sure?' Aziza suggested.

'I think it might be a good idea,' Margaret agreed, walking back over to her chair but hovering, as if unsure whether to remain standing or to sit back down.

'I'll go and get one,' Ray offered, leaping up from the seat which seemed too small for him, as if glad for the opportunity to do something, to help. Aziza wasn't sure how much he was actually helping, however; as soon as he had leapt out of his chair, he fell over his own feet and then stumbled into the chair next to him where Aziza was sitting, and almost pushed her chair over. He managed, however, to stop her chair (and her) from falling and regain his balance before leaving the room in large, clumsy strides.

Aziza watched affectionately and as he left the room, mused, 'How can he be so graceful and athletic during a game of rugby, but then so clumsy off the pitch?'

Andrew paused, remaining motionless and listening. If he wasn't mistaken, he was sure he had just heard a change in the usually constant beeping. It sounded as if it had suddenly become faster and higher-pitched, although it was only for an instant and it had now returned to its usual slow pace. He waited, unsure if he had imagined the change.

Rose replaced the stethoscope around her neck after briefly examining Andrew.

'He seems fine,' she smiled reassuringly, 'but this printout definitely shows an anomaly in the pace and pattern of his heartbeat.'

Rose tucked a stray strand of her deep crimson hair behind her ear, studied the sheet of paper she held in her hand, which was the printout from the ECG monitor beside her, and traced the sudden peak in Andrew's heartbeat with her index finger, an expression of curiosity on her face.

'Is this a good thing or not?' Margaret asked. 'You seem unsure yourself as to the meaning of it.'

Rose lifted her gaze from the printout to meet Margaret's eager stare.

'I don't think it's any cause for concern,' she replied in her distinctively soft voice, 'but we'll definitely be monitoring him more closely. You were right to let me know and I urge you to do so if it ever happens again.' Rose smiled gently around the room and headed towards the door, the soles of her grey plimsolls padding softly across the floor.

'What does it mean if it happens again?' Margaret asked as Rose reached for the door handle.

Rose turned around to face Margaret and smiled at her with eyes filled with compassion and an expression of understanding. 'I can't say for sure, but it may be a problem with Andrew's heart. This might be a symptom of a heart condition or injury, but it is probably just pressure on his heart due to the injuries he has sustained. However, it is more than probable that it's just a one-off, and I must stress that this sort of anomaly is perfectly normal and *not a cause for concern*,' she emphasised.

Margaret paled slightly but kept her composure. 'Thank you.'

Rose nodded softly and with one last sweeping smile around the room, opened the door and closed it gently behind her.

The word 'Genesis' was echoing around Andrew's mind. He knew that he had heard it before and that he understood its meaning. He also knew that it was important, somehow, to understanding his predicament.

'What could Genesis mean?' he pondered aloud. 'It could be someone's name . . . or maybe the name of some*thing*, as opposed to someone,' he mused as it suddenly dawned on him. 'Genesis is the name of a case,' he exclaimed, nodding slowly to himself. 'Of course,' he muttered. 'Of course.'

Resisting the urge to pace around the room, Andrew half-closed his eyes and tried to recall exactly what Genesis entailed. It was then that his eyes hit upon the photographs he had been studying and pondering the day before (or was it the day before that?) on a small table near to where he was sitting. His eyes snapped wide open when he saw the photograph of himself and another man at what appeared to be a wedding. Only this time, when he looked at the picture, he didn't feel confusion. He felt understanding and sadness, deep sadness. Last time he had felt this emotion he hadn't understood it, but now he did. Now Andrew knew who the groom was and why his face brought with it such intense waves of sadness.

'Baxter,' Andrew whispered. 'Chief Inspector Dave Baxter.'

Ten minutes later, he had remembered the basic outline of the Genesis case and he also remembered Baxter: training with him, working alongside him ... and finding his body in Domsville Park. The memory of Baxter's unavenged murder caused Andrew to feel anger as well as pain. He gritted his teeth and clenched his fists. It wasn't until he began to calm down that he realised the significance of his clenched fists – he could move his hands. Andrew's whole body relaxed as he felt excitement soar through his body. He slowly unclenched his fists, unsure if it was a figment of his imagination, and looked on enthusiastically as he managed to unclench his fists and then clench them again. He began to grin to himself, but then he was reminded of all he still had to figure out. Remembering the basics of Genesis, and being able to move his hands were thin slivers of hope, but there were still a lot of pieces of the jigsaw that didn't fit together.

Andrew experimented with his movement abilities, but soon discovered that the only movement restrictions that had been lifted were the ones restraining his hands. The rest of his body (with the exception of his head, which he had always been able to move freely) was still tethered to his armchair. This small change gave Andrew hope and suddenly, he recalled a memory of trying fruitlessly to move his hands, but he couldn't remember why.

'All of my efforts so far have been to gain information,' he mused. 'Information about where I am and what I'm doing here.' He paused, unsure of where his current train of thought was headed. 'What information could my hands provide me with?' he asked, puzzled, as he glanced down at his hands, the fingers of which he was happily drumming in celebration of their movement returning. And then he abruptly stopped moving his hands. 'Of course,' he whispered.

Andrew moved his gaze down to his left hand and held it there. Then, in eager anticipation, he slowly turned his hand over so that his palm, which was currently facing downwards, would be facing him. He sat in silence, staring at the palm of his left hand, and laughed out loud. The word staring back at him was *Genesis*. He remembered struggling in vain to turn his hand over, because he knew that something was written on the other side. He also knew, correctly, that what was written on his hand was important somehow. Now that he had finally managed to turn his hand over, it confirmed what he had just figured out. Genesis was important.

'I knew we hadn't imagined him laughing before,' Aziza exclaimed.

'Chuckling,' Margaret corrected with a grin.

Aziza nodded and laughed. 'Chuckling,' she repeated. 'Are you having any luck?' she asked, using the interruption from their work to check on any progress that Margaret might have made.

Margaret shook her head and rubbed at the back of her neck.

'You're tired.'

Margaret smiled, aware that Aziza's comment had been a statement and not a question. She wondered who Aziza had inherited that air of authority from.

'I'm fine.'

Aziza looked disapprovingly at her mum. 'That's not what I asked.'

'Technically you didn't ask anything,' Margaret smiled.

Aziza began to speak but Margaret held a hand up to stop her. 'I am *not* sleeping at home.'

Aziza sighed. 'You can't be comfortable sleeping here. I mean, look at yourself; you're tired and aching. Why don't we take it in turns?' she suggested. 'I can stay here tonight and you can sleep at home. I'll call you if there's any change.'

Margaret shook her head firmly. 'No. I am staying here and that is the end of it. If you want to stay then that is your choice, but I am not going anywhere. I am not leaving him.'

Sensing defeat, Aziza nodded softly.

'Now,' Margaret began, the determined edge from her voice gone. 'Why don't we get back to work and see what we can do to help Caley and William ... and your dad.'

'I know all about Genesis,' Andrew pondered. 'I know who was killed and who was suspected of killing them. What I don't know is why it is written on my hand.' He studied his hand intently, staring at the word Genesis, almost as if he was waiting for it to vanish from his hand completely. As if he had imagined it.

'Surely, I would only be familiar with the case if I worked it?' He furrowed his brow in frustration as he pondered aloud. 'I remember working on the case, trying to figure it out. Yet I know, somehow, that it wasn't my case. I wasn't in charge. So who was?' He began drumming his fingers along the edge of his armchair as he searched frantically through the archives of his memory. 'Maybe I investigated this case because of what happened to Baxter,' Andrew suddenly exclaimed, as the thought came to him. 'I know that Baxter's death deeply upset me and I am sure that it wasn't resolved, at least not in my mind. So maybe I investigated the case myself, on the QT, in the hope of avenging Baxter's death?' he suggested then laughed humourlessly. 'That does sound like something I would do.'

The room was silent for a few minutes, silent except for the incessant and unexplainable beeping, the murmured voices, which Andrew had currently tuned out, and the sound of his fingers tapping the edge of his armchair.

'Or maybe that wasn't the reason I investigated,' Andrew added doubtfully and sighed heavily. 'Either way, I know that I investigated this case, that I cared about this case ... and that I still do. So why can't I remember who *did* investigate Genesis?' he wondered a few moments later then relaxed his fingers and laid his head on the back of his armchair. He knew that he had some serious thinking to do and he was sure that if he could only solve Genesis, then his current predicament would be solved too.

Andrew began to drift off, somewhere that was half devoted to sleep and half devoted to his thoughts and to solving the mystery that had presented itself to him. When he opened his eyes briefly half an hour later, he wasn't fully awake. His eyes were only partially open and the first thing he noticed, through his narrow vision obscured by his own heavy eyelids, was the bag of golf clubs in the corner of his living room. His brow furrowed automatically, but he was too weary to open his eyes fully. What was a bag of golf clubs doing in his living room? Andrew sighed and shook his head and as he shut his eyes once more, he muttered to himself, 'Just another piece of the ever-growing puzzle.'

8

Here We Go Again

'Here we go again,' Caley complained, sighing heavily as she twisted the key in the lock of the door in front of her. The lock clicked to announce that she was free to enter and she placed her right hand on the door handle.

'Now would be where I'd say something really deep and meaningful, but encouraging and uplifting at the same time,' William commented.

Caley turned slightly to face him, a bemused grin on her face. 'What are you talking about?'

'Well, it's just that you don't want to break Andrew's privacy *again* by going into his office *again*, and I should really have something to say. You know,' he continued when Caley still looked nonplussed, 'something that makes you realise that we have to do this.'

'Thankfully, however, you don't have anything like that to say,' Caley replied with a laugh.

'Yeah, so basically man up and open the flipping door.'

Caley elbowed William gently in the ribs and still laughing, pushed the door to Andrew's office at the Domsville Police Headquarters, which was situated on the edge of Domsville Town, which housed those within the police force who were higher up in the ranks than the mere likes of Caley and William.

Caley stood in the doorway until William pushed her to one side.

'What-oh, it's so tidy,' he exclaimed, as he realised the source of Caley's shock.

'I know,' Caley replied, shutting the door to Andrew office and striding over to his desk. 'Mum would love this place,' Caley laughed, noting the shining surface of Andrew's wooden desk, bare except for a photograph of the six of them (including William and Ray) at a New Year's Eve party at their house from the year before; a computer, along with a keyboard and mouse; a small lamp; a stationery pot; and a practically empty, extremely neat in-tray.

'I'm not so sure,' William disagreed. 'There's nothing for her to do. Nothing to tidy.'

Caley laughed and pulled on one of the drawers in Andrew's desk.

'What's wrong?' William asked, noting Caley's frown.

'It's locked.'

'Do you want me to try?' he suggested, flexing his muscles.

Caley's fit of laughter was so severe that genuine tears escaped from her eyes and rolled down her cheeks.

'Hey, there's no need to laugh so hard,' William complained, swatting her with a book from the thin wooden bookcase on the wall opposite the door.

Once Caley had finished laughing she turned to William. 'Where do you think he keeps a key for his desk?' she asked.

'On a chain around his neck?' he suggested sarcastically.

Caley rolled her eyes and began wandering around Andrew's moderately sized office in search of his hiding place. Meanwhile, a typically nonchalant William studied Andrew's modest collection of books. Most were work-related and William ran his index finger along their spines in search of an interesting title. His sudden laughter captured Caley's attention.

'What's so funny?'

'This,' William replied, taking a book from Andrew's bookcase and showing its cover to Caley.

'The Key to Policing,' she read aloud with a grin.

William held the book firmly by its spine and shook it. A small silver key fell into the palm of his hand. With a laugh, he tossed the key to Caley who took it over to Andrew's desk.

'This just doesn't feel right,' she pondered aloud.

'What do you mean?' William asked, replacing the book and strolling over to her.

'It's just too . . . neat,' she explained. 'It's not like Dad at all,' she added as she twisted the key and pulled open the first of Andrew's desk drawers. But then she began to laugh. 'Now this is more like it,' she grinned, pointing to the contents of the drawer, which was overflowing, piled high with documents and stuffed to the brim with rubbish. The other drawers were exactly the same as it appeared that Andrew had simply tidied his office by hiding the mess.

'I'd suggest that you try this, to tidy up your cave, I mean, office,' William corrected his intentional mistake with a grin, 'but I don't think the drawers in your desk are big enough.'

'Nothing on Genesis,' Caley confirmed.

William nodded and gathered a stack of papers from the floor in front of him and threw them into the middle drawer of Andrew's desk.

'I know,' William replied. 'I didn't find anything either.'

'What about TLC?' Caley asked with a smirk.

William grinned, appreciating the fact that she had adopted the abbreviation. 'No, at least nothing interesting. There are a few reports and the like, but nothing extra.'

Caley nodded half-heartedly. 'Just as we expected then. I'm assuming that his mobile phone isn't here either.'

'Not that I've seen,' William replied. 'That was definitely expected, though.'

Caley nodded once more. 'Which means that whoever attacked Andrew took his phone.'

William lowered himself onto the edge of Andrew's desk and looked into Caley's eyes. 'What are you thinking?' he asked.

'Oh, just about why they, whoever *they* are, took his mobile.'

William nodded slowly and prompting a response, asked, 'And . . . ?'

'It means that Andrew's phone had important information on it, evidence against whoever attacked him.'

'Which implies that Andrew contacted his attacker, or vice versa, because then the evidence in question would simply be the record of this communication.'

'Exactly,' Caley agreed, 'and although they could have deleted the record, there's always the chance of it being recovered.'

'It's just easier to take it,' William agreed as he and Caley worked in their usual style of bouncing ideas off one another.

Caley grimaced. 'That points us towards the rather uncomfortable thought that Andrew knew his attacker.'

'Or at least they knew him,' William suggested.

'What do you mean?'

'Well, if it was someone whom Andrew had sent to prison, or whatever, then they might have remembered him and found out his contact information. That would enable them to contact him, but he wouldn't necessarily know them.'

Caley nodded. 'But then why would Andrew agree to meet up with them?'

'He wouldn't,' William replied simply.

'Which sends us back to square one,' Caley replied with a roll of her eyes.

'What if it was a professional hit?'

Caley's attention snapped back into place and focused on William.

'Well, it's something that we pondered before. It makes sense in some ways and explains the motive, not that it really narrows down the suspect list.'

'I suppose it is possible,' Caley mused.

'I'm not saying that's what I think happened; it's just a possibility.'

'I understand,' Caley replied. 'I agree actually; it's quite a likely possibility. It would explain why they took his phone for one thing.'

'But not why he met up with them,' William pointed out.

'Okay,' Caley announced. 'It gives us something else to think about certainly,' she added, pushing herself up from the chair and moving across the office. As she reached the door, William closely behind her, she paused and winced, surveying the room.

'What's wrong?'

Caley shook her head. 'I just feel like we're missing something. I mean, Andrew kept his desk locked, which implies that there is something important there, something worth locking up. Yet, we didn't find anything.'

'Maybe whatever he has deemed important enough to lock away isn't pertaining to Genesis, TLC or his attack. Or maybe he just likes his privacy.'

Caley nodded. 'I guess I just feel like there's something we're missing.'

William waited a few moments before adding, 'We've checked all of the desk drawers, the filing cabinet and his computer.'

'I know,' Caley replied, her hand still resting on the door handle, her face still doubtfully scanning the room.

'We can go through his desk contents again if you want,' William suggested.

'No. It would just be a waste of time.' Caley sighed and seeming to have admitted defeat, was about to turn the door handle when she suddenly froze.

'What is it this time?'

'What was in the drawers we searched?' Caley asked.

William looked at Caley as if to say 'Seriously?'

'Look, just humour me.'

William sighed and backed away from the door slightly. 'I don't know, erm, lots of paperwork,' he shrugged.

Caley leant back against the door, arms folded stubbornly across her chest.

It was only genuine respect for Caley that evoked a reply. 'Paperwork on cases, mostly reports etcetera, and a lot of it pertaining to the most recent cases in the department, such as TLC. There was also some information on staff in the Homicide Department, understandably as that is the department that he oversees. There was also a file on each police officer in the department in his filing cabinet.' William paused, but Caley motioned to continue so, with an obvious sigh, he did. He had listed several other things from the desk drawers, all of no significance, when Caley interrupted him.

'What did you just say?'

William winced as he tried to remember. 'An annotated copy of *What Makes a Killer?*' he guessed.

Caley's eyes widened. 'That's it!'

William didn't say anything; he didn't need to, he simply raised one eyebrow.

'Can you find that book again?'

'Sure.' William nodded apathetically. He then strolled over to the bookcase and retrieved the key for Andrew's desk drawers from *The Key to Policing*, and unlocked the drawers. After a few minutes of rooting around in various drawers, William returned to Caley, who was still leaning against the door, apparently deep in thought, with the book in his hand.

'Thanks,' she replied, taking the book and placing it in her bag while William relocked the desk drawers and returned the key to its hiding place.

William looked at Caley questioningly when she put the book in her bag with no explanation, but when he opened his mouth to speak she put her index finger to her lips. William, miraculously, picked up on the hint and didn't speak. Caley then proceeded to open the door and hold it behind her for William, who followed her out of the office and into the corridor. As soon as William stepped into the corridor, he saw why Caley had hushed him; there were two men a few doors down from Andrew's office, whose voices she had no doubt heard.

The two men were both dressed in expensive, pin-striped, power suits and were communicating in hushed and secretive voices, which seemed to suggest that no one else was important enough to be a part of their discussion.

The first man turned to face Caley and William at the sound of Andrew's office door shutting, and both Caley and William instantly recognised him as Chief Superintendent Richard Taggart.

'Good afternoon,' Taggart greeted Caley in an authoritative voice, stepping forward as he spoke.

'Good afternoon, sir,' Caley replied with a slight nod of her head.

The man with whom Taggart had been conferring stepped out from his companion's shadow and with a brief nod to Caley and William, and an even briefer comment muttered to Taggart as he passed, he strode off down the corridor and out of sight.

Taggart returned his attention to Caley. 'And what brings you to this side of Domsville?'

'We have just come from the superintendent's office,' Caley replied with a side glance at Andrew's office door, all but wincing as she tried to second-guess Taggart's response.

Taggart nodded his head slowly, as if trying to convey emotions of empathy and understanding. 'Yes, I heard about what happened to your father,' he replied in a grave voice. 'I have already been round to see him. I hope your mother is well?'

'Yes, thank you, sir,' Caley replied, expertly hiding her surprise.

'Yes, very unfortunate business. Your father is an excellent police officer and of course, a wonderful man. He is deeply missed here.'

Caley was about to respond when Taggart suggested, 'Perhaps we could just step into my office for one moment, so that we can continue this conversation in more discreet surroundings?'

*

95

Taggart's office was notably larger than her dad's, which Caley presumed was a result of his chief superintendent status, as opposed to Andrew's rank of superintendent.

'After you,' Taggart gestured to William to follow Caley into his office.

'Thank you . . . sir,' William added bitterly in a falsely polite tone which bordered on sarcasm. 'I didn't think you'd noticed me,' he muttered under his breath as he entered the office and once he was out of earshot of Taggart.

'Take a seat,' Taggart offered the two burgundy leather armchairs in front of his desk. The desk was made from mahogany and gleamed so much that William subtly checked out his reflection as he sat down. Taggart shut the door, which was padded and therefore ensured their privacy, marched purposefully over to the leather chair behind his desk and sat down, which meant that he was sitting in a place that provided him with authority over Caley and William. Caley and William's chairs, in addition, were lower down than Taggart's which added to his appearance of authority.

'I understand that you have been at work these past few days.' Taggart aimed his comment at Caley and rested his elbows on the desk while steepling his fingers.

'Yes, sir,' Caley replied, wondering why he was asking, while William was wondering what business it was of his.

Taggart nodded and smiled softly. 'I know how difficult it is for you.'

William scoffed, but thankfully for William, bearing in mind that Taggart easily outranked him, he didn't hear him. Caley did, however, and carefully avoided William's gaze, instead staring directly at Taggart, feigning interest.

'Give sorrow words,' Taggart recited in a soft and elegant voice, 'the grief that does not speak, whispers in the overwrought heart and bids it break.' He paused, a sad smile on his face and then added, 'Shakespeare. It is from Hamlet.'

Caley acknowledged Taggart with a gentle nod, biting her

cheeks as she did so for she had heard what Taggart had not: William muttering, 'Macbeth, not Hamlet, you stupid, supercilious man.'

'Thank you, sir,' Caley smiled softly, 'but Andrew *will* wake up.'

'Let us hope and pray that he does,' Taggart replied with a patronisingly sympathetic smile. There was a brief pause while he shifted in his chair slightly. 'As I was saying,' he continued, 'you have been working since your father's . . .' He paused while he seemed to search for an appropriate word. 'Accident?'

'You make it sound like he wet himself,' William grumbled to himself, his expression similar to that of a petulant child.

'Yes I have,' Caley replied determinedly.

'You do know, of course, that you are more than welcome to take time off work. It is allowed, advisable even.'

'I know. Thank you, sir,' Caley replied slightly more brusquely than previously as she struggled to keep her tone respectful.

William smirked at the stubborn set of Caley's jaw and in his mind, urged Taggart to keep going, to keep pushing. He didn't, however, which was definitely the more sensible choice and instead asked, 'May I enquire what you were both doing in your father's office?'

'Yes, but we're not going to tell you,' William mumbled, still sulking.

Caley, ignoring William, replied in an even tone, 'We were simply checking his office. We can't have spent more than five minutes there, and we just checked that everything was in order and that there wasn't anything that would be beneficial for the current investigation.'

'I see,' Taggart rested his chin lightly on his steepled fingers. 'I hope that I don't have to remind you that you, both of you, are assigned to your *own* department and your *own* cases. The investigation into Superintendent Arling's attack is being investigated by another department.' He spoke in a formal tone that bordered on reprimanding.

'You don't, sir.'

Taggart met Caley's gaze for a moment or two before breaking it with a brief nod. His voice returned to its usual soft and elegant tone. 'I am glad; I do not want to have to lecture you. I am fully aware of what an excellent police officer you are. You certainly take after your father. You make a superb inspector and I am positive that one day you will make an equally superb chief inspector. You just need to ensure that you focus on your own department and your own investigations. We have a perfectly capable team of police officers working on your father's attack.'

Taggart smiled at Caley and using his desk, pushed himself to his feet so that he towered even further over them. William, who was never very good at playing 'politics, mind games and all that twaddle', as he referred to it, stood up too. This meant that William was 3 inches taller than Taggart. The latter frowned slightly and hurriedly tried to hide his annoyance. He soon had further cause for annoyance, however, when Caley, who was rather amused by the scene playing out in front of her, stood up too and although she wasn't quite as tall as William, she was a clear inch taller than Taggart.

'I had better let you two go; I am sure you have lots of work to be getting on with, as have I,' Taggart smiled, ushering Caley and William towards the door. 'I am sorry if you feel this has been a little rushed, it is always a pleasant change to talk to an officer such as yourself, especially when I spend so much of my time with people whose jobs are now closer to resembling that of a politician than a police officer,' he laughed.

William strolled past Taggart, his hands in his trouser pockets as usual. 'Sir,' he acknowledged Taggart with a brief nod as he passed him and then he continued out of the door.

'Thank you for your time,' Caley smiled as she passed Taggart, who stretched out his hand and firmly shook Caley's.

'The pleasure is all mine, and please pass on my regards to your mother,' Taggart replied, shutting the door softly behind them.

William waited until Caley had followed him out onto the corridor and then headed down to the small car park in front of the office block. When he reached the car park, he noticed a young police officer admiring his Ferrari. He smirked and meandered over to his car. The officer, who couldn't have been more than twenty-two and who Caley actually thought wasn't a police officer at all, but a child in a Halloween costume, blushed when he noticed William and Caley approaching.

'Is this yours?' he asked William in awe.

'She certainly is,' William replied proudly and with a smirk.

'Wow!' the officer mouthed as he examined the car more closely.

Caley stood slightly behind William, which meant that neither William nor the officer saw her roll her eyes.

'How can you afford this? I mean, I didn't think that police earned that much, even when they *are* higher up in the force,' the naïve officer asked, still awestruck.

'No, I couldn't afford her on my wage,' William replied with a grin.

'Especially not the way he spends money. I don't think he ever has enough money in his bank account to earn interest and if he does it's gone too fast to actually get it,' Caley interrupted sarcastically.

'I inherited the money.'

'Oh,' the officer stopped examining the car and blushed again. 'Sorry, I didn't realise.'

'Don't worry about it,' William replied easily. 'It was my granddad who died, and it was quite a while ago now.'

The officer smiled bashfully. 'How come your parents didn't get the money?'

'They were already dead.'

This time, instead of blushing, the officer visibly paled. 'I'm so sorry.'

William shook his head genially. 'Don't worry about it,' he laughed. 'To lose one parent may be regarded as a misfortune;

to lose both looks like carelessness.' The officer simply gaped at William, so he added, 'Oscar Wilde.'

'So you're not bothered that your parents are dead?' he asked in disbelief.

William laughed bitterly. 'My parents weren't the sort of people one misses easily. To quote Oscar Wilde once more, some cause happiness wherever they go; others *when*ever they go.'

'Oh,' the officer once more appeared to be at a loss for words.

'My parents were very tedious, stuffy and pompous people. My mother married my father when she was only very young and he was a doctor which apparently meant that my mother was superior to her own family. She disowned them. She didn't even attend the funeral when my grandmother died,' he added bitterly. 'That was when I first met my granddad and we kept in touch, secretly of course. We used to send one another letters and we even met up now and again. Anyway, my dad was a doctor and he had his own practice. He expected us, my brother and me, to follow in his footsteps.'

'You didn't?' the officer guessed, a slight grin on his face.

'I didn't,' William repeated. 'I was always in trouble, something of a miscreant. Hard to imagine now I know,' he smirked, ignoring Caley's sardonic laughter. 'And I never really fitted in with the rest of my stuck-up family. Anyway, when I joined the force it was the final straw.'

'In what way?' the officer asked, enthralled by the story.

'They wrote me out of their wills and kicked me out of their house.'

The officer gasped.

'I went to live with my granddad, so I didn't care,' William laughed.

'So how come they died?'

'They went on holiday and the plane crashed,' William laughed humourlessly. 'My brother was looking after the practice and inherited the whole lot.' William shrugged. 'Nothing to do with me.'

'But your granddad left you his money when he died?'

William nodded. 'He left me everything. Hence how I managed to afford this beauty,' he grinned, running an admiring hand over the shiny red metal of the sports car he was perched on.

Fifteen minutes later, William and Caley were on the way down the familiar corridors of Domsville Hospital.

Caley sighed, 'I'm sick of this place. When Dad wakes up, I never want to return, with its sickly smiles and mint-green walls. Yuck!'

William laughed. 'I know what you mean.' After they had walked a little bit further, habitually following the twists and turns of the hospital, to the room in which Andrew was temporarily residing, he added, 'What are our plans for tomorrow, oh mighty one?'

Caley turned to William, one eyebrow raised. 'Oh mighty one? It's Inspector to you. I thought we'd go back to my office and decide our next move.'

William nodded. 'What about what Taggart said?'

Caley smirked. 'What about it?'

As they reached the door leading into Andrew's room, Caley paused.

'What's wrong?'

She sighed. 'I know this sounds terrible. I just hate the atmosphere in here. I know we're all upset because of what has happened to Dad, but I just hate how gloomy everyone is. We always have to start reminiscing and everyone starts crying and we all talk about our emotions. Yuck!' she exclaimed for the second time within the space of about five minutes.

William smiled. 'I know, but it helps them, you know, to talk about it.'

'Why?' Caley complained.

'Suppressed grief suffocates, it rages within the breast and is forced to multiply its strength,' he replied simply.

'Oscar Wilde?'

'Ovid.'

Caley laughed. 'Here we go again,' she murmured, half to herself and half to William, as she pushed open the door.

9

The Centre of the Universe

Caley was sitting in an ancient armchair, which was originally green but had faded over time. It was covered in patches where Caley had 'mended' various rips and tears and it had a hole in the top right corner, which she used to pull the stuffing out if she was feeling thoughtful, upset or frustrated. Her feet were resting on the coffee table in front of her, she had a mug of coffee in her right hand and open on her lap was the book that she had 'borrowed' from her dad's office at work. It was entitled *What Makes a Killer?* and its content was obliterated with his distinct and practically indecipherable annotations, which were accented with fragments of highlighted text in various colours and underlined text.

Caley jolted slightly as she heard the sound of her phone vibrating against a nearby surface. She wedged a nearby scrap of paper into the book at the page that she had reached and put both the book and her mug of coffee on the table. She then searched fruitlessly for ten minutes for her phone and eventually gave up and rang it. She traced the sound back to her armchair, where she found her phone down the side of the cushion. She sat back down and read a text from William: *I know that Oscar Wilde said that 'punctuality is the thief of time', but he also said that 'The only horrible thing in the world is ennui*

. . . That is the one sin for which there is no forgiveness.'

Ten minutes later, Caley jogged into her office where she found William sitting in her chair, his feet resting on her desk and two mugs of coffee beside his size twelve shoes.

'I managed to decipher your text; basically I was late and consequently, you were bored.'

William laughed and removed his feet from her desk. 'Pretty much.'

Caley grinned and gestured for William to move out of her chair.

'Sorry I'm late, not that it's a surprise I'm sure.'

'I know you too well for it to be a surprise,' William teased as he swung his legs over Caley's desk and collected his mug of coffee en route.

'Thanks for the coffee too,' Caley added as she gulped a mouthful down.

'Well, I figured, seeing how well I know you, that you'd have a half-drunk cup of coffee at home which you would have been forced to abandon when my text made you realise that you were late.'

Caley laughed. 'You've got me there!'

'So, what are our plans for today?' William asked, leaning against the office door as he addressed Caley, who was standing opposite him on the edge of her desk.

'I thought we could forget about Genesis and everything else for a while, and just address the case as if it was just that – a case.'

William nodded and drank some more of his coffee.

'How about we start at Domsville Park?'

'Sounds good to me,' William agreed. 'I know we're forgetting Genesis for now, but not only is Domsville Park where Andrew was attacked, it is also where Baxter was killed.'

'I know. It seems too much of a coincidence doesn't it? I was thinking that we could interview the people in the businesses around the park. Maybe they know something.'

'It would be helpful to track down some of the people who were in the park at the time too.'

Caley nodded. 'Maybe we could meet in the park tomorrow morning to do that; we'll catch the people who usually come in at that time then.'

'Definitely, as long as you get there on time,' William laughed.

Caley kicked him playfully and William frowned. 'Don't forget who made your coffee.'

Caley laughed. 'We'd better get going. Let's see if we can find out why Domsville Park is so important.'

William gulped down the rest of his coffee before answering. 'Maybe it's the centre of the universe.'

'Just think, if Domsville Park is *actually* the centre of the universe, then right now we are stood right in the earth's core,' William mused.

Caley looked at him in disbelief. 'Sometimes I wonder how I'm still sane, working with you all day long.'

'Who said you were sane?' William muttered in reply.

Caley and William were standing in the middle of Domsville Park, beside the boating lake, scanning the surrounding area.

'So there's the station,' Caley pointed to the police station where she and William worked, which was stood directly behind them, over the road from the park gates. 'There are a few houses over there,' she continued, pointing to their left where a handful of terraced houses stood. 'However, the majority of buildings surrounding the park are all businesses,' she concluded, pointing to the rest of the buildings around the park's perimeter. The businesses looked like Victorian terraced houses and were identical in appearance to the cluster of houses; the only difference was that the businesses had signs over their front doors.

'So where are we starting?' William asked. 'And if you even dare to say at the beginning I *will* throw my coffee over you,' he added, referring to the cup of takeout coffee, which he had bought from the police station's vending machine.

'No you won't; you wouldn't waste your coffee,' Caley smirked and then added in a more serious tone, 'I thought we could start with the businesses.'

William nodded, 'Let's go.'

As they approached the first of the businesses surrounding Domsville Park, William asked, 'What are we going to say?'

'What do you mean?'

'Well, are we going to tell them that we are investigating Andrew's attack or reopening the Genesis case, seeing as we *are* from the Cold Cases Department, or are we just going to say that we're from the police and want to ask them a few routine questions?'

Caley stopped walking momentarily. 'I hadn't thought of that. I thought we could just wing it.'

William shrugged and took advantage of their brief pause to throw his empty polystyrene cup into a nearby bin. 'Why not? After all, "the best laid schemes o' mice an' men gang aft a-gley",' he quoted in his best, which was actually pretty terrible, Scottish accent.

Caley rolled her eyes and continued walking. 'You seem to be quoting people an awful lot more recently. Is there any particular reason? Are your own words not good enough?'

William grinned. 'It makes me sound intelligent.'

Caley snorted. 'If that is your aim then I think you need to quote people a lot more.'

Caley strode purposefully towards yet another one of the businesses surrounding the park.

'What are you waiting for?' she demanded of William, who was lagging behind.

'Honestly, I'm not sure whether these interviews are making our job harder or easier,' he replied, briefly pressing his fingers to his temple.

Caley sighed and William saw, with her guard momentarily down, the emotion in her face.

Inwardly cursing himself, William hurried over to Caley's side. 'Right, Favel and Sons. Do we think they're *the one?*' he teased.

Caley shook her head in exasperation, but William saw some of the worry slip out of her mind.

'So far we've got a few people who have no alibi, they all have easy access to the park, but I'm just not sure about any of them,' Caley mused.

'Well, let's get this interview over with, and then we can discuss it. What do you say?'

The reception area of Favel and Sons was painted in varying shades of what Caley could only describe as beige. Although she was sure that the paint tin was entitled 'café au lait' or 'butterscotch' or maybe even 'cinnamon'. There was a leather sofa stretched along one wall with several people waiting on it. The sofa was, naturally, beige, as was the carpet upon which Caley strode towards the reception desk.

The woman sitting behind the reception desk was slender, dressed in a beige (for what other colour would it have been?) suit, and had blonde hair which Caley could only describe as being *fluffy*. She was wearing apricot nail varnish, peach lip gloss and probably had a brain the size of a grape, or at least that was William's summary.

When Caley approached the desk, the woman stopped filing her nails and fixed her false smile on Caley. Caley thought the smile was actually quite creepy, but she was sure that others found it welcoming.

The woman barely hid her disdain for Caley as she interlinked her apricot-tipped fingers and smiled scarily at her. 'Do you have an appointment?' she asked, in a voice so sickly sweet that Caley didn't need much imagination to imagine it dripping with honey.

'No,' was Caley's brusque reply. 'I need to speak with your employer. Is he in today?'

'I am sorry, but I am not at liberty to divulge that information,' the woman replied, the artificial smile still in place, but her evident dislike for Caley showing in her eyes; she seemed to be eyeing Caley as if she was something she had just scraped off the bottom of her (undoubtedly beige) shoe. 'If you would like to make an appointment then I am sure that–'

'I am with the police and I need to ask your employer some questions,' Caley stated irately, pulling her police badge free from the pocket of her beloved leather jacket. 'I do not need an appointment, as *this*' – at this, she jabbed her badge ferociously – 'means that I can ask whatever I want to ask without asking *your* permission beforehand.'

The receptionist's nostrils flared and she stood up and placed her excessively manicured hands on the desk. She placed a hand on Caley's police badge, pushed it towards her and said, 'Mr Favel is extremely busy–'

'Madam,' William interrupted, strolling over to the receptionist and speaking in an extremely relaxed and suave manner, which he added to with his laid-back gait and charming smile.

The receptionist immediately stopped speaking and turned her attention to William. She, completely forgetting about Caley, fluffed her blonde hair with her hand and smiled (not the creepy smile that she had directed at Caley, but a genuine and slightly flirtatious one) back at William.

'Sir, can I help you?' she asked somewhat breathlessly, dropping back down into her chair.

William nodded briefly to Caley, who stepped to one side reluctantly, and stood where Caley had previously been standing, leaning over the desk towards the receptionist.

'I am with the police, you see,' he began, flashing his police badge to the receptionist, 'and I need to take up a few minutes of Mr Favel's time. It is extremely important and I'm sure you wouldn't mind,' he added, smiling charmingly at the receptionist once more.

The receptionist laughed, a high-pitched and artificial laugh that made Caley shudder, and fluttered her eyelashes at William. 'Of course,' she replied, picking up the phone beside her elbow as she spoke. Once she had hung up the phone she turned her attention back to William, who flashed his thousand-watt smile at her. 'Mr Favel will see you now,' she explained. 'If you'd just like to follow me,' she added, standing up and leading William and Caley down a spacious corridor and to the doors of the corner office. Her voice was as sickly sweet as ever as she added, 'If you need anything just give me a shout.'

'Thank you,' William replied, dazzling her once more with his suave manner, elegant tone and charming smile.

The receptionist fluffed her hair with her hand once more, before rapping her knuckles daintily on the doors in front of her. She then pushed the doors open and, with an elegant wave of her hand towards William and Caley, announced their presence to Mr Favel before leaving. She didn't leave, however, without one last flirtatious flutter of her eyelashes towards William.

'You loved that didn't you?' Caley muttered between gritted teeth as the receptionist glared at her and left the room, shutting the padded doors firmly behind her.

'Yes,' William replied with a smirk.

'Mr Favel,' Caley began, stepping towards the man in question, her hand outstretched. 'I am Inspector Arling and this is my colleague, Sergeant Aaron.'

Caley and Mr Favel shook hands firmly with one another.

'Please take a seat and feel free to call me Max; I get called Mr Favel all day long by junior associates and hare-brained receptionists,' Max smiled and offered two chairs to Caley and William.

'Thank you,' Caley replied, sitting down as she spoke.

'Now, what exactly is this all about? My receptionist wasn't very clear on the phone.'

109

'We're just making some routine enquiries into an incident that happened in Domsville Park,' Caley explained.

'I see. Well, of course, anything I can do to help ... After all, I am always complaining that people aren't compliant enough with the police force. I am happy to do anything I can to aid your investigation and any other police investigation for that matter.'

'It would help matters, thank you,' Caley replied.

'If only more people had that attitude,' William added, having gotten comfortable in the chair beside Caley.

Max Favel had steel grey hair and an expensive suit to match. His face was lined and his eyes had a cunning gleam to them. Although he smiled generously and frequently, his smile didn't seem to reach his eyes, which were a cold shade of blue and it seemed to be merely a façade. His personality was the sort that made you wonder what about him was genuine and what wasn't. At the end of a conversation with Max Favel, you were often left wondering if you really knew him at all and more importantly, if you really wanted to.

'Can I ask what department you are with?' he enquired.

'The Cold Cases Department,' Caley replied, lifting up her police identification badge for Max to see.

Max nodded slowly and William realised that this was an interview they were going to have to play carefully, not least because they weren't supposed to be there in the first place.

Caley smiled broadly at Max and he returned the smile. However, William observed that neither of their smiles were genuine. He knew that Caley's smile wasn't, simply because of how well he knew her, and he guessed that Max's wasn't, although he also guessed that he would probably never know. William also deduced that Caley and Max were both grinning so enthusiastically at one another that they looked as if they had slept with clothes hangers in their mouths, so that they both appeared to be truthful and open. This meant that they had no intention of being either of these things.

110

'Now, there's no reason to worry,' Caley began, the idiotic grin still plastered across her face. 'We're only here because we think that *you* might be able to help *us*. This is simply due to the locality of your business; as I mentioned earlier, the incident we are currently investigating happened in Domsville Park, which your business and your office overlooks,' Caley added, glancing out of the large window that spread across the corner on which Max's office was situated and provided a picturesque view of the park.

'I understand perfectly,' Max replied. 'Questioning me and of course any other members of staff at Favel and Sons is a logical course of action,' he added, inclining his head slightly. 'Can I inquire as to the nature of the incident? Obviously, being in the business of law myself, I am aware of certain rules, certain boundaries which may prevent you from sharing any details with me. However, seeing as how this investigation is a cold case, I don't think any of those rules apply. It might be helpful, you see, to jog my memory. I am, after all, very well informed of incidents such as these, especially one so close to home.'

Caley lightly nudged William's foot with her own. 'It's an excellent idea, sir, and one we may exercise if necessary. However, at this stage, I think it might be more beneficial for our investigation if you don't actually know specific details. Studies have shown that if the interviewee knows lots of details regarding the incident then their answers are more likely to be biased. This isn't intentional bias; it is merely down to the mind and the way it organises information and recalls memories. So I think at this stage, the less you know about the specific event the better really. This way the mind is more of a blank slate, so to speak, which is easier for the interviewer to manipulate. This is just part of our interview process, to aid us in our investigation. However, if you feel that you would prefer to know the details of the incident in question . . .' William tailed off, leaving the unasked question in the air.

Max smiled broadly and falsely once more. 'No, no, not at all. It is interesting actually,' he replied, addressing William, 'to get some insight into the police force and their processes and techniques. Obviously, I work alongside the police on a day-to-day basis, but I always find studies like that particular fascinating, especially ones that are psychological in nature.'

'I quite agree, sir,' William responded, as confidently and fluently as he had previously. 'I think that part of the fascination with the human psyche is its mystery. I mean, we are extremely unlikely to ever be able to fully understand the human mind and the way it works, and I must say that I personally think this is a positive thing. I think that to understand it fully would be to take away its main charm and maybe in a sense, its main purpose.'

Caley tapped William's foot with her own once more; this time as a signal that she was to regain charge of the situation. She adjusted her position in her seat slightly to gain Max's attention, so that she was sitting up slightly straighter and portrayed more of an authoritative appearance. She then began to question him. Her questions were fairly routine; she asked the usual questions of, 'Have you seen anyone acting suspiciously?' or 'Have you seen anything that you thought was slightly unusual?' These questions didn't get Caley very far and Max's answers mostly consisted of, 'If I had then I would have, naturally, in my duty as a law-abiding citizen and a law-enforcing businessman, informed the police.'

Caley then subtly found out whether or not Max Favel had an alibi on the morning of Andrew's attack, and on the night before Andrew and Caley found Baxter's body, and the morning that they found him too. She did so, however, without providing Max with any more details about the case, even a rough timeframe or approximate date, because she jumped around in time so much; she was enquiring about Baxter's death and Andrew's attack simultaneously. She also tried to ascertain whether or not he had a motive to either kill Baxter or attack

Andrew and whether or not he had any connections with the Genesis case, or even TLC. She then managed to get a list of people who might consider Max as their enemy and although he claimed that there weren't many people and that all of them will have been through his work, Caley thought that everyone Max had ever come into contact with would probably be on the list.

'Thank you very much. You have been a great deal of help,' Caley concluded twenty minutes later, having exhausted her list of questions.

'Don't mention it,' Max replied, which William thought was superfluous as Caley already had mentioned it. 'As I mentioned earlier, I am always more than happy to do anything in my power to assist law enforcement officers in their work. Although,' he added, 'it is rather difficult to tell if one has been of help or not if one does not actually know what one is supposed to be helping with.'

Caley smiled broadly. 'I understand, but we do know what we require help with and I can assure you that you have been most helpful.'

'Well that's marvellous,' Max replied, standing up as he spoke. 'And if that's all then allow me to show you out.'

Once Caley and William had left Max's office and he had shut his office doors firmly behind them, William muttered, 'Was that in case we had forgotten where the door was?'

'I think he just wanted to make sure we left,' Caley replied with a smirk.

'Well he's a jerk,' William stated.

'Definitely,' Caley agreed. 'A pompous, supercilious jerk.'

'But is he a murderer?'

'That is definitely the real question,' Caley mused. 'I didn't like him and I don't trust him, but that doesn't make him a murderer. By the way,' she added with a grin. 'Excellent improvisation!'

'Thanks,' William laughed. 'You did know that over seventy-five per cent of all statistics are made up on the spot, right?'

Caley laughed and they began walking back up the corridor.

Suddenly a phone began to ring, and Caley gestured for William to wait, retrieved her ringing phone from her pocket, and pressed it to her ear.

'Hello . . . Oh hi, what can I do for you? . . . No, we're out at the moment, but tell me anyway . . . Really? . . . No, that is helpful, very helpful . . . Thanks . . . See you later . . . Bye.'

William waited for an explanation while Caley returned her phone to her pocket, a slight smile on her face.

'Max Favel has just been upgraded. As far as I'm concerned, he's officially on our list of suspects,' she whispered, aware that they were still stood outside Max's office.

'I didn't realise we had a list of suspects, but why the sudden promotion? I mean, I didn't like the guy either, but–'

'That was Aziza on the phone,' Caley interrupted. 'I asked her to look through Malcolm Wood's files, just because I feel as if we're not really getting anywhere, and you'll never guess what she found? Malcolm asked to be represented by Favel and Sons.'

'But they didn't represent him, or I would have found that in his files when I glanced through them, before we met him.'

'I wonder why he turned Malcolm down,' Caley mused.

'What time is it?' Caley asked as she and William strolled through Domsville Park.

William lifted up the sleeve of his suit jacket slightly and glanced at his watch. 'Twelve o'clock.'

Caley nodded slowly. 'Do you fancy discussing our thoughts over lunch?'

William froze and began pinching himself repeatedly on his arm.

'What on earth are you doing?' Caley demanded.

'Pinching myself,' William replied, continuing to do so.

'I can see that, but why?'

'Because I can't believe that this is happening! Caley Arling is actually suggesting that we eat lunch!'

Caley punched him lightly on his arm and kept walking. 'We don't have to go if you don't want to,' she teased.

'No you said it now, you can't take it back. I'm sure our good friend Max Favel will tell us all about the consequences of a verbal contract,' William replied sarcastically, walking alongside Caley.

Caley laughed. 'I think it would just be easier to go for lunch.'

They walked through the park for a while without speaking; the only sounds were twigs snapping and leaves crunching underneath their feet.

'It's a red carpet especially for me,' William teased, breaking the silence, as he pointed at the carpet of deep-red autumnal leaves they were walking on.

Caley grinned and deeply breathed in the crisp autumn air. 'I love this park,' she smiled.

'It does have everything . . . including a golf course for Favel and his chums,' William laughed, pointing to the park's golf course as they passed it.

'It's even better first thing in a morning,' Caley commented a few minutes later as they neared the park gates.

'Well, I guess we'll find out tomorrow,' William replied with a shudder at the thought of rising so early, referring to their plan to meet at Domsville Park in the morning to see and hopefully talk to some of the people who were usually there at that time. After all, someone must have seen something.

10

The Little Black Book

'I have worked with you too long to still be amazed by how much you can eat,' Caley stated as she watched William eat in astonishment.

William shrugged while he swallowed and then smirked as he added, 'Yet I still have such an impressive physique.'

Caley laughed loudly and sardonically in response.

'So, now we've eaten shall we get down to work?' William asked when he had finished, rubbing his hands together in anticipation.

'Definitely,' Caley replied. 'I think we should start by formulating our opinions of Max Favel.' She smirked, fully aware of William's opinions of him, not that she was overly fond of him herself. She then reached into the thin briefcase, which she used for work, and produced a black leather notebook. 'This,' she began, slamming the notebook onto the coffee table between her and William, 'is my little black book.'

William surveyed the notebook with a grin. 'I haven't seen this in years,' he exclaimed. 'Since I first joined the Domsville force and started working for you.'

Caley grinned. 'I still use it on cases, but I've just never needed to share its contents with you until now.'

Caley's 'little black book' was a black, leather notebook,

which she used to make notes on cases, in particular on suspects in cases. The notebook contained information about the suspect, why she suspected them and evidence against them. She had an entire crate full of them in her apartment, as she used a new one for each new case, each one identical to the last. She then labelled the covers with the case name, the date and any necessary and additional information, and stored them. She wasn't sure why. It was a habit she had gotten into when she was studying, when she had taken up on some of Andrew's advice on note-making.

'Max Favel,' Caley read aloud as she wrote his name in her book. Once she had jotted down some basic notes on him and her impressions of him, along with the fact that Malcolm requested that Favel and Sons represent him in court, which seemed too much of a coincidence to miss out, she passed the notebook to William to read through. 'See what you think,' she commented as she slid the book across the highly polished table to him. 'And feel free to make any *appropriate* suggestions.'

William grinned. 'You say that as if I'm likely to make *in*appropriate suggestions.'

Once William had passed the notebook back to Caley with his nod of approval, she scanned it through briefly and, with a sigh, used a rubber to get rid of the definitely inappropriate comment that he had added in pencil, in his distinctive italic handwriting, which evoked envy in Caley, whose own handwriting, William claimed, would be a disgrace to a four year old.

'So, seeing as we're going back to basics, what are the three main factors when considering suspects?'

'Means, motive and opportunity,' William replied, counting them off on his fingers. 'Do I get a gold star?'

Caley, not even bothering with a reply, placed the end of her pen in her mouth as she thought.

'Opportunity,' William began, 'could stem from the location of Max's office; it's so close to the park and because of the time he usually arrives at work, it fits time-wise too.'

Caley nodded slowly, an indication that she was thinking, and scribbled something down in her little black book.

'What about motive?' William asked. 'After all, it is probably most important. Without it you would have a *pretty* long list of suspects, including every other numpty who works in one of the businesses around the park.'

Caley sighed and said, 'The main motives.'

William raised one eyebrow and replied bluntly, 'Sex and money.'

Caley grinned. 'Subtle and sympathetic as ever.'

William shrugged. 'Well, I suppose there are others: jealousy, which is linked to sex, revenge, usually linked to sex or money or both, and killing to keep a secret, usually money and sometimes sex.'

Caley laughed. 'Jealousy doesn't have to be linked to sex.'

'It usually is,' William replied, unperturbed.

'Okay, so how do they link Max and Andrew, or Max and Genesis?'

'I thought we were forgetting about Genesis?'

'I was going to,' Caley mused, 'but then I decided that it was too strong a link.'

'Money could link Max to Genesis,' William suggested. 'I imagine that Max has quite a lot of money and would do just about anything to acquire more ... or prevent himself from losing it.'

'What about drugs?'

'What *about* drugs?'

Caley rolled her eyes. 'Didn't you have a theory about Genesis linking to drugs?'

William snapped his fingers. 'I did!'

Caley laughed. 'What *was* your theory?'

William snapped his fingers again. 'I have no idea!'

'Excellent.'

'Wait a minute,' he murmured. 'I'm just thinking ... Got it!'

THE LITTLE BLACK BOOK

Caley rolled her eyes. 'Well?'

'I thought that it was unlikely that this murder was the result of a "family feud",' he began, using quotation marks to illustrate his point, 'and I thought that it could have been related to drugs. Drug smuggling or selling and an argument that got out of hand.'

Caley nodded. 'I think I like it.'

'I think that there was actually a compliment in there . . . you just had to dig to find it.'

Caley thought for a few moments before William suggested, 'Do you want me to ring Ethan?'

'Which one is Ethan?'

William raised his eyebrows in disbelief. 'The one that works in the bookies. That's why I was going to ring him about this.'

'I was kind of asking for that, wasn't I?' Caley laughed. 'Okay, so I'm guessing that Ethan works in the Drugs Department?'

'Yes,' William laughed.

'It sounds like a good idea,' Caley agreed. 'Meanwhile I will add some more notes in my little black book. I like Max for this; so far it all seems to be fitting into place, but I'll also make some notes on the other business owners we spoke to this morning.'

Fifteen minutes later, William strolled back into the café, his mobile phone pressed to his ear,

'No, I'm not actually free then, sorry. Were you thinking darts or snooker? You know I'd destroy you at both.'

Caley glared at him and made an aggressive, cut-throat gesture.

'Sorry, Ethan, I've got to go . . . Yeah . . . Okay then . . . See you later. Sorry about that,' he grinned as he strolled over to Caley, slipping his phone into his pocket as he did so.

Caley rolled her eyes. 'Have I *really* been sitting waiting for you for *fifteen* minutes while you arranged to meet up with Ethan to play *darts*?'

'Or snooker.'

Caley stood up. 'I need another coffee,' she stated brusquely and headed over to the counter.

'I'll have a cappuccino,' William called after her.

Approximately two minutes later, a large mug of black coffee in her hand, Caley sat down opposite William, who was contentedly sipping the froth from the top of his cappuccino. 'So did you find out anything interesting from Ethan?'

William nodded. 'They don't have any concrete proof, but they suspected that the Smiths and Joneses were smuggling drugs into the country and then selling them on. A lot of the family members had criminal records and they all had suspicions attached to their names, and a lot of them were related to drugs.'

'Well Markston *has* got a harbour,' Caley mused, referring to the town where the Smiths and Joneses lived.

'Ethan said that when they first set up shop, they bought and sold drugs on the streets.'

'Hardly uncommon in Markston.'

'Exactly,' William agreed. 'The competition was fierce and they needed to up their game. Ethan reckons that is when they merged.'

'Became Smiths and Joneses you mean instead of *the* Smiths and *the* Joneses?' Caley clarified.

William nodded with a slight smirk at Caley's phrasing. 'The thing that doesn't completely add up is how they organised it all. Ethan reckons that they were starting to get big; they were importing some serious drugs and they were getting good at what they did.'

'When suddenly Dominic's body turned up in their back garden,' Caley added.

William nodded. 'But Ethan says that they're sure that someone else was involved: the brains of the operation if you like. They needed someone to organise it all.'

'Not to mention, someone to clean up the mess,' Caley stated bitterly.

'There's a body count of three,' William agreed.

'Someone wanted it to be four.'

A large grey cloud hovered over the coffee table where William and Caley were sitting and silence rained down.

'There's also Malcolm to consider,' Caley added after a few moments. 'He asked for Favel and Sons to represent him in court, but they turned him down. What if it was because Max was the head of this drugs ... operation, and he knew that Andrew was overseeing Malcolm's case?'

'I suppose, it just seems a bit of a ... tenuous link, sorry.'

'No, you're right,' Caley sighed, 'but so far Max is still our most likely suspect for being the head of the drug smuggling, and if he was the head, then that means that he was responsible for Genesis.'

'And if Andrew thought the same way as us, then that explains why he was attacked.' William sipped thoughtfully at his cappuccino and Caley gulped down her coffee, unaware that she was burning her mouth as she did so, trying to divert her thoughts from her dad.

'Are you thinking what I'm thinking?' Caley asked after what felt like a lifetime of silence.

'I doubt it.'

Caley frowned slightly at William's bemusing response. 'Why?'

'Because I'm thinking about that woman over there,' was William's blunt reply.

Caley rolled her eyes, shifted slightly to look at the woman then shrugged apathetically. 'She's not really my type,' she commented as she turned to face William again.

William grinned. 'So what were *you* thinking about?'

'Max Favel.'

'Yeah, I suppose that would make sense,' William agreed.

'I think that he would be able to orchestrate the operation and it would tie him in nicely to Genesis; he's certainly got the brains to organise a drug smuggling operation like in Genesis, and we agree that whoever organised that, is responsible for the three murders.'

'Not to mention Andrew's attack . . . even though I just did,' William added. 'The only other problem being *why* he turned Malcolm Wood down. Maybe he just thought that TLC was too open-and-shut; that there was too much evidence against Malcolm, and it would ruin his sparkling reputation?'

Caley nodded slowly and gulped down the remains of her coffee.

'Are you finished already?' William asked incredulously.

Caley nodded and tilted her mug towards William to prove it.

William peered into his half-full mug and mumbled something which sounded remarkably like, 'Cast-iron mouth.'

'But the only link we have so far between TLC and Genesis, other than drugs, is if Max *was* at the head of Genesis and the whole drug smuggling thing. That would connect him to both, because he refused to represent Malcolm, who was convicted of TLC.'

'So if Max was involved with Genesis, that would provide him with a motive,' William stated.

'It would if Andrew had found out that he was involved with Genesis . . . not only involved but that he orchestrated the whole thing really and especially that he was the one who murdered Dominic and Daniel and more importantly, Baxter.'

William nodded. 'We already know that he doesn't have a solid alibi for the murder of Baxter or Andrew's attack, thanks to your subtle interviewing skills.'

Caley inclined her head modestly at the compliment. 'How would Andrew find out that Max was involved with Genesis, though? I mean, I can't imagine the Smiths and Joneses telling him, can you?'

'No, definitely not, especially considering they lied in the initial investigation.'

'Presumably under Max's – if the Genesis ringleader really was Max – orders,' Caley added.

'Presumably,' William agreed.

There were a few minutes of silence, except for the metaphorical sound of the cogs of both Caley's and William's brains working.

'I'm guessing that we need to have another word with Max,' William suggested after another sip of coffee.

'It's probably a good idea,' Caley agreed, 'but I think that we need to decide what to ask him first.'

'Yeah, that's probably a good idea, as opposed to my strategy of simply jumping in with both feet.'

Caley laughed. 'That sounds about right . . . except for when it comes to paperwork.'

William shrugged. 'I learnt from the master.'

Caley responded instinctively by kicking him under the table. 'I'm *not* as bad as you. For one thing I don't hate deadlines.'

'I don't hate deadlines. On the contrary, I love deadlines. I love the whooshing noise they make as they go by.'

At Caley's raised eyebrow, William added, 'Douglas Adams.' Then at Caley's bemused expression he shook his head and explained, 'Author of *The Hitchhiker's Guide to the Galaxy*.'

'That reminds me . . .' Caley exclaimed and suddenly reached into her work bag. She produced a book from her bag and slammed it down excitedly onto the coffee table.

William reached across the table without moving the rest of his body and retrieved the book.

'Honestly, your arms are so long that I'm sure that you're related to orang-utans,' Caley commented, which led to William's best impression of an orang-utan. Once he had finished his impression, he examined the front cover of the book.

'What makes a killer?' he read aloud. 'A little bedtime reading?' he asked sarcastically, placing the book back on the table.

Caley was about to respond when William interrupted, 'I know, it's from Andrew's office. I was just kidding,' he grinned, aware that this investigation was taking Caley's mind off Andrew, despite the fact that the case centred around him, and he hoped that his humour was making things better for her rather than worse.

Caley sighed exasperatedly. 'This is what I was doing this morning when I got your text: reading through this and trying to make sense of it.'

'Did you have any luck?'

'Not really,' Caley admitted. 'Andrew has highlighted, annotated and underlined as if it was going out of fashion, but I can't really see a pattern to the pieces of text that he has selected or make any sense of his annotations ... or at least the ones that I can read,' she teased.

'Tell me about it,' William muttered sarcastically. 'Can I have a look?'

'Sure,' Caley replied and slid the book, which she had been flicking through while talking, back across the table to William.

After about five minutes, William stopped reading and put the book back on the table.

'What's the matter?' Caley asked. 'Have you given up already; are there not enough pictures for you?' she taunted.

'As a matter of fact, I think I've cracked it,' William replied in a mock-superior voice. 'But if you're not interested ...'

Caley laughed. 'I apologise. Go on.'

'Well, Andrew has highlighted sections all through the book that describe a killer, but not just any killer – our killer.'

Caley leaned over and pushed the book back to William. 'Read me some of it; show me what you mean.'

William flicked through the book until he settled on a page and began reading aloud: 'This type of killer is extremely organised. He, or she, is meticulous and will orchestrate operations and crimes easily and effectively. They will have a high-powered and controlling job where they often show their authority, which they will do frequently.'

Caley grinned. 'Keep going,' she encouraged.

William found a different page and once more read extracts

aloud. 'Although you may think that this type of person would get someone else to kill for them, as the previous type will, they will kill themselves to exercise their authority and maintain their control.' William then continued from a page later on in the book. 'This type of killer will be supercilious as they feel that others are inferior to them and will often treat people they feel are beneath them, often people who work for them or underneath them, in a degrading way.'

'What do you think?' William asked, snapping the book shut.

'I think you're right; you've cracked it. You've found our killer . . . and I think that this time I'm not the only one who's thinking of Max Favel.'

'Only because that woman has left,' William grinned.

11

All Roads Lead to Golf

Caley ran towards Domsville Park gates, partially because she was ten minutes late and partially because she could hear William singing at the top of his voice; not just singing, but singing Bonnie Tyler's 'Holding out for a Hero' – in a Welsh accent. When she reached the park gates she saw William leaning against a nearby tree and realised, mortified, that he was not only singing but dancing too – very badly.

Caley stopped him in his tracks, literally. 'What are you doing?' she demanded.

'Amusing myself while I waited for you,' he smirked.

Caley's reply was to simply stare incredulously at her colleague for a few moments, his smirk still plastered across his face, until turning around and walking away muttering to herself. William laughed and followed her down the footpath, which weaved around Domsville Park, calling after her.

Caley rolled her eyes, but slowed down her strides slightly to match William's pace.

'So where are we starting?' he asked.

Caley shrugged. 'I'm not sure yet. We agreed that we wanted to talk to people who usually come in at this time. I thought that we could just walk around the park, get more of a feel for it and see if there's anyone we want to talk to.'

William nodded in agreement and then asked, 'Does this mean that you haven't been for your morning run today?'

'I woke up early and was going to come, but it was really dark and I just didn't have the energy,' Caley admitted. 'I did go to the gym instead, though.'

'Slacker,' William muttered sarcastically. 'Anyway, don't you usually come in at this time?'

'Yes, but I don't walk around making notes about everyone who passes me,' Caley replied, as if William's question was completely ridiculous, 'I'm usually concentrating on other things.'

After about five minutes, a dog came running around the corner, straight towards them. William heard a woman shouting 'Honey!' repeatedly and he deduced that she was calling the yellow Labrador running towards them. William stretched his hand out towards the dog, who bounded towards him excitedly, and then he deftly grabbed its collar while stroking it; the dog was enjoying being fussed over so much that she didn't seem to notice that William had hold of her collar.

'Thank you,' a breathless voice called out, as the woman approached where William was crouching.

'It's okay,' William smiled, releasing the dog as the woman fastened the yellow lead in her hand, which matched the collar around the dog's neck.

'I don't know why I call her,' the woman laughed. 'She's completely deaf.'

The dog looked happily upwards at her owner, unaware of what was happening and wagged her tail enthusiastically.

'I haven't had her for very long,' the woman explained, 'and I was just letting her run around in a fenced-off area when someone else came in and left the gate open,' she added exasperatedly.

'I'm actually glad that you're here,' William replied. 'We're with the police,' he began, gesturing towards Caley and showing his police badge to the woman. 'It's nothing to worry about; we're just asking some routine questions following an incident that happened in the area.'

'Oh, well is there something I can help you with?' the woman asked, straightening up after crouching beside Honey, the latter whining softly in protest.

William briefly glanced towards Caley who took a step towards them. 'Do you come in the park regularly?' she asked.

'Yes, practically every morning. I've always had dogs and they need their exercise as much as I do,' she laughed.

'So you always come at this time?'

'Yes, it's the best time for me to come because I'm so busy. You know,' she continued, 'I don't work so people think I just sit around doing nothing!' She laughed incredulously, as if she had never heard anything so ridiculous. 'I wish!'

Caley smiled, which prompted a smirk from William as he could tell how forced her smile was. 'My sister always says the same thing. She doesn't work either, but she and her husband have three children and she's always busy with them. There's always some fete or parents' and teachers' meeting, or mums and tots, or something!'

The woman laughed. 'I feel the same way. Only, I don't have children; I have dogs!'

Caley laughed: laughter as fictitious as the sister she had just invented.

'I'm sure that if you had seen anything or anyone unusual or suspicious, that you would have already contacted the police?'

'Oh yes,' the woman replied enthusiastically, so enthusiastically that Caley initially thought she was being sarcastic.

Caley beamed enthusiastically in response. However, her enthusiasm was sarcastic. This remained undetected by the woman, but the same could not be said for a smirking William.

'We're interested in the sort of people who come to the park at this time. Obviously there are dog walkers such as yourself and a few joggers,' Caley added as a man jogged past them to the beat of his iPod. 'What other types of people come at this time?'

'Well, the majority of people at this time are people walking dogs or coming for a morning run, or sometimes power walking,' the woman replied with a laugh, as two women strode past them, arms swinging so excessively that they had to walk several feet apart so that they didn't hit each other, power walking around the park. 'But there are some other types of people, too. Occasionally mums or dads come in with children, usually small children: either in a pram or toddling around, but usually they come a bit later.'

'Right, so why do these people come with their children at this time?' Caley asked curiously.

'Basically because everyone else comes later. To avoid the rush,' the woman laughed. 'And if the children aren't at school and the mums don't work then they can come in at this time.'

'Right, but they wouldn't walk around would they?' Caley asked. 'Surely, they would go to the park or maybe the boating lake?'

'Usually, but sometimes they walk around the park; if they only have a little baby, and then they walk around the park with a pram.'

'I see,' Caley replied, realising that she was steadily veering off track. After all, she doubted that anyone would kill while they were accompanied by a child. 'What about other people who come to the park at this time regularly?'

'Well, there are the businessmen from around the park,' the woman suggested, gesturing to the businesses around Domsville Park: the likes of Favel and Son.'

'What about them?' Caley asked, expertly giving nothing away in her tone.

'Well, they usually come into the park of a morning to play golf. They should be here now,' the woman added, checking her watch before she spoke.

'Just businessmen from around the park, or do others come too?'

'Primarily those from around the park, but often others join them. Someone once told me that the best business is done over a game of golf. I don't understand what all the fuss is about personally, but they certainly take it very seriously,' the woman laughed. 'One time, the park was shut because the boating lake had flooded. You should have heard the comments! Do either of you play golf?'

Caley merely shook her head in reply, whereas the ever-eloquent William replied, 'I regard golf as an expensive way of playing marbles.'

The woman laughed. 'Who said that?'

William turned to look behind him and then turned back to face the woman. 'Me,' he smirked and then added with a laugh, 'G.K. Chesterton.'

The woman laughed again but Caley responded with a customary roll of her eyes.

'Well, thank you for your time and information. You've been very helpful,' Caley smiled. 'And sorry for keeping you, and especially you,' she added to Honey who was sitting patiently beside her owner.

'No problem,' the woman beamed. 'I'm only too happy to help.'

As the woman left in the direction from which she had come, an excited Honey bounding beside her, eager to be active once more, Caley and William continued along the path towards the golf course.

'She was loquacious,' William grinned.

'If you mean talkative why don't you just say it?' Caley commented sardonically.

William laughed. 'That is certainly interesting, though, isn't it?'

'It certainly is,' Caley agreed. 'Especially the fact that our dear friend Max never mentioned playing golf in Domsville Park of a morning, even when I questioned his whereabouts at this time on various days,' Caley commented, pointing Max out of a group of men standing on Domsville Park Golf Course, slightly further up the path.

When William didn't reply, Caley turned to face him. He was surveying the golfers with a look of absolute disgust on his face.

'The wind will change you know, and you will be stuck like that.'

'Is that what happened with you?'

Caley hit him on the arm and then asked, when he still didn't alter his expression, 'What is wrong with you?'

'Golf was originally restricted to wealthy, overweight Protestants, today it's open to anybody who owns hideous clothing,' he replied, adding, as he turned to face Caley, 'Dave Barry.'

'Is that what you're so disgusted with?' Caley asked incredulously. 'Not that one of these people is probably a killer, but that they have no sense of style?'

William adjusted the black leather lapels of his dark-blue suit jacket and replied simply, 'Yes.'

Caley rolled her eyes and began walking in the opposite direction of the golf course.

'Are we not going to talk to Max?' William asked, following Caley down the leave-strewn path.

'No, not yet,' she replied. 'He's bound to be suspicious after yesterday and I don't want to heighten his suspicions anymore . . . not yet anyway, not until we have more to go on.'

William shrugged. 'I suppose that would be the sensible thing to do.'

Caley laughed. 'That's probably why you don't want to do it then.'

They continued to walk around Domsville Park, discussing ideas as they went, and spoke to a few people, but didn't learn anything new. About ten minutes later, they rounded a corner and reached the golf course once more. William looked around him, clearly bemused.

'The golf course again?'

'Apparently so,' Caley replied, turning around and walking away in a different direction. 'I didn't realise the course was that big.'

As they walked away from the course they heard someone yell, 'Fore!'

William eyed the golf course with distaste. 'No wonder people don't understand golf; it's a game in which you yell fore, shoot six and write down five.'

Caley laughed. 'Go on then. Who said that?'

'Paul Harvey.'

Caley shook her head as they continued to walk. Crisp autumn leaves crunching underneath their feet and equally crisp autumn air swirling around them, causing William to constantly rearrange his wind-swept hair.

'Your memory is phenomenal,' Caley told him. 'If only it was for remembering useful things.'

Five minutes later, they found themselves at the fence separating the park grass from the golfing green once more.

'What is going on?' Caley asked exasperatedly.

'All roads lead to golf,' William suggested with a shrug as Caley marched away from the golf course for the third time in fifteen minutes.

'Come on, let's get out of here,' she called to William who was happily strolling behind her, heading towards the park gates.

'At least they'll be fit,' Caley commented, 'playing golf every day and on a course which is apparently so big.'

'You're kidding me, right?'

'Why?'

'Golf isn't exercise. It's a day spent in a round of strenuous idleness.'

As Caley strode out of Domsville Park gates, rolling her eyes at yet another golfing quote, William called after her. 'William Wordsworth!'

*

When Caley and William arrived back at the police station they went straight upstairs to Caley's office. As they reached their department door, however, a woman in police uniform stepped in their way.

'Police Constable Triggs,' Caley acknowledged her. 'What can we do for you?'

'Sir,' Triggs replied with a brief inclination of her head towards both Caley and William. 'I'm not sure whether I, well, whether I should be telling you this.'

'Telling us . . . what exactly?' Caley asked in bemusement.

'Deputy Chief Constable Steinmann is waiting in your office for you,' Triggs blurted.

Caley's brow creased while William grimaced.

'Thanks, Triggs.' Caley smiled as she headed towards her office, muttering to William as she passed, 'Just what we need.'

As Caley opened the door in front of her, William whispered to Triggs, 'We didn't hear it from you.'

Triggs smiled and walked away, back to her bullpen, happy that she had done the right thing.

Caley hesitated before she reached the door to her office, glanced behind her briefly at William, who winked reassuringly at her, straightened her stance, toughened her shoulders, steeled her eyes, shook her head back defiantly and opened the door.

Steinmann is a German name, which (like most German words) has a literal translation: stone man. Caley and William squeezed into Caley's box-like office and William struggled to shut the door behind them; three is most certainly a crowd in Caley's office. Steinmann was leaning against Caley's desk. He didn't so much as flinch when Caley and William entered, neither did Caley upon entering her office and seeing her superior officer already there waiting for her.

Steinmann took up a lot of space in Caley's already-small office as he stood in the most authoritative position he could muster. William imagined that he would have ordinarily sat in Caley's chair and therefore, had the position of authority in a more traditional way, but as William was fully aware, such an action was certainly easier said than done and William could not imagine Steinmann vaulting over Caley's desk. In fact, William *could* imagine such a scenario and expertly masked a smirk at this image.

Steinmann appeared to be as wide as he was tall, which was saying a lot as he was only a few inches under six foot. Although William was easily taller than him (and Caley was actually slightly taller herself), Steinmann's build made him look taller than he was and William would not have liked to get on the wrong side of him. Between his broad shoulders and steely glare, he certainly lived up to his name.

'Sir.' Caley was the first to break the silence. Her back was as straight as her poker-face expression and she acknowledged Steinmann with a respectful inclination of her head.

'Inspector Arling,' Steinmann replied. 'Sergeant Aaron.' His emotionless, dark-brown eyes, which were so dark that they appeared to be black and were impossible to differentiate from his pupils, hovered over William for a fraction of a second too long. William, however, stood his ground and although he didn't stand to attention as Caley had done, his gaze did not waver from Steinmann and he set his jaw defiantly; he had the impression that Steinmann would rather speak to Caley alone, but he was not prepared to let this happen. This he made clear. Steinmann acknowledged this with an extremely slight inclination of his head and William wondered why the language of politics was not spoken through words, but through inclinations of the head, firm handshakes and penetrating glares. Usually when people addressed police officers with their ranks, such as Steinmann had just done with Caley and William, it implied respect and importance. Steinmann's words had the opposite effect. Instead of reminding Caley and William how high up the police ranks they had come, the four words he had spoken and the way he had spoken them reminded Caley and William how low down the ranks they were in comparison to him. They clearly reminded Caley and William that *he* was the ranking officer, the superior officer, and the man in charge of their 'meeting'.

'I do not enjoy making these visits,' Steinmann began and in common with most things that he said, it was a firm statement. 'You know why I am here and I will not insult your intelligence by presuming that you do not understand my presence in your office.'

While Steinmann spoke, Caley was thinking about his voice and his body language, and how dominant he was in the room. Although he was not wearing a power suit or a high-ranking police uniform, it was clear that he was the superior officer: that he was in charge. When he spoke, he demanded everyone's attention. His voice was as hard as steel or perhaps, more accurately, stone. He fixed his equally stony glare on Caley and William while he spoke and although he spoke slowly and clearly, and left large gaps between his sentences and even his words, neither Caley nor William even thought of speaking.

William, however, while Steinmann spoke, was thinking about how Steinmann had described Caley's cupboard as an office, and wondering what make and model of car Steinmann drove.

'Superintendent Andrew Arling is subject to an on-going investigation: an investigation into his attack. I understand your personal interest in the case. I do not understand your professional interest in the case.'

Steinmann did not speak loudly, as one might expect, due to his demeanour, but he actually spoke relatively softly; this meant that the people he was addressing had to concentrate on what he was saying and only on what he was saying. His audience always consisted of rapt listeners. Even in press conferences, eager reporters and nosey journalists did not shout questions and hurl accusations at him. He spoke in such a way that his words could not be misconstrued. Caley and William, therefore, understood exactly what point he was making. Although they had already guessed the nature of Steinmann's visit as soon as Triggs had informed them that he was in the office.

'You are not spending personal time developing your personal interest, however, you are spending professional time developing your personal interest.'

Although Steinmann didn't make any specific threats or give any specific warnings – he didn't, for example, tell them that what they were doing wasn't allowed, and he didn't warn them that their actions could result in them being fired, or at least suspended, from their jobs – he made all of this perfectly clear.

'I do not want to have to repeat this visit,' he concluded, fixing his glare of stone on Caley and William in turn. 'Do we understand each other?'

'Perfectly, sir,' Caley replied, inclining her head once more.

Steinmann and Caley then turned to face William expectantly.

'Sir,' William stated briefly. He made no further comment and Steinmann kept his gaze on William for a few moments longer. William, as stubborn as ever, didn't add anything further, but kept his gaze locked on Steinmann's and his jaw set arrogantly. His hands didn't even leave his trouser pockets. Steinmann inclined his head slightly towards William, as if to say, 'So be it,' and Caley managed to refrain from rolling her eyes.

'I trust that the next case you undertake will be as successful as your last.' Steinmann spoke directly to Caley as he outstretched his hand towards her.

Caley shook his hand firmly with a final inclination of her head in acknowledgment of Steinmann's praise. Steinmann then shook William's hand, equally as firmly, with William feeling as though he was gripping a block of granite, and then exited without another word.

'That was stressful,' Caley sighed deeply.

'I know, to send in the big guns . . . must be serious,' William mused.

'That's the second time we've been told to stop investigating Andrew's attack by a senior officer.'

'This was a formal warning, too,' William added.

Silence filled Caley's office, not that there was a lot of space for it to fill, as they both dwelled on the seriousness of what had just happened and the consequences of their actions if they, foolishly, decided to continue with their investigation.

'We are going to keep investigating, though, right?'

'Of course,' Caley replied simply.

William raked a hand through his hair and then automatically straightened it back out with his other hand.

'We should probably clear this lot away,' William suggested, gesturing to all of their information on the case.

'Good thinking,' Caley agreed. She glanced at her watch. 'That lot dealing with Da . . . Andrew's attack will be over here soon to see if we have any information that's of use to them.'

'We could do with a box or something,' William commented and turned to leave Caley's office to find one.

'Hold on,' Caley replied before he could leave. 'We need to be more subtle from now on.'

William grimaced. 'Subtlety never was my strong suit.'

'Really?' Caley asked sarcastically and then added in a more serious voice, 'It was never mine really either.'

William laughed. 'What are we doing?'

Caley laughed, too - she found that laughter often hid her true feelings better than a blank expression, and it did more to take her mind off her worries – and then suddenly clicked her fingers. 'Triggs.'

William, a bemused expression on his face, clicked his fingers together too and called out, 'Poker.'

'Poker?' Caley asked curiously.

'Triggs?' William replied simply.

'Police Constable Triggs,' Caley explained and then looked to William for an explanation of his outburst of 'Poker'.

William shrugged. 'First thing that came into my head.'

This time Caley didn't refrain from rolling her eyes. 'Do you have Triggs' number?'

'Yes, actually I do,' William replied, retrieving his mobile phone from his pocket. 'I'm not sure why,' he mused.

'It doesn't matter why,' Caley sighed. 'Just send her a text and get her to come in here . . . and see if she can bring a box or two for us to use.'

Before a minute was up, Caley and William heard someone knocking on their door and a beaming Triggs stuck her head around it.

'Can I come in?' she asked.

William grinned and opened the door wider then wedged his foot in front it so that it remained open. Triggs stood in the doorway, one cardboard box underneath each arm. Her usual grin was plastered across her face; William thought that she looked as if she had hooked the corners of her mouth onto her ears. He loved her for it, though.

'What are these for?' she asked.

'We're relocating,' William replied, while Caley thanked Triggs, took the boxes from her and began filling them with pieces of paper, files, folders and various other knick-knacks from her office, accumulated while investigating Andrew's attack.

'Oh,' Triggs replied, her confusion evident.

'It's hard to explain, but we're officially stopping our current investigation.'

'That's a coincidence, seeing as how you've just had a visit from Deputy Chief Constable Steinmann,' Triggs grinned.

'It certainly is,' William replied, taking a full cardboard box from Caley and resting it on his hip, underneath his arm.

'What about, unofficially?'

'If I told you, I'm afraid I'd have to kill you,' William replied with a wink, 'and that would be a shame.'

Triggs laughed again.

'Could you do me a favour?' William asked her as Caley finished packing the second box.

'It depends what it is,' Triggs replied with a laugh.

'Could you get hold of the medical analysis of Superintendent Andrew Arling and email it over to me?'

Triggs hesitated slightly.

'Don't worry. It will be easy to do and you won't be doing anything wrong,' William reassured her. 'You can access it easily from your computer and nobody will even notice. Besides, if they do I'll just say that I ordered you to do it as your superior officer,' William grinned. 'I won't let you take the fall.'

Triggs beamed sunnily once more. 'Okay then. I have your email address. I'll get it for you straight away. Although . . . couldn't you just access it yourself?'

'Yes, but let's just say that our recent visit from Steinmann wasn't a social call. It's complicated-'

'It's fine,' Triggs interrupted happily, 'I'll do it, I just wondered.'

Thanks,' William smiled. 'Now I definitely owe you one.'

'Why can't we take my car?' William whined.

'Because we have to put these boxes somewhere,' Caley replied, loading the two cardboard boxes into the boot of her car. 'It's not my fault that your car is so small that there's nowhere to put them.'

William scowled and sulkily climbed into the passenger seat of Caley's car. Caley laughed, slammed the boot shut and slid into the driver's seat.

'Where are we going?' William asked as Caley started the engine.

'I was thinking of the hospital,' she replied, reversing out of the parking space.

'Good idea,' William replied with a candid nod of approval.

As Caley sped out of the car park, she asked, 'What if anyone comes looking for us? I didn't think to tell anyone that we were leaving. That's going to look really suspicious if Steinmann checks up on us.'

'Don't worry,' William replied. 'I'm in control.'

'And that's not supposed to worry me?' Caley laughed.

'I left a Post-it note on your office door saying, *Out on enquiries.*' William laughed and then winced as Caley almost collided with a lorry. 'Why do I let you drive?' he muttered to himself as he released his grip from his seat and his knuckles gradually returned to their usual colour as opposed to ghostly white.

'Stop complaining!'

'Well then concentrate on the road!' William complained in return. 'Your driving is either going to send me prematurely grey or kill me!'

Caley laughed and swung the car into the hospital car park. 'Stop being such a woman!'

12

The Sword of Rebellion

Andrew felt as if he had been sitting in his armchair for an eternity. He had been left for too long with only his thoughts for company. He thought about his family, whom he could hear as if from a radio: slightly distorted and he had the ability to tune in and out. In normal circumstances, Andrew would have been glad to be able to tune out of his family and their conversations, but this wasn't a normal circumstance. No matter how hard he thought, however, he still hadn't figured out what exactly his current circumstance was. His thoughts also concentrated on Genesis and the fate of Baxter.

In the silence, Andrew's thoughts began to develop and he often sat for hours at a time (or at least he guessed that it was for hours, as he had lost complete track of time) trying to remember what had happened to him. This was what he was currently doing. His head was leant back against the armchair, his eyes were shut and his fingers were spread out along the edge of the arm of his chair. He was completely relaxed. He emptied his mind of all thoughts and worries, well, at least as much as he was able to, which was actually a lot more than usual.

Watching the memories play out in his mind was bizarre; it

was like watching a film or dreaming or, better still, remembering a dream. Everything about Andrew's life at the moment felt like a dream. His memories were distorted, the faces of people blurred and they seemed to belong to someone else. But although he could recall images, he didn't seem to actually be able to remember them.

He walked down corridors of his imagination in a dream-like trance. He could see the familiar gates of Domsville Park and stopped to look around. He couldn't see himself. Why couldn't he see himself? He furrowed his brow, but the image began to slip away from him and he began to tune back into his surroundings; he started to hear Margaret's dominant voice and he could hear Caley and Aziza too.

Andrew quickly relaxed; he loosened his firm grip on the arm of his chair, released his clenched jaw and cleared his mind. The image sharpened slightly again, although it was still blurry, but now no more so than before. He stood watching as two women jogged past and through the park gates, talking breathlessly and laughing carelessly. Andrew looked down at himself to see if he was wearing his running clothes. Maybe he was going for his morning jog with Caley? He was wearing his running clothes, but he was also wearing . . . a pair of brown leather shoes. Andrew exhaled air angrily as his hatred of the shoes augmented. He then sighed deeply to calm himself. Once more the image around him became slightly more focused and Andrew knew that what he was wearing in the dream, he was wearing in . . . his living room – for surely that was a dream too? This gave him no clue as to what he was doing at the park.

He suddenly noticed that it was raining and the reason that he hadn't noticed before was that he wasn't getting wet. He looked upwards, towards the heavy grey sky and frowned. Why wasn't he getting wet?

He was about to leave the park entrance and take a walk around the park to see what he could find, to see if he could recall any useful memories, or any memories at all, when Caley jogged around the corner. She was wearing her running clothes too and as she reached the park gates, she checked her watch. When she saw the time she grimaced and then looked around her. She looked straight at Andrew and he yearned to walk over to her, to talk to her, to embrace her, to even make her see him, but he knew that she had no idea that he was there. So he waited. He watched Caley check her watch anxiously several times and glance up and down the road. She often stared to her left, in the opposite direction in which she had come, and Andrew knew that was where his house was. That was where he usually came from when he came to the park, usually for his morning jog with Caley. He looked at Caley now. She was leaning against the park gates and looked perfectly at ease. She didn't feel the desperation he felt. He knew that he (the 'he' from the memory) wasn't going to come, but he didn't know why. She had to go and find him.

Caley glanced at her watch once more and shook her head with a laugh. 'Like father like daughter,' he heard her laugh.

Andrew shook his head ferociously and strode over to Caley. He stretched his hand out and tried to touch her arm, but he went straight through her, like ghosts do in films. Andrew furrowed his brow and began yelling at Caley. 'Come on! We have to go! I'm not going to come, you need to find me! You need to help me!'

As Andrew uttered the words, 'Help me,' Caley suddenly frowned. She furrowed her brow and Andrew felt as if he was looking into a mirror. He peered over her arm as she looked at her watch again and saw that it was quarter to seven. He knew that they were supposed to meet at half past six.

Caley pushed herself away from the park gate on which she had been leaning and began striding purposefully down the path, which wove all around the park. Andrew strode alongside her, growing frantic as he did so. Caley stopped when she reached the bandstand at the edge of the boating lake. The rain was growing heavier and Andrew could hear the bullets of rain hitting the roof of the bandstand. He watched as Caley climbed up the steps and looked around it. It was empty. She rummaged into the pocket of her trousers then produced a mobile phone from it. Andrew realised that she was going to call him, he realised that she had gone to the bandstand because she didn't know where he was. She thought that he might have been waiting at the bandstand because it was dry.

'But I wouldn't do that,' Andrew whispered. He could hear the frantic edge to his voice. He was scared. He didn't know what had happened to him. He didn't know where he was. He knew, however, that he was about to find out and he wasn't convinced that he wanted to know.

Caley was just about to dial a number into her phone, presumably Andrew's number, when a woman screamed. Both Andrew and Caley tensed momentarily and then dashed towards the source of the noise. Andrew relaxed; it was only a woman whose child had gotten too close to the water. Andrew rolled his eyes. 'Children,' he muttered, thinking that the parents were often just as bad, if not worse.

Caley relaxed too when she discovered the source of the scream, at the same time as Andrew. She was about to retrieve her mobile phone from her pocket once more, where she had stashed it when she hurried to investigate the woman's scream, when she froze.

Andrew watched her like a hawk, although his eyes appeared to be less like a hawk's and more like those of a rabbit startled by car's headlights. He watched as Caley sprinted over to a bush beside the boating lake. Bewildered, he ran after her. He saw her run into a bush beside the water. It was only when he got closer to the bush that he saw a pair of shoes sticking out of the bush. The shoes were the same pair that were sitting in his living room. Andrew shook his head violently.

Caley stood beside the bush, her phone pressed to her ear. Andrew could hear her barking her location down the phone, but her words didn't register. He forced his way into the bush and immediately wished he hadn't. His blood froze. He had found himself ... lying on the floor face-down in a pool of blood. He had seen scenes like this before, too many times before. Forcing himself to stay where he was, he looked around him frantically, desperate to find a clue. He didn't even know what he was looking for. Out of the corner of his eye, Andrew saw someone walking away from the clearing. It looked like a man, but his outline was blurry as if it was a memory, as if it wasn't happening in the same time as everything else. A memory inside a dream? Andrew shook his head and squinted at the man. The man was pulling something behind him, something which looked like a dark-green golf club bag. Andrew froze. He slowly turned to look down on his own body. He could feel himself being pulled away, like being roused from sleep and pulled from that dream, but he forced himself to move closer to the ground. The blood was on his head. He had been hit on the back of his head, and he didn't have time to examine the wound properly, but he would bet money on the fact that he had been hit ... with a golf club.

Andrew opened his eyes and found himself back in his living room; the shoes he had just seen sticking out of a bush were lying a few feet away from him. He felt a tear roll down his cheek. He had presumed the worst, or what he had thought was the worst, that he had gone mad or that he was ill. He had not guessed, even for a second, that he was dead.

Andrew saw the photograph of his family beside him and began to cry.

'You have mail,' William imitated the automated voice of his laptop. 'You have mail,' he repeated. 'You have – Ow!' he complained as Caley hit him on the head with a bottle of water.

'Is it from Triggs?' Caley asked, struggling to hide the interest in her voice.

'Maybe. Maybe not,' William replied sulkily, trying to make her smile.

William's 'ploy', however, didn't work.

'I'm going for a coffee. Do you want one?' Caley suddenly asked, jumping out of her seat.

'Yes please,' William replied hesitantly, glad of the opportunity to read the medical report alone, but slightly confused by Caley's reaction. She wasn't usually one to delay doing something. William frowned as he considered the possibility that Caley was hiding her true feelings more than he had realised.

When she returned to the room five minutes later she asked, in a voice that made William wonder if she had been debating whether or not she wanted to know, 'What does the medical report say?'

William silently passed Caley the laptop, taking his coffee from her as he did so. Caley placed her own coffee on the floor and the laptop on her knee, visibly steeled herself, and began to read the email from Triggs.

Caley was quiet for a while as she studied the email, and William sat very still, the images from the report running through his mind, very aware that the same images were now running through Caley's.

'The shape of the wound is unusual,' she commented after what seemed like an eternity.

'Slightly rounded, almost cylinder-like, but in a short line,' William summarised the medical jargon.

Caley nodded slowly. 'Look what else is written here,' she pointed to the screen. 'It was inflicted by a golf club, the edge of a golf club.'

'You don't know that,' William replied warily, 'that is just one possibility.'

Caley frowned at him. 'Whose side are you on?' she asked.

William rolled his eyes. 'Yours. I agree completely,' he reassured her. 'I'm just saying that we shouldn't jump to conclusions.'

Caley nodded. 'You're right,' but her voice didn't sound convinced, and William eyed her warily.

'I know that we "shouldn't jump to any conclusions",' she said, mimicking his earlier comment.

'But . . . ?' William prompted.

'But . . . wouldn't that provide the perfect cover?'

William paled slightly as the idea dawned on him. 'It would,' he agreed.

'I mean, Max – and I'm not jumping to conclusions here – would have been able to blend easily.'

'Anyone who saw him would have assumed that he was going to play golf with the other morning businessmen golfers and he might well have done.'

Caley's jaw tightened slightly at this comment as she realised the truth behind it. She allowed herself a few moments to calm down and when she spoke again, her jaw was relaxed once more. 'It would provide him with an alibi, just in case anyone did suspect him.'

'Not that they would,' William commented wryly.

'Exactly,' Caley agreed. 'Or at least that is what he would have thought,' she added with a raised eyebrow.

'Of course!' William exclaimed.

Caley turned to him questioningly.

'We were contemplating how anyone would have been able to walk around Domsville Park with a baseball bat under his arm covered in blood, and no one would have noticed.'

Caley's eyes widened as she came to the same conclusion as William. 'He would have just put his golf club back into his . . . golf club bag,' she added hesitantly. 'Or whatever those things are called.'

William nodded. 'What about his clothes? Do you think that they would have had blood on them?'

'Possibly,' Caley replied. William could practically hear the cogs turning in her mind as she pondered the question. 'He could have got changed.' She suddenly shattered the silence as she found an answer to William's question.

'Where could he have gotten changed without drawing attention to himself?'

'In the bushes,' Caley replied, her jaw stiffened once more.

William closed his eyes momentarily. 'So, Max attacks Andrew with a golf club and then places the golf club back in his golf club bag. He then changes out of his clothes and into . . .'

'Golfing clothes presumably,' Caley replied with a shrug.

William nodded. 'He could have been wearing golfing clothes originally and simply changed into an identical pair of clothes in the bushes.'

'That would make sense,' Caley agreed.

'Then he just walks away and goes to play golf,' William added bitterly.

Caley closed her eyes and pressed her fingers lightly to her forehead. William had the opposite approach; he leapt out of his chair and began pacing the room, kicking any objects that got in his way, and a few that didn't.

Margaret and Aziza strode down the hospital corridor together, arms linked like teenage girls, sharing the latest gossip and trying to divert their thoughts and increasing worries from Andrew. When they reached the door to Andrew's room, Margaret smiled.

'Caley is here,' she announced to Aziza. However, her smile faded when she opened the door and saw Caley sitting in a chair with her head in her hands.

'What's wrong sweetheart?' Margaret asked, rushing over to comfort her. She sat in the chair beside her and wrapped a gently strong arm around her. Caley shook her head and straightened in her chair, shrugging Margaret's arm off her.

'I'm fine,' she lied.

Margaret simply stared at Caley, eyebrows raised, in a way that said, 'Don't lie to your mother.'

'Is William not here?' Aziza asked, her soft voice easing the tension in the room.

Caley turned her attention to Aziza. 'He was. He left a few minutes ago.'

'I'm back,' a voice called from the doorway. William walked into the room, looking more composed and smelling distinctly of tobacco.

'What's going on?' Aziza asked cautiously.

'It's not your father is it?' Margaret asked, frantically rushing towards the foot of his bed.

'No, no,' Caley replied, 'it's just a theory.'

Aziza and Margaret exchanged a puzzled glance.

'I don't understand why this is getting to me like this, I do this all the time. I do this for a living!' Caley exclaimed jumping out of her seat.

In the end it was William who explained the theory to Margaret and Aziza.

William strolled over to where Caley and Margaret were sitting and he and Aziza stood opposite them, forming a sort of circle. He frowned and reached for his cup of coffee. 'It will be cold by now,' he complained. He gulped some down and grimaced. As he replaced the cup on the floor, however, he grimaced again but this time more of a grimace of pain than disgust.

'What's wrong?' Caley asked.

'Nothing,' William replied, hastily stuffing his right hand into the pocket of his suit trousers, wincing as he did so.

Caley eyed him suspiciously. 'What's wrong with your hand?' she demanded.

'Nothing,' William insisted.

Aziza placed her hand gently around William's wrist, her small hand not quite reaching all the way, and gently tugged on his wrist, pulling his hand out of his pocket. William sighed and allowed his hand to be removed from his pocket. Aziza gasped when she saw it; the knuckles were bruised and crusted with dried blood, blood which had run down his hand. There was hardly any skin left on his knuckles and his hand looked extremely painful.

Caley sighed sadly. 'What did you vent your anger out on? And I *am* presuming, and hoping, that it was a "what" and not a "who"?'

William shrugged and mumbled, 'A wall.'

'I'll go and see if I can get some bandages or something for you,' Aziza offered, heading towards the door. She returned only a few seconds later with Rose. Rose had a small first-aid kit under one arm and a clipboard under the other. She placed the clipboard at the foot of Andrew's bed and ushered William into a nearby chair, where she administered to the injuries on his hand.

'Thanks,' William smiled gratefully, hiding his embarrassment from everyone but Caley, although this exception was not intentional.

'No problem,' Rose smiled. 'It's what I'm here for.'

'Idiots punching walls? I don't think so,' William smiled ruefully.

Rose laughed quietly and stood up. 'I was on my way here anyway,' she replied. 'I've just come to see how Andrew's doing.' She smiled at the protective gathering of people around Andrew's bed. 'Has there been any change?'

'No,' Margaret replied, biting her lip as she struggled to retain her composure.

Rose nodded compassionately, as if she felt the pain that Margaret felt, and perhaps she did. She then leant over to collect her clipboard from the foot of the bed. As she did, a stray strand of her deep crimson hair (the shade of red that conjured thoughts of expensive red wine) fluttered into her face. As she stood up again, the clipboard clutched under her arm, she used both hands to tuck the rebellious strand of hair back into the clutches of her ruby-studded hairclip.

While Rose checked up on Andrew, studying various monitors

and charts, jotting notes on her clipboard in indecipherable medical shorthand and observing Andrew himself, Caley and William were having a whispered conversation.

'We need to talk to Max,' William whispered to Caley.

Caley shook her head. 'You just want to talk to Max because you want to yell at him ... and possibly more,' she added in an undertone as her eyes caught the bandages around his hand.

'Don't you trust me?'

'Of course I trust you, but I also understand you. I feel the same way about Max; I barely trust myself with him. Besides, we need to do this properly. Think about it,' Caley urged. 'Max is bound to have lots of highly influential friends, including very expensive lawyers who will be able to set him free like that.' Caley clicked her fingers to demonstrate her point.

'Not to mention people in the force,' William added. 'Especially if we're right about Max being the one who got us formally kicked off the case.'

'That's another reason not to talk to Max until we're one hundred and ten per cent sure ... and no comments about my maths skills, thank you,' Caley commented at William's smirk. 'We're not even supposed to be investigating this case,' she whispered.

'You're not supposed to be investigating the case?' Margaret interrupted in a loud whisper.

'What do you mean? I thought that you were investigating Dad's attack officially?' Aziza asked, her whisper the only one so far that was actually quiet enough to qualify as a whisper.

Caley rolled her eyes. 'We're trying to have a private conversation here,' she whispered irately.

'Hence the whispers,' William pointed out sardonically.

'You call that a whisper?' Margaret demanded in her quietest voice, which wasn't actually very quiet at all.

'Kettle calling pot black,' Caley muttered.

'Stop ignoring the question,' Margaret demanded. 'Why are you not supposed to be investigating this case?'

'We were only investigating it on the QT to start with,' Caley admitted, still whispering. 'We're Cold Case, remember?'

'I can't believe you two!' Margaret exclaimed in the loudest whisper of the conversation so far.

'This is something that is very important to me,' Caley protested.

'To both of us,' William corrected her in a whisper.

Margaret smiled despite herself and then hurriedly turned the smile into a disproving frown. 'You could get yourselves into trouble.'

'You're already in trouble aren't you?' Aziza whispered gently, observing the guilty looks on both of their faces.

Margaret sighed exasperatedly. 'You are just like your father,' she muttered.

'Look, we're getting somewhere,' Caley persisted.

'How much trouble are you in?' Aziza asked.

When Caley didn't reply, William whispered, 'We've been officially kicked off the case ... and been given a formal warning.'

Caley elbowed him sharply in the ribs and William simply shrugged in reply. 'You would be rubbish under torture,' she complained in an angry whisper.

William muttered, 'This *is* torture. Her stare creeps me out,' he added, gesturing to Margaret with a slight incline of his head.

Caley grinned before seeming to remember the sombre atmosphere of their hushed conversation and returned to her previous straight face.

'So what are you going to do now?' Aziza asked.

'I am assuming that you are *not* going to stop investigating this,' Margaret whispered. However, she wasn't angry anymore; Caley and William's actions reminded her too much of Andrew's for her to be angry. She shook her head as she remembered how she had never been able to get annoyed with Andrew ... not properly anyway.

'That would be a correct assumption to make,' Caley replied stubbornly.

'So, what are you going to do?' Aziza asked softly.

'Erm,' Rose's hesitant interruption diverted their attention momentarily and all four of them turned their attention from their whispered conversation in the corner of the room. 'Sorry to interrupt,' she began with an apologetic smile. 'I'm all finished here, but I'll be around if you need me.'

'Thank you, Doctor,' Margaret smiled.

'Rose, please,' Rose returned with a friendly smile. She then turned and padded across the room, through the door and down the corridor; the sound of her grey plimsolls tapping against the hard floor could still be heard until the door clicked shut.

'What *are* you going to do?' Margaret demanded in a whisper, repeating Aziza's earlier unanswered question.

'Keep investigating,' Caley replied in a hushed but stubborn voice.

'Naturally,' William added in a whisper then he suddenly frowned, surveyed the room and asked in a whisper, 'Why are we still whispering?'

Margaret, Aziza and Caley each looked around the room, observed that it was empty except for themselves and Andrew, and shrugged. Caley sighed and headed towards one of the four empty chairs scattered around Andrew's bed.

'Come on, let's sit down and talk about this properly.'

William sat down next to her and stretched his long legs out in front of him. Aziza then sat down opposite him, and Margaret next to her.

'This is better,' Caley commented, discarding her leather jacket as she spoke and throwing it carelessly onto the floor, the heavy material landing with a thud.

'So you're really going to keep investigating, even though you have been told not to, and even though you could get into a lot of trouble if anyone finds out? I mean, you could get fired,' Aziza asked incredulously.

'Maybe we're going to keep investigating *because* we've been told not to, and *because* we could get into a lot of trouble,' William suggested dramatically, undoing his tie as he spoke. He then folded it neatly and laid it on the back of his chair. 'I hold it that a little rebellion now and then is a good thing and as necessary in the political world as storms in the physical – Thomas Jefferson.'

Caley surveyed him affectionately. 'You ruined that by folding up your tie; you should have thrown it to one side.'

William turned to face Caley, his expression aghast. 'That's a nice tie, thank you very much.'

Caley laughed and the bellowing expulsion contrasted with Aziza's gentle laugh, which resembled the sound of a wind chime in the soft breeze.

'Was that supposed to be rebellious?' Aziza asked, between peals of laughter.

'Thomas Jefferson?' Margaret asked with a grin. 'Very rebellious,' she added sarcastically.

William smiled slightly to himself, as the tension in the room visibly eased.

'You're lucky that he was quoting a politician as opposed to a poet,' Caley mocked with a grin.

'Poetry is man's rebellion against being what he is,' William replied and then added over the laughter, 'James Branch Cabell.'

'Surely a rebel should be someone more . . . dangerous,' Aziza teased lightly.

'Yes,' Caley agreed. 'Someone who does something . . . exciting . . . world-changing . . .'

'Ah, but what is a rebel?' William replied. 'A man who says no,' he added in an exaggerated masculine voice, about an octave lower than his usual voice, banging the arm of his chair with his fist.

Once the laughter had subsided, Margaret was the first to speak. Wiping the corners of her eyes with a lace handkerchief, she smiled, 'I feel like a teenager again, when I was dating your father,' she added with a laugh. 'He used to always joke that he never knew whether I was laughing with him or at him,' she smiled reminiscently.

'He still does,' Caley grinned.

Margaret sighed deeply. 'I can see that you have decided to keep investigating your father's attack. I understand and I just want you to know that I support you all the way.' She gently placed her hand on Caley's knee.

'We both do,' Aziza added. 'I just can't reach your knee.'

Margaret laughed and replaced her hand on the arm of her chair.

'Thanks,' Caley replied.

'If there's ever anything we can do to help . . .'

'We know,' Caley smiled.

Andrew smiled to himself as he sat in his armchair; he could hear the laughter of the people close to him, both physically and emotionally, and he was happy. He shared their joy. He was glad because he knew that this had not been easy on them. He still didn't know what had happened to him and although there was the lingering worry that he was . . . dead, he pushed it to the back of his mind.

'I know who did this to me,' he stated confidently. 'I *will* remember, I *will* work it out and when I do, this will all be over. If I am still alive then I can get justice for myself and send them to jail, where they belong. I can return to my family,' he added with a smile. 'And if I'm not,' he mused sombrely, 'then I will still find out who did this; if not for myself, then for them, for my family.'

Andrew's eyes settled upon the bag of golf clubs in the corner of his living room. They had been there for some time now and up until today he had no idea why they were there. He thought that he was losing his mind, that he was simply dreaming, imagining, that his mind was playing bizarre tricks on him. However, he had heard Caley and William (and Margaret and Aziza) talking about golf. He smiled. He was reassured that the golf clubs were there for a reason.

'They're not mine,' he thought aloud. 'I don't play golf.' This thought triggered another. 'Who played golf? I know someone used to play golf, someone I knew ... or perhaps someone I just met?' He shook his head. It was no use; he couldn't remember. He did, however, remember the man who appeared as what seemed to be a memory in a dream, the man who was walking away from his own unconscious body, with a bag of golf clubs in tow.

'In the dream I'd been hit with a golf club, I'm sure of it. Or else, why would the man be walking away from me, and not helping me? I'm still missing something.' He frowned. 'This is so frustrating!' He sighed deeply and tried from a different angle.

'Golf. Golf. Golf.' He repeated the word as the thought repeated in his mind. As his gaze wandered around the room, his piercing green eyes suddenly hit upon the watercolour painting of Domsville Park gates and lit up with excitement.

'Of course, there's an enormous golf course in the park. I see it all the time when I'm in the park.' He started then to think about Domsville Park and about his morning run with Caley. 'That person I know who plays golf,' Andrew mused, his brow furrowed in concentration. 'They played in the morning. Businessmen.' Andrew nodded slowly. 'Businessmen play golf in the park in the morning, in the park's golf course. People have asked me to join them before now, but I always turned them down, partially because I have no real interest in golf, but mainly because I go for my run with Caley at that time. I can't be in two places at once, and I would much rather be with Caley than with some supercilious morons playing a game of expensive marbles,' he mused and started to think about the morning that he had found himself in his armchair. He knew that he had gone for his morning run and he thought he knew that Caley had found him lying in the bushes beside the boating lake. He had met someone that morning. Whom had he met? What did they have to do with golf?

156

'The man walking away from me, if he did attack me, maybe I met him? Who *was* he? He has to be important. The golf course, he had golf clubs with him, maybe he was going to the golf course . . . and it was early in the morning, so maybe he was one of the businessmen. Yes,' he nodded, 'that fits . . . But it means that I *knew* him, I *know* the man that attacked me.'

This thought both hurt and confused Andrew as he struggled to remember something, anything useful. He only had more questions.

Why was he wearing brown leather shoes?! Andrew studied the bag of golf clubs and the hideous brown leather shoes on his feet in turn. He then turned over his hand and studied the word 'Genesis'. What was going on?

'It's Max Favel we're looking for, right?' Margaret confirmed, several folders spread across her and Aziza's laps.

'That's right; it's somewhere to start. He has opportunity, he has a link to TLC, and it's a hunch I have,' Caley replied.

'Well, you've now got a link to Genesis,' Margaret stated, handing Caley a piece of paper.

William read it over her shoulder at the same time as Caley read it.

'Favel and Sons represented Dominic when he was arrested ten years ago, when he was seventeen, for stealing a car,' William read aloud. 'What's this from?'

'Some notes on Genesis. It's only mentioned because either Andrew or David was looking into Dominic and Daniel's criminal records. They've got quite a list between them.'

Caley banged her fist on the arm of her chair in frustration. 'This is still all circumstantial.'

'Let's talk it through,' William suggested. 'If it was Max, he could have represented Dominic because he was orchestrating the drugs operation, or he could have come into contact with them through that.'

'It's one more link at least,' Aziza commented.

'We thought before that Max could have turned Malcolm down, because of the drug connection and the connection with Da-*Andrew*,' Caley corrected firmly. 'But maybe it was because he had already represented Dominic, and Andrew would have recognised his name from looking at Dominic's criminal record?'

'It's starting to sound less tenuous,' William commented optimistically.

'It still wouldn't stand up in court though,' Caley commented wearily.

'You think that Max was involved in Genesis?' Margaret clarified. 'You think that he was this ringleader that would have been necessary, that Ethan told you about?'

'Yes, we think that Favel was that ringleader for the Genesis drug smuggling and the murders, and we think that he still is,' William replied.

'Still is?' Aziza asked.

William nodded. 'Favel solved the problem that Dominic and Daniel, presumably, had caused. They probably wanted more money or more power so Favel killed them. He then killed Baxter to solve the problem once and for all. He wouldn't go to all of that trouble only to stop the operation – that was Ethan's take too.'

'Only that created another problem,' Margaret interrupted. 'Andrew.' It was impossible to miss the pride in her voice.

'Exactly,' Caley agreed.

'It's unlikely that after all of that work,' William continued, 'they would simply stop their operation. It had been extremely successful except for that one problem, which Favel thought he had dealt with and if anything, it probably made it even more successful because the others knew what happened when you messed with Favel; they weren't likely to demand more money or power after that.'

'It doesn't even have to be Max,' Caley sighed, 'but at least we have a theory, now we just need a murderer.'

A comfortable but rather sombre silence fell upon the room

as each individual was left to his or her own thoughts.

'I'm going for a cigarette,' William announced, standing up and heading towards the door.

Margaret pursed his lips disapprovingly as William passed her, and Caley expertly disguised a laugh as a cough.

As William headed towards the door, he turned and noted how tired and depressed they all looked. They had only just started the investigation really, and if they were going to succeed, then they would have to remain more up-beat and more focused.

'Don't worry, though,' William stated, turning to face them all. 'This isn't just a rebellion; it's a war and I for one will not be surrendering. I will not give up, even if it means looking death in the eye.' William was speaking in an unusual accent. Caley couldn't quite place its intended origin, but it was a deep and dramatic voice. 'I *will* find who did this . . . even if it's the last thing I do! For, as the wisdom of our ancestors declares through this old English proverb, when the sword of rebellion is drawn, the sheath should be thrown away!'

At the end of William's little speech, there was silence in the room.

'I was actually expecting a round of applause, possibly even a standing ovation,' William commented in his usual voice.

'Sorry, we're all trying not to laugh,' Caley told him.

'Were you talking?' Aziza teased, looking at William expectantly.

'If I stand up to push you out of the room, does that count as a standing ovation?' Margaret asked.

William flicked his hair extravagantly, straightened the lapels of his handsome crimson suit jacket and strolled out of the door, hiding his smile. It was a temporary solution at least.

'Make sure you don't stab yourself with your sword of rebellion!' Caley called after him.

Andrew studied the bag of golf clubs in the corner of his living room and then the brown leather shoes on his feet. There was a connection and he was determined to find it. As he sat in silence, brow furrowed (Margaret always joked that this movement activated his brain), he thought about that morning when he had found himself in his armchair, unable to move, unsure about what had happened, and he also thought about the dream he had recently had about Caley finding his body in the bushes by the boating lake. He wondered if that was what had really happened. That was when he remembered. He remembered the brown leather shoes and the bag of golf clubs and where he had seen them before. The person he had met in Domsville Park that fateful morning, for he was sure that he had met someone, had carried with them a bag of golf clubs just like the ones sitting in his living room. It was the same bag as he had seen the man, his attacker (he corrected himself sombrely) carrying.

Andrew turned his attention to the brown leather shoes. He had finally remembered. The brown leather shoes were the last things he had seen before he had woken up in his armchair.

13

Olive Branch

'That's a very vibrant outfit,' Aziza smiled as William strolled into Andrew's hospital ward.

William was wearing an aubergine-coloured suit, a white shirt, black leather shoes with a matching black leather shoulder bag, and a slim black tie.

'Thank you,' he grinned, sauntering over to an empty chair beside Aziza. 'Someone has to look fashionable out of Caley and me,' he added with a wink.

Aziza laughed and smoothed her pale pink pencil skirt down with her hands, with nails painted to match, and replied, 'Tell me about it.'

'Good morning, William,' Margaret called from behind her knitting.

'Morning, Margaret,' William replied. 'What are you knitting?'

'A jumper for Andrew,' she replied, staring at William as if he should have been able to tell.

Before William could respond, however, the sound of someone jogging down the corridor reached their ears. 'Here comes Caley,' he announced with a smirk, adjusting his deep purple cufflinks as he spoke.

A few seconds later, the door burst open and Caley jogged

into the room. She saw William sitting beside Aziza and, furrowing her brow, checked her watch.

'You're late,' William called across to her. 'As usual,' he added with a grin.

'Oh,' she replied with a frown. 'I thought I was early.'

'Did you really? Why were you running then?' William asked, placing his shoulder bag on the floor beside his chair as he spoke.

Caley furrowed her brow once more, this time in annoyance instead of out of concentration.

'Oh, for heaven's sake, would you stop doing that!' Margaret exclaimed. 'You are going to end up with more wrinkles than me by the time you are thirty!'

'That wouldn't take much doing,' William winked at Margaret. 'You know the first time I met you and Andrew, Aziza wasn't there and I thought that *you* were Caley's older sister.'

Caley grimaced and mimed throwing up, while Margaret replied, with a smile, 'Why *older* sister?'

Caley was standing in front of the door, her expression sullen. She was wearing a white shirt tucked into a pair of faded jeans, but her shirt collar was stuck up on one side, visible over her battered black leather, knee-length jacket.

'Honestly!' Margaret exclaimed. 'Sometimes, you look exactly like your father.'

Caley's frown deepened as she looked down at her outfit and seeing nothing wrong, shrugged, strode over to Margaret and threw herself down into the chair beside her.

'Did you get dressed in the dark?' Margaret asked, placing her knitting on her knee as she surveyed Caley's outfit with distaste.

'What's wrong with what I'm wearing?'

'It is less of *what* you are wearing, and more of *how* you are wearing it,' Margaret sighed. 'Your hair looks as if it has been electrocuted, and your shirt collar is sticking up on one

side. I understand that not everyone is interested in style,' she
continued, carefully brushing her hand over her cornflower
blue, cashmere blazer, her dainty sapphire earrings glinting in
the light as she did so. 'That doesn't mean that you shouldn't
wear it properly,' she concluded, reaching over to straighten
Caley's shirt collar, but Caley pushed her hand away irritably.
Margaret sighed and resumed her knitting.

'Are you two going to be here more often?' Aziza asked.

'Probably,' Caley replied, attempting (unsuccessfully) to
flatten her hair with her hand.

'We shouldn't really work on this over at the station,' William
added. 'Not that I don't enjoy taking risks,' he winked.

Caley rolled her eyes and raked her hand through her hair,
unintentionally adding to its volume.

Caley and William were discussing various theories, bouncing
ideas off each other in their accustomed way, with occasional
interruptions from Margaret and suggestions from Aziza, when
the door opened. Caley glanced up, disinterested, expecting to
see Rose or another nurse, or possibly one of Andrew's many
friends or colleagues, but she was shocked to see Taggart standing
in the doorway.

'Good morning, sir,' she announced loudly, alerting William
to his presence. She then strode over to Taggart and stood
directly in front of him, making small-talk, while William hastily
shoved his laptop and their notes into his shoulder bag. William
sighed in relief as he managed to get everything suspicious out
of sight, just as Caley stepped to one side, then he suddenly
saw Caley's little black book sitting on her chair. He quickly
caught Margaret's attention and gestured to the book. As quick
on the uptake as ever, she leant over Caley's chair and
straightened her leather jacket, which had been haphazardly
thrown over the back of the chair, swiftly picking up the book
as she did so. She then stood up, placed her knitting on her
own chair and walked across the room, expertly passing Caley's

little black book to William, who stuffed it into a side pocket of his bag, as she passed him.

'Good morning,' Taggart smiled as Margaret approached him. Taggart shook Margaret's hand firmly and offered her his sincerest condolences as he did so. 'I was going to bring flowers, but I thought that you were probably overrun by them.' Taggart glanced around the room and added, 'I can see that I was right.' The small hospital room was covered in posies, bouquets and baskets of flowers: from cheerful sunflowers to elegant lilies, and deep red roses to bright red tulips. 'I did want to bring *something* though,' he continued in his smooth and evidently educated voice, 'So I brought this for you. I hope it is to your liking,' he smiled, passing Margaret a bottle of expensive red wine. 'It is a favourite of mine and I always keep some in my house in case an appropriate occasion arises. Of course, one does hope that it is a more cheerful occasion than this.'

'Thank you,' Margaret replied, taking the bottle of wine and studying its label. She smiled appreciatively as she did so. 'Yes, this is a particular favourite of mine too. It is one of my many indulgences,' she laughed, straightening her blazer as she spoke, the many rings on her fingers catching the light as she did so.

'And mine,' Taggart replied with a smile.

As Margaret returned to her chair, the bottle of wine in her hand, Taggart caught Caley's eye and asked, 'Caley, would it be possible to borrow you for just a moment?'

Caley, hiding her instinctive grimace, nodded. 'Of course,' she replied, starting to follow Taggart out of the door.

At Taggart's question to Caley, William had protectively leapt out of his chair and stood at his full height of six foot. He didn't say anything, but simply looked at Taggart.

'Of course you are more than welcome to join us,' Taggart addressed William, inclining his head slightly as he did so.

Aziza hid a grin behind her perfectly manicured hand and exchanged a swift glance with Margaret as Taggart led the way out of the room, followed by Caley and flanked by William.

Once they were in the hospital corridor, Taggart waited momentarily for the door to shut and then spoke.

'I come in peace,' he smiled. 'My olive branch is in my briefcase,' he joked, gesturing to his brown leather briefcase. 'On a more serious note, however, I *am* aware that Deputy Chief Constable Steinmann spoke with you, both of you,' he corrected, acknowledging William as he did so. 'Just as I am aware of what he spoke to you about.'

'The same thing that you spoke to us about,' William replied. 'The only difference is that his voice is deeper than yours,' he muttered. 'And you sound more arrogant than he did,' he added even more quietly.

Taggart smiled and gracefully inclined his head towards William. 'You are right, of course. However, I am not here today to repeat those words of warning, nor am I here to monitor you, to see if you are still working on the case . . . which I have no doubt that you are.'

Caley began to speak at this point, but Taggart smiled and held up his hand slightly in protest.

'I would be disappointed if you were not still working on the case,' he continued.

William glanced at Caley with wide eyes and shrugged.

'Now I know what you must be thinking,' Taggart continued, 'but I was sitting in my office yesterday evening and I was remembering all of the times that I worked alongside your father, alongside Superintendent Arling. I remember that he always helped me when I needed it, I remembered what an excellent police officer he was and I recalled what excellent police officers you were too, both of you,' he added. 'I want to help.'

Caley and William simply stood in shocked silence for a few moments before Caley responded to Taggart's unexpected offer.

'You mean that you want to help us investigate Andrew's attack?' she clarified.

'Even though we're not supposed to be investigating it,' William added.

'That is exactly what I mean,' Taggart replied. 'Look, I know that this must be a lot for you to take in, but why don't I take you both out for lunch and we can discuss this further.'

Caley nodded slowly, thoughtfully, but William was still frowning. He eyed Taggart suspiciously.

'How do we know that we can trust you?' he asked.

Caley rolled her eyes, but Taggart smiled and replied, 'You don't. That is why I want to take you both out for lunch, to persuade you. I have some documents you might find interesting,' he added, gesturing to his briefcase: light brown to match his suit. 'So what do you think?'

'I think it's an excellent idea,' Caley replied with a grin, extending her hand towards Taggart, who shook it firmly and enthusiastically.

Taggart and Caley then turned expectantly towards William who was still frowning slightly, but he looked at Taggart thoughtfully and asked in a serious voice, 'Where are we going for lunch?'

Caley rolled her eyes once more, but Taggart laughed and replied, 'Wherever you want to go. Wherever you want to go,' he repeated as he shook the hand that William had proffered.

Once William and Caley had explained to Margaret and Aziza where they were going, and Margaret and Aziza had turned down Taggart's gracious offer of taking them to lunch too, they headed out of the hospital and towards the car park.

'What happened to my little black book?' Caley whispered, suddenly realising that she no longer had it with her.

'Here,' William replied, retrieving it from the side pocket of his shoulder bag and passing it to her.

'Shall we all go in our own cars and then we are free to go wherever we want to after lunch?' Taggart asked, stopping in front of a white Jaguar XF.

'We'll share,' Caley replied, gesturing to William.

'Are you sure?' Taggart asked. 'You are free, of course, to share my car.'

Caley shook her head gently and smiled, 'No, it's fine, thanks.'

Taggart started to reply, but was interrupted by William shouting, 'Bagsy we take my car!'

Taggart smiled, while Caley, naturally, rolled her eyes. 'Which one is your car?' he asked, surveying the car park and probably expecting to see a battered Vauxhall Corsa or possibly a Ford Escort.

'This beauty,' William replied, strolling over to his gleaming red Ferrari F430, which was parked a few cars away, and standing by it proudly.

Taggart hid his surprise, but not his admiration. 'Impressive! Especially on a police salary.'

'That's what everyone says about me,' William replied with a wink, adjusting the lapels of his aubergine suit jacket as he did so.

Taggart laughed, retrieved his car key from his pocket, unlocked his car and was about to get in when he suddenly stopped. He stared at William's car for a few moments, looking at it very strangely, then shook his head, laughing and finally got into his car. As soon as his car door slammed shut, Caley strode over to William.

'Stop rolling your eyes at me,' he complained. 'What have I done now?'

'For one thing you're wearing a purple suit!'

'Purple in more ways than one,' William replied, accessorising his words with an exaggerated wink and sliding into the driver's seat of his Ferrari.

Caley gritted her teeth, shook her head exasperatedly, rolled her eyes and then, laughing, slid into the seat next to William.

'Plus there's your registration plate.'

'Not that again!'

Caley shifted in her seat to glower at William. 'Did you see Taggart's reaction to it?' she asked, trying to prove her point.

William grinned and swung out of the car park behind Taggart, the powerful engine of his car roaring as he sped away from the hospital. 'Well I like it,' he replied obstinately and as he drove away, the registration plate of his car clearly read, *SEXY SGT*. 'Besides,' he added, 'I *am* a sexy sergeant.'

The restaurant that William had chosen was called The Olive Branch and as the name connoted, it was both friendly and Greek.

'I am guessing that you come here a lot,' Taggart laughed as the waiter addressed William by his name and asked if he wanted his usual table. This assumption was added to when the waitress serving them asked if William wanted to see a menu, or if he just wanted to order his usual.

Although hadn't replied to Taggart's comment, he hadn't thought a reply necessary, Caley had laughed and responded with the sardonic comment of, 'I wouldn't be too surprised; all of the restaurants, bars, pubs, cafés, and coffee shops in Domsville know William by name.'

Once they were seated at William's usual table in the corner of the room – a spacious table intended for two, to which the waitress had brought another chair to accommodate three – and had ordered their food, Taggart started the discussion.

'As I said earlier, I know that you are not supposed to be investigating the attack on Andrew, but I understand why you are. Not only that, but I want to help; I have always respected Andrew as a colleague and I hope, as a friend, and I know that he always helped me whenever I needed it. Now I feel that he deserves the same courtesy in his time of need.'

Neither Caley nor William replied while the waitress brought their drinks over to them, and some olives, Greek flatbread and olive oil.

'Thanks Alexandrina,' William smiled as she placed their starters and drinks down on the table.

Once Alexandrina had left, Caley sipped her black coffee,

nodded approvingly and then spoke. 'Thanks. Your offer is very generous and your help is definitely appreciated.'

Taggart smiled appreciatively.

'You said that you had some interesting documents to show us,' William reminded Taggart with his usual diplomacy.

Taggart laughed. 'That I did.' He began to reach towards the floor for his briefcase, but then remembered that he had handed it in when they arrived at The Olive Branch. 'I will just go and retrieve it,' he explained, standing up.

As he headed towards the entrance and the cloakroom to the side of the main doors, William leant slightly closer to Caley and whispered, 'Are we going to tell him everything?'

'I haven't decided yet,' Caley replied. When William frowned, she added, 'You still don't like him, do you?'

'I have come to the conclusion that my impressions of people are usually accurate.'

Caley rolled her eyes. 'He's offered to help us investigate this case, even though he won't get anything out of it, and at great risk to himself and his career. I think that we should be honest with him.'

Now it was William's turn to roll his eyes.

'He can't help us unless we tell him everything that we know,' Caley pointed out.

William sighed. 'I'm still not convinced.'

'Look, he was the investigating officer in the Genesis case, which we're sure is linked to the attack on Dad. Maybe he can help us with the case, look at it from a different angle, with closer focus on the Genesis case?'

'How can we find out about the Genesis case without telling him everything?' William asked and then quickly added, 'Wrap it up; he's coming back,' in a mumbled voice.

'Let's just improvise,' Caley replied.

'It's what we do best,' William muttered, sipping his Martini as Taggart reached the table.

Taggart slid into his seat and opened his briefcase on his lap.

'Here we go,' he murmured, mostly to himself, as he pulled three rather slim files out of it. He placed the files on the table and locked his briefcase once more.

Caley reached for the files and then hesitated slightly. 'I'm assuming we're okay to look at them,' she checked with Taggart.

'Of course,' he replied. 'That is what I brought them for,' he added, picking up his glass of white wine as he did so.

William placed his glass back on the table and retrieved a handful of olives from the small bowl on the table. He then popped them into his mouth one-by-one as he studied the files that Caley had placed in between them. The first was the medical analysis of Andrew, which Caley and William had already seen. It showed the type of wound that Andrew had received and made some observations and theories about how the injury had been sustained, particularly in reference to the type of weapon that had caused the near-fatal blow. The closer images of the wound and the more detailed analysis of it merely added to Caley and William's suspicions that Andrew was struck with a golf club. Caley quickly flicked through that file and then, after checking with William, shut it again; they had already seen its contents.

The second file was a forensic report of Andrew's wound, body and the area where he had been found: the clearing beside the boating lake in Domsville Park. It wasn't very useful, other than to show that whoever had attacked Andrew knew what they were doing; there were no fibres or fingerprints, or anything else left behind by the attacker.

The third and final file was a brief report summarising the current investigation into Andrew's attack. They had looked into his past: specifically cases that he had investigated, people he had arrested and enemies he had made. They had interviewed a number of people, including prisoners who were in prison because of Andrew (these were the ones who were considered 'dangerous criminals'), ex-convicts who had recently been released from prison, and also Malcolm Wood.

Caley nudged William gently and pointed to the notes about Wood and TLC, specifically the notes referring to the interview with Wood.

'He was probably beside himself with excitement,' William muttered. 'Two separate interviews with police officers.'

Caley laughed quietly, so as to not attract Taggart's attention, and replied in a mutter. 'He'll have been confused if nothing else. We questioned him about Genesis and they questioned him about Andrew's attack.'

William laughed, but muffled his laughter into his Martini glass as he took another sip.

'Have you found anything interesting?' Taggart asked, looking up from the menu in front of him, which was open on the dessert page.

'It was certainly an interesting read,' Caley replied, 'but I don't think that there's anything particularly useful.'

Taggart nodded. 'I know what you mean. I just thought that I would bring them in case.'

'Well, I'm glad you did,' Caley smiled, passing the files back to Taggart, who began to put them back into his briefcase. Taggart suddenly hesitated and looked to William for confirmation. William, however, was happily biting the olives off the cocktail stick in his martini. Taggart, therefore, replaced the documents in his briefcase, which he put back on the floor.

An hour later, Taggart, Caley and William left The Olive Branch and headed towards the car park at the back of the restaurant.

'That was definitely a good choice,' Taggart called to William as he retrieved his car keys from his briefcase.

William grinned. 'I like it there. I shouldn't have told you two about it, though; now when I try and go there for a hot date, you'll be in there waving at me from across the restaurant.'

Taggart laughed and headed towards his car. 'I doubt it,' he replied. 'By the time you are in there with your hot date, I will probably be at home tucked up in bed or if I am having a late night, then I will be in the bath with a cup of herbal tea.'

William laughed and slid into the driver's seat of his Ferrari.

'Should you be driving?' Caley asked.

'I barely had any alcohol,' William replied with a laugh. 'Besides, I ate food with it.' When Caley still looked dubious, he added, 'Look, it's my car and you're not driving it. No one drives my car except for me and besides, I have seen how you drive. Okay, so I had a few martinis. What are you going to do about it, arrest me?'

Caley was too tired to argue and as she got into the passenger's seat, Taggart drove towards them and opened his window. He leaned out of it and Caley opened hers to greet him. 'What's wrong?' she asked.

'We didn't decide where we were going.'

Caley realised that Taggart was right and asked, 'What were you thinking?'

'I would understand if you wanted to go back to the hospital, but you could always come to mine. We could discuss the case some more,' Taggart suggested.

Caley looked at William who shrugged apathetically. 'Okay,' she replied, 'why don't we go to yours then. We can talk about this a bit more and then William and I can head back over to the hospital later. We should probably tell work something, too,' she mused.

'There is no need to worry about that,' Taggart replied. 'I will sort it for you. Are you okay to come to my house and we can discuss this a bit more?' he asked, addressing William directly.

'Can I assume that we will be discussing this over a whisky?' William asked. 'Perhaps a Macallan Whisky?'

Caley rolled her eyes, but Taggart's eyes lit up.

'How does a Macallan 1962 sound?'

William revved the powerful engine of his Ferrari and replied with a wink, 'I'll race you there.'

*

Taggart's home was not the stately mansion that William was expecting. Taggart drove to the outskirts of Alexia, in the most expensive part of Domsville's closest city, and parked in the car park beneath a classy apartment block. William parked beside Taggart's Jaguar XF and slid out of the car, followed by Caley, who seemed to climb out of the car a lot less gracefully than William.

'Your car's too small,' she complained as she strode towards the car park's exit, following Taggart's lead.

William frowned at Caley as she walked away and leaning towards his car, whispered, 'You're not too small. Don't listen to her. You're perfect,' he purred, pocketing his car keys and strolling after Caley and Taggart.

Taggart's apartment was on the top floor, but Caley and William refused to take the lift, opting instead for their preference of walking up the stairs. Taggart, however, announced that he was too old to walk up that many stairs and would meet them at his apartment.

The spiral staircase was elegant and William admired it, and the building up which it swirled through, as he strolled.

'Wait for me,' Caley complained, jogging up to where her was standing.

'Why are you going so slowly?' he asked.

'Because,' Caley replied, jogging to keep up with him, 'you're taking the stairs three at a time.'

'Oh,' William replied, glancing down at his feet and then at Caley's. 'You mean that you can't do that?'

Caley glowered at him, and William strolled up the stairs slower, keeping pace with her.

'Thanks.'

William shrugged and then commented, 'Some place, huh?'

'Yeah, it's pretty nice isn't it?'

'Pretty nice?' William mocked. 'But then again, I suppose growing up in that palace of yours makes most places seem small and dingy.'

Caley rolled her eyes and jabbed William in the ribs with her elbow.

'Hey,' William complained, dodging her elbow by jumping up three steps. 'So, have you decided how we're going to tackle this?' he asked, once she had caught back up with him.

'Well, the situation should be made a lot easier if you're stone cold drunk,' Caley replied sarcastically.

'Stone cold sober,' William corrected.

'Well, what's the word for drunk then?' Caley asked, bemused.

'Drunk. Or, if you prefer: legless, annihilated, hammered, three sheets to the wind, smashed–'

'That's quite enough, thanks. I get the picture.'

William grinned. 'So, getting back to the point . . .'

'What was the point?' Caley asked, but before William could reply she exclaimed, 'Oh, I remember! I was thinking that we could bring up Baxter. We could mention about a friend and colleague of Dad's whom he met when they were both studying to become police officers. We could describe him and say how close he and Dad were; we could talk about how Dad was best man at Baxter's wedding.'

William grinned. 'Good thinking. Then it will be Taggart who brings Baxter up. Then we could ask what happened to Baxter.'

Caley nodded, continuing William's train of thought, 'We could say that he was murdered, but we can't remember the details.'

'And, of course, Taggart will then inevitably bring up Genesis, without us having to mention that Andrew had "Genesis" written on his hand, until you wiped it off, and opening a whole can of worms.'

'Exactly,' Caley grinned. 'So what do you think?'

'I think that it sounds like a plan,' William replied with a wink.

As they reached the top of the spiral staircase, where Taggart's apartment was situated, William glanced upwards at the chandelier hanging from the ceiling through the centre of the spiral staircase.

'Impressive, isn't it?' Caley commented, noticing William's admiration.

'It certainly is,' William replied. 'A bit low, though,' he added, as he reached the top and noted that it was too close to the top of his head for comfort.

'You shouldn't be so tall then, should you?' Caley joked.

'Kettle calling pot black!'

Caley laughed and then, as she reached the door that separated the staircase and the hallway from the apartments and the corridor, turned to William, a more serious expression on her face. 'Look, you *will* be nice to Taggart, won't you?' she asked, her hand on the door handle.

William rolled his eyes. 'It's like being back in nursery. Don't worry, we'll play nicely.'

Caley sighed. 'I'm being serious. When he came to see us in the hospital, he took a big risk. His career is important to him and he's risking it to help us. He extended an olive branch to us this morning and I think that we should return the gesture.'

William frowned slightly and jammed his hands into the pockets of his aubergine suit trousers. 'Fine,' he replied reluctantly.

As Caley opened the door, however, William muttered under his breath, 'She didn't specify where to stick the olive branch.'

Once Caley and William were settled on Taggart's cream, leather corner suite – Caley with a mug of strong black coffee from which a rich and tantalising aroma was emitting in swirls of steam, and William with a glass of Macallan 1962 whisky – and Taggart was settled into a matching armchair opposite the sofa, a glass of whisky in his hand also, Caley brought up the topic of Genesis.

'Do you remember that friend of Dad's?' she asked, addressing William. 'Oh, what was his name?'

William hesitated and swirled his whisky while he thought. 'Do you mean the blonde one?'

Caley shook her head. 'No, the one he studied with. They were both very young when they met, only just becoming police officers.'

'Oh, I know who you mean,' William replied. 'I can't think of his name.'

There were a few moments of silence and then William added, 'Didn't he get married?'

'Yes,' Caley replied, as if she had just remembered that he had. 'Dad was his best man.'

'Of course, that was it. I remembered someone getting married,' William responded slowly, as if deep in thought. 'He worked with Andrew, didn't he?'

'Yes,' Caley replied. 'In the Homicide department. You don't know who we mean, do you?' Caley asked suddenly, turning to address Taggart.

Taggart frowned slightly as he pondered the question. 'I probably will have known him, but I am not sure who you mean.'

Caley sipped at her coffee while she thought. 'Was it Baker?'

William clicked his fingers loudly, 'Baxter!'

'That was it,' Caley exclaimed. 'Chief Inspector Dave Baxter!'

Taggart grimaced slightly at the name and pressed his lips together sombrely. Thinking that neither Caley nor William had noticed, he closed his eyes momentarily and then took a deep swig of his glass of whisky, emptying it completely. As he placed the empty glass onto the coffee table beside him, he sighed deeply and sadly.

'Did you know Baxter?' Caley asked him.

Taggart nodded his head slowly. 'Yes I did. I worked alongside him several times. He was a good man and an excellent police officer.'

William frowned slightly. 'He was murdered wasn't he?' he asked in his usual blunt way.

Caley rolled her eyes. 'Yes, he was. I remember how upset Dad was about it. Was his killer ever caught?'

'No, he wasn't,' Taggart replied, his voice practically a whisper.

Caley's eyes suddenly widened, as if she had just remembered that Taggart was the investigating officer in Baxter's death, but William still appeared to be oblivious.

'I can't really remember,' William replied. 'You must have an impressive memory. I have a memory like a sieve,' he laughed, finishing off his whisky and placing his glass on the coffee table next to him.

'I remember,' Taggart replied in a quiet voice, 'because I was the investigating officer. It was me who didn't catch Chief Inspector Baxter's killer.'

Silence crept up on the room, like a predator to its prey, and then attacked, suddenly and violently.

Taggart was the first to speak. 'I have been with the police force for a very long time. I have worked my way through the ranks and I think that I do a good job. Obviously I make mistakes, everyone does, and I am only human after all.' Taggart smiled briefly and humourlessly. The atmosphere in the room resembled that of a funeral – except for William's aubergine suit. 'I always remember the cases that I feel I failed in. In some cases the person responsible got a lighter sentence than they deserved. In other cases, people died that I felt I should have protected, their deaths preventable. The case of Chief Inspector Baxter has haunted me ever since it happened. It was resolved, but not in the way that I would have liked. It is not an open case, but nor is it really a closed case. The thing that I regret most about it is Baxter's death . . . a death that I should have prevented.'

Caley shook her head slowly. 'It's not your fault. Like you said, you're only human; you make mistakes like the rest of us.'

Taggart smiled sadly. 'Thank you, it means a lot to me. I still regret it, though, and I think that I always will.'

'Can I get a refill?' William asked, holding up his empty whisky glass.

'Yes, help yourself,' Taggart replied absentmindedly; his mind was clearly on other things.

William picked up his glass and headed towards the kitchen, collecting Taggart's glass en route. William retrieved the bottle of Macallan 1962 from the wine rack in Taggart's kitchen and admired the expensive and impressive collection of alcohol that Taggart boasted while he did so. William then opened the bottle and poured liberal amounts of the whisky into both his glass and Taggart's. Instead, however, of returning to the living room straight away, William stood leaning against the kitchen counter. He surveyed the minimalistic kitchen, his glass of whisky in his hand. He then began to wander around the kitchen, investigating the contents of various cupboards and drawers as he did so. He then noticed a door off the kitchen. With a quick glance behind him that confirmed that both Taggart and Caley were still in the living room, deep in conversation, and had no intention of leaving it any time soon, William opened the door and strolled through, closing it quietly behind him.

He found himself in a corridor, with doors off it on either side, and began to stroll, peeking into each room as he went. When he reached Taggart's study, he hesitated, swigged down half of his glass of whisky and strolled inside.

Taggart's study didn't fit the decorating scheme in the rest of the apartment. All of the other rooms that William had seen were minimalistic and didn't appear to be lived in. They contained few personal items; William had yet to see a photograph of a family member for instance. The study, however, had a more personal touch; it was a lot more ornate with lots of furnishings, possessions and various trinkets. The colour scheme was also a contrast to the minimalistic décor in the rest of Taggart's apartment: dark, rich and full of decorative patterns and fabrics. William guessed that this was where Taggart spent the majority of his time. The hardwood floor, desk and bookshelves were all made of dark walnut and the chair behind the desk was dark brown and made of padded leather. There was a large rug covering the majority of the floor, which was decorated in ornate swirls and patterns, and was varying shades of brown, dark green and deep red. There were two dark-brown, padded-leather armchairs in the corner of the room with a small walnut table in between them and an expensive marble chess set on the table. One wall of the room was devoted entirely to bookshelves, from floor to ceiling, and Taggart had a set of ladders (walnut, of course), which ran along this wall; the books on these bookshelves were thick and heavy with expensive binding; not what William would call light reading. Heavy curtains covered the window behind Taggart's desk and the curtains were decorated in intricate patterns similar to the rug. A painting of a racecourse hung beside a painting of a golf course on another wall and there was a walnut shelf on the final wall where the door was, which was laden with the various awards, medals and trophies that Taggart had acquired over the years, which stood proudly side-by-side. William headed straight for the bookcase ladder, which reached from the floor to the ceiling, and spent five minutes rolling back and forth on it. Once he had finished, William strolled over to Taggart's desk, finished off his glass of whisky and placed the glass carelessly on the desk. He then headed round to the other side of the desk and sat down in Taggart's chair. Although he was tempted to roll around the room on the chair, he realised that he had already wasted five minutes on the ladder and that Caley and Taggart would soon start to wonder where he was. Resisting temptation, therefore, he began to flick through neat piles of paper on Taggart's desk. Most of the papers were work-related and were, therefore, relatively dull; although William was pleased to see that an officer he didn't like was under investigation and he made a mental note to gloat next time he saw him. William then found a bank statement. He was about to flick past it when he noticed something unusual. Taggart had been receiving rather hefty payments regularly and he had also been paying quite large sums of money into another account.

'Who are you paying money to?' William murmured as he studied the bank statement. He then left it in the middle of the desk and began to search the drawers which were, thankfully, unlocked. Taggart probably didn't feel the need to lock them; he lived in a high-security building on his own.

After about five minutes, William found another bank statement and within ten minutes, he had finished searching all of the drawers in Taggart's desk and had found five different bank statements: all for different bank accounts. Although there was no law against having multiple bank accounts and in fact, many people did have several bank accounts, William thought it was slightly unusual and placed them all on Taggart's desk. He then began to study them. He was no expert with money, other than how to spend it, as Caley often pointed out, but he thought that the amounts of money that Taggart had in his accounts were unusually large, and that the patterns in the statements were odd too; quite large sums of money were regularly being paid into various accounts, from accounts which William didn't recognise. Furthermore, the sums of money that had been paid out of the first account for which William found a statement were being paid into another one of Taggart's accounts, which he also thought was strange.

Unsure as to what to make of it all, William took pictures of all five statements with his mobile phone, tidied Taggart's desk by replacing the statements where he had found them and rearranging the papers slightly so that they were in the same order. He then slipped his phone into the pocket of his suit trousers and left the room, his empty whisky glass in his hand, and tiptoed down the corridor and back in the kitchen. He refilled his glass with the Macallan whisky and tried to think of an excuse as to why he had been absent for so long. Suddenly, thinking of an excuse, he retrieved his mobile phone from his pocket once more, pressed it to his ear and strolled into the living room.

'Yeah,' he spoke into the mobile. 'I will do . . . Like I said, I'd just lost your phone number . . . Yeah, of course I will . . . See you then . . . Bye.' William then slipped his phone back into his pocket and strolled back to his seat.

Caley looked at him with one eyebrow raised, but it was Taggart who spoke first.

'Could you not find the whisky?'

William turned to face him and sighed, 'Drat! I forgot. Sorry. The one thing I went in there for,' he added with a laugh, heading back into the kitchen. 'I did have a fascinating conversation instead, though. I won't be a minute,' he called to Taggart as the door shut behind him.

Once in the kitchen, William leant on the counter and waited for a few seconds before collecting the full glasses of whisky from the kitchen and carrying them back into the living room.

'Do you want anything?' William asked Caley after he had given Taggart his drink.

'No thanks,' she replied. 'I saw how long it took you to get the whisky. I'll have died of boredom by the time you make the coffee,' she laughed.

'Who were you on the phone to?' Taggart asked and then suddenly added, 'I am sorry. That was very rude of me. Of course, it was private.'

'It's fine. It was just someone I met about a week ago. We went out for a meal and she gave me her number, but I didn't call her back,' he shrugged apathetically. 'I told her that I'd lost her number and had been trying to get hold of her, but with no success. I said that she should be the police officer instead of me, tracking me down first,' he added with a laugh.

Caley shook her head exasperatedly. 'You have *got* to stop telling people that. One of these days, you'll use it on someone with a friend that you've already used it on. You'll get found out one of these days,' she laughed.

William grinned and drank some of his whisky. 'Did I miss

anything interesting?' he asked, placing his half-full glass of whisky on the coffee table beside him.

Taggart smiled. 'Hardly; I am afraid that I was simply boring Caley with stories of my past. When she mentioned Chief Inspector Baxter earlier, I began to reminisce. I was telling Caley all about the case and how much I regret the whole sorry affair. I am still trying to figure out what went wrong, what actually happened.' Taggart sighed deeply and shook his head sadly. 'I am afraid that I may never know.'

'I thought the case had all been resolved though?' William asked. 'I know that it wasn't a perfect ending, but it isn't a cold case, is it?'

'No,' Taggart replied. 'There was a young man that I felt was responsible, but someone obviously tipped him off that we were going to arrest him; either that or he just realised that we were onto him and he ran. We did find him, but it was too late; by that time Baxter, who was the investigating officer into the case, was dead and the culprit was dead too.'

'How did he die – the one responsible, I mean?' William asked.

'He hung himself,' Taggart replied in a melancholy voice.

The room was silent for a while and both Taggart and William finished their glasses of whisky.

'I think that we should probably go,' Caley announced, breaking the silence. 'I hope we're not leaving you in too dismal a mood,' she laughed softly.

Taggart smiled. 'No, not at all. I think that I will have a cup of tea and go to bed,' he replied, consulting his watch to confirm what the darkness outside the window and the tiredness inside his body had already told him.

'Will you go to the hospital?' Taggart asked.

'Yes, I think so,' Caley replied. 'Even if to just say goodnight to everyone.'

Taggart nodded and stood up, preparing to see Caley and William out. As they reached the door and began to walk towards the staircase, Taggart called behind them, 'If there is ever anything you need, you know where I am.'

'That wasn't too bad, was it?' Caley asked as she and William walked down the stairs, Caley striding purposefully, as usual, and William meandering, as usual, but taking the stairs three at a time so that they were actually walking together.

'No, it was actually quite interesting,' William replied, deciding for the time being not to tell Caley about the bank statements. After all, he would only be in trouble for snooping around and lying, and he was sure that Caley would manage to explain the whole thing rationally and reasonably. So, he decided instead to wait and either confirm his suspicions or disprove his paranoia the next day. He thought that Caley would be particularly annoyed after her little speech about extending an olive branch to Taggart; William had simply snapped the olive branch in two, but he really didn't like Taggart; he was too supercilious for William's liking, and he had misquoted Shakespeare, which, in William's eyes, was the eighth deadly sin.

14

If One Door Closes

Caley paced up and down the room, her mobile phone pressed to her ear. 'Come on, William. Pick up your phone,' she muttered as she paced. After a few seconds, she removed it from her ear with a deep sigh. 'Voicemail . . . again!'

Margaret was sitting beside Andrew's hospital bed, a deep blue, cable-knit jumper folded neatly on the table beside her and a pair of knitting needles in her hands.

'Morning, Mum,' Aziza called out cheerfully as she opened the door.

'Morning, sweetheart,' Margaret replied, striding over and enveloping her in a loving embrace. 'How are you holding up?'

'Forget me,' Aziza replied. 'What about you? Have you been here all night?'

Margaret sighed wearily and stepped back slightly from Aziza. 'I have told you before: I am not going to leave him.'

Aziza sighed. 'You're not leaving him; there are nurses and doctors here all the time and if there is any change then they will call you . . . straight away,' she added emphatically. 'You need to sleep; you're no use to Dad if you're ill,' Aziza continued. 'You've got shadows under your eyes; it's clear that you haven't been sleeping properly.'

'Thanks,' Margaret replied. 'That really made me feel better.'

Aziza started to argue back, but Ray placed his large hand on her shoulder. 'You know she's not going to change her mind,' he murmured. 'Why don't you compromise?' he suggested. 'We could always take her out for lunch later.'

Aziza turned to Ray with a smile. 'You're right,' she replied.

Aziza strode over to Margaret who had resumed her knitting, her high heels clicking against the hard floor.

'Have you finished the jumper already?' Aziza asked in astonishment, laying a perfectly manicured hand on top of the deep blue, knitted jumper.

'Yes,' Margaret replied absentmindedly. 'I am knitting him a scarf now,' she explained, knitting as she spoke.

Unsure of what to say in response, Aziza strode over to Ray, an exasperated smile on her face. 'Why don't you sit down?' she suggested gently, steering him towards a chair and sitting down next to him. 'This may sound like it has a rather obvious answer,' she began again, 'but is Caley not here?'

Margaret smiled and placed her knitting on her lap. 'She was, but then she stepped outside to call William. She said that she had some things to discuss with him and you are obviously not allowed to make calls in the hospital,' she added, gesturing to a conveniently placed, *Please switch off all mobile phones* sign nearby.

Caley abruptly ended her conversation with William's voicemail service, interrupting William's recorded message:

'Hi! William speaking . . . Just kidding. I'm not here really. You're lucky enough to have my mobile number, obviously, but I'm not here right now, which probably means that I'm out somewhere having a better time than you. The beep is due any minute now; you know what to do. Ciao!'

Caley frowned as she checked the time on the screen of her phone: it was ten o'clock. She knew that William liked to sleep in and also that he had drunk a fair amount of alcohol the day before, but she would have expected him to have answered his phone by now. She sighed and was about to go back inside the hospital when she saw that she had an email. With a bored expression, expecting it to be junk mail, she opened up the message. When she saw that it was from Taggart, she headed over to a nearby bench and sat down. Then, phone in hand and brow slightly furrowed, she read:

I am sorry to interrupt you, which is why I did not call, but I just wanted to let you know that I have cleared your time off, and William's naturally, with work. You are officially off on 'compassionate leave' and you are free to have as much time off as you want and/or need. Do not worry about it; I have sorted it all out for you and if you receive any grief off your senior officer then just let me know. While I am on the subject, if you need anything – and I mean anything – then just let me know and I will see what I can do for you. That includes advice, information (such as any official documents that you cannot get hold of), or simply someone to listen. I am fully at your service. I will now sign off as I have taken up more than enough of your time, and please give my most sincere regards to your mother and sister.

Yours faithfully, Richard Taggart.

Caley smiled and closed the message. Her smile quickly evaporated, however, when she saw that her mobile phone had a full signal, but no messages from William. It was half past ten already.

'Where *is* he?'

The record keeper slammed the top drawer of a filing cabinet shut. William winced and pressed his fingers lightly to his forehead. He blamed it on the whisky, although it could have been the martinis.

'Can you please be a bit quieter,' he murmured as John plodded over to him, the sound of his feet hitting the concrete floor ringing inside William's head.

John merely grunted at him in response. 'Hangover?' he asked, although it was more of a statement than a question.

'I always thought that the word "hangover" was an understatement.'

'Funny, I always thought that the word "hangover" was an exaggeration . . . for a headache.'

'A hangover is not a headache,' William retorted. 'A hangover is the wrath of grapes.'

John shrugged and dropped the files onto the table, the sound accompanied by a wince from William, and spread them out so that William could see them all clearly. 'Which one do you want to see first?' he asked.

William was feeling slightly worse for wear and, consequently, looking the same way. His usually clean-shaven face was covered in stubble and although it was only one day's growth, his combination of olive-brown skin and chocolate-coloured hair made it seem several days' longer. Furthermore, in contrast to the aubergine-coloured suit that he had worn the day before, he was wearing . . . a black suit. However, being William, it wasn't an ordinary black suit; he was wearing a crisp white shirt underneath a black suit jacket, which he was wearing fastened, and the white cuffs of his shirt were folded over his black cuffs, which were halfway between his wrist and his elbow. He wasn't wearing a tie, but the collar of his shirt was folded flat and stood straight against his neck above his jacket lapels. Finally, just for that 'William touch' as Caley called it, he had a thin white rectangle sticking slightly out of his breast-pocket.

William sighed heavily and pulled a chair over to John's desk, where John was sitting with the files he had retrieved spread out in front of him. 'Let's see what you've got for me.'

John opened the first folder but then hesitated. 'I'm not sure about this,' he frowned, the papers in his hand.

William sighed, 'Aw, come on! I thought we'd been through this already?'

187

John's frown deepened; so much so that his eyebrows were in danger of engulfing his eyes.

'Look, I told you why I was doing this. I showed you the statements.' He supported this argument by waving his phone in his hand. 'And I told you that whatever I found out would stay between these four walls' – William then hesitated and counted the walls to ensure that there were four – 'until I had something concrete . . . If I get something concrete. No one will know where I got the information from.'

John's eyebrows rose slightly and he looked at William's face: his golden-coloured skin, the stubble on his face showing the effects of the night before and the piercing blue eyes that dominated his perfectly proportioned features. Most of all, however, John saw honesty and he saw a face that he could trust. 'Fine,' he replied brusquely, taking the papers out of his hand and placing them on the table in front of William. 'As you pointed out, the amounts in his accounts are unusually high and have unusual patterns. I am still running the searches on those accounts, but I think you'll find that they're all legit and that all of the amounts paid in are from one of his other accounts.'

'Don't you find that in itself suspicious?'

John shrugged. 'I don't want to get involved,' he mumbled.

'Come on,' William complained. 'I dragged myself out of bed for this.'

John shook his head. 'You shouldn't let your drinking interfere with your work.'

'At least my work isn't interfering with my drinking,' William retorted.

'What's the difference?'

'If drinking is interfering with your work, you're probably a heavy drinker. If work is interfering with your drinking, you're probably an alcoholic.'

John laughed briefly, but loudly, a deep, booming laugh, and then straightened his face once more. 'You came to me because you needed information, right?' he confirmed.

'Yes,' William agreed. 'That and because I am hopeless at stuff like this, whereas I thought that it would be right up your street,' he added with a wink.

John sighed and held his hand out reluctantly for William's mobile phone.

William grinned and passed him the phone. 'If I wasn't hung-over then I would be doing a celebratory dance right now.'

John rolled his eyes. 'In that case I should be glad that you *are* hung-over.'

There was silence while John studied the photos that William had taken the evening before. 'I'll agree that it is unusual to have this many bank accounts, unless they're for specific reasons or if you have a lot of money that you want to invest,' John commented. 'And not only are these amounts unusually large, but the patterns are unusual too.' John hesitated. 'Are you sure that you're not just doing this because you hold a grudge . . . or something?' he added, showing his lack of knowledge of human nature.

'Okay, so I don't like him. I think that he's a supercilious jerk . . . who misquotes Shakespeare,' William added, clenching his fist briefly at the memory, 'but that doesn't mean that I'm wrong.'

John shrugged and turned his attention to his computer. 'The searches are finished,' he announced and began to scroll through various files and documents on the screen.

'What exactly am I looking at here?' William asked in bemusement at all of the different numbers flashing before his eyes on the vast computer monitor.

'These are records on the bank accounts that Taggart has,' John explained. 'As you can see, they are all high in interest, which isn't unusual, especially considering the amounts that Taggart has in the accounts.'

William nodded. 'Anything else?'

John studied the screen for a moment. 'He is being paid large sums of money at regular intervals and in quite unusual patterns, as you observed with the bank statements that you . . . found. However, this is occurring with all of his bank accounts and if I'm right . . .' He hesitated slightly while he confirmed his thoughts using the information in front of him. 'Then the majority of the money isn't coming from any bank accounts other than his own.'

William frowned slightly. 'What do you mean? If they're not coming from other people then who *are* they coming from?'

'Well some are from other people – his wage for example – but the rest are from him.'

William did not need to ask for an explanation; his bemused expression made it clear that an explanation was necessary.

'These sums of money being paid into his account here, here and here,' John explained, gesturing to different amounts, 'are from another one of his bank accounts. I know,' he continued, pre-empting William's next question, 'because I've compared the account numbers in his statements with the numbers of his accounts.'

William nodded. 'So how does that work? I mean, where is he getting the money from; if he was just paying himself constantly, surely his money would just be going round in circles?'

'He regularly receives cash payments into this account,' John explained, pointing to a specific account, 'as you can see from the bank statement, and he only does so to the one account . . . from what I can tell from the bank statements you've brought me, anyway.'

'So, Taggart is getting paid large amounts of money, regularly, in cash and is transferring it from one account to another?' William confirmed.

'Yes, that's about the bare bones of it. The cash payments only go to one account, but then the money is transferred into various accounts: a different one each time. This could simply be to avoid raising the alert on his accounts or there could be a specific pattern to it; without knowing what the money is for, I couldn't confirm this pattern one way or another.'

William didn't reply to John's comment; instead, he sat, immersed in his own thoughts. Eventually it was John who spoke again; the silence was making him visibly uncomfortable as was not knowing what William was thinking.

'Does this help you?' he asked.

'Yes,' William replied. 'Yes it does. Thanks. It helps a lot.' He frowned slightly as he tried to organise all of his thoughts.

'Do you want to talk any ideas through?'

'If you don't mind,' William replied earnestly. 'My head is getting a bit cramped at the moment; there are too many thoughts up there. Not that it takes much,' he added with a grin.

John shook his head exasperatedly and William began to talk.

'Taggart likes expensive things and he must be getting the money from somewhere. I mean, he can't earn *that* much as a Chief Superintendent.'

John rolled his eyes. 'People could say the same thing about you and you're on even less money.'

William grinned. 'Okay, so I have an expensive car, but I inherited that money and I know that I have expensive clothes,' he continued, brushing the shoulders of his designer suit jacket as he spoke, 'but I have an extremely cheap apartment. I spend my money on my car and my wardrobe, because that's what matters to me,' he shrugged. 'I just think that Taggart is . . . dodgy, but I can't put my finger on it,' he added with frustration.

'Maybe he's a "bent copper",' John suggested, using quotation marks. 'I know that people have been arrested for that before and I'm hardly part of the grapevine,' he snorted. 'So you must definitely know officers like that. Maybe he accepts bribes; it could have started off small at first, like, you know, for the odd case, and then developed? Maybe that's where the money's coming from?'

William snapped his fingers so enthusiastically that he almost fell off his chair, 'John, you're a genius!' He then leapt up and pulled his mobile phone out of his pocket. Bemused, he held it in front of him.

'You won't get a signal down here,' John called over from his desk.

'Oh, of course,' William replied, stuffing his phone into his pocket. 'I forgot that I was in the Labyrinth.'

John shook his head slightly at the nickname for his office and began to study his computer screen once more.

'Well, in that case, I think I'm done,' William mused as he slipped some papers that John had retrieved from the archives into his black leather shoulder bag.

'Didn't you come here with a woman last time?' John asked suddenly, as William tided various documents away . . . and John then tidied them himself.

William rolled his eyes. 'Have you only just noticed I'm on my own?'

'No,' John replied unconvincingly. 'I forgot you came with someone else last time. Who was she then?' he asked. 'She had a black leather coat. I remember now, down to her knees. A coat it was, not a jacket; it had a collar and everything.'

William grinned. 'Yeah, that's Caley: Inspector Caley Arling.'

John nodded, grunted and then returned to his work. Taking that as his cue to leave, William was about to head out of the door when John called out, 'Do you not want this then?'

William frowned slightly and turned back to face him. 'Do I not want what?' he asked, meandering back over to John's desk as he spoke.

'When you and, erm . . .'

'Caley,' William prompted.

'That was it. When you and Caley came here last time you looked at some files, but you also asked me to run a search. You never came back for the results.'

William raised his eyebrows and sat back down beside John.

'What search was that?' he asked, trying to remember.

'Now who's got the bad memory?' John muttered and then added in a louder voice, 'You wanted to see who had checked out the Genesis file.'

William's eyes widened. 'Do you have the results here, then?'

'Yes, I was waiting for you to come back,' John replied, passing William a piece of paper.

'Thanks,' William replied and scanned the sheet. It contained a list of names and dates, showing people who had taken the Genesis file out of the archives. Caley and William were right at the top. Taggart's name was also on it, unsurprisingly; he had told Caley and William that he kept raking over the case because in his mind it was unsolved. It made sense, therefore, that he would check the file out. William's piercing blue eyes widened, however, when he saw one name in particular: Superintendent Andrew Arling. He stared at Andrew's familiar scrawled signature. Andrew had checked out the file, which confirmed his and Caley's suspicions that he was investigating Genesis.

'Thanks,' William repeated. 'I can take this, right?' he asked as he strolled out of the door, not even waiting for a reply. As he was escorted back through the Labyrinth and into the station once more, he pondered the list he had just been given. Whoever attacked Andrew obviously did so because he was getting too close to the truth about Genesis, as he and Caley had suspected. Andrew had reinvestigated the case because he was upset about Baxter's death. It fit with their suspicions about Favel, too, William thought excitedly as he followed a member of IT support through the subterranean passageways. His train of thought, however, suddenly hit a brick wall as he realised that Max wouldn't have had access to the list and so wouldn't have known that Andrew was investigating. Who would have had access? 'Taggart,' he whispered to himself.

If John was right and Taggart had been accepting bribes, which William wouldn't put past him, then maybe someone bribed him to find out if Andrew was actually investigating Genesis? Maybe even Max?

William's pace quickened as he realised that he had to find Caley and share his thoughts and findings with her. He looked at his watch and saw that it was almost half past eleven. She would probably be at the hospital; that was where they had agreed to meet.

Outside, as he slid into the driver's seat of his Ferrari, he wondered how much Taggart knew. If he had been bribed by Favel, which William thought was more than plausible, then maybe he suspected that Favel had attacked Andrew. Maybe he even felt guilty and that was why he had offered to help.

'Favel and Taggart probably know each other,' William muttered as he placed his bag on the passenger seat. 'They've probably met at one of these black-tie dinners. They probably get together and misquote Shakespeare,' he muttered angrily, clenching his fist around the steering wheel as he sped out of the station car park and headed towards the hospital.

Caley parked her car in one of the 'guest' parking spaces beneath Taggart's apartment building. As she climbed out of her car, she checked her mobile phone. It was eleven o'clock and she had still not heard from William. She shrugged, remembering the note that she had left for him at the hospital telling him where she was, not to mention all of the missed calls on his mobile. With a sigh, she locked her car and shoved her car key into the pocket of her jeans. She then strode towards the car park exit with only a brief glance back at her battered 4x4, which stood out amongst the Jaguars, BMWs and occasional Aston Martins like a sore thumb.

'But how much does a sore thumb actually stick out?' she mused as she signed in at the reception desk and began to stride up the stairs. 'Oh shut up, Caley,' she muttered. 'You sound like William. Next you'll be quoting Oscar Wilde, Ovid and Shakespeare,' she added with a roll of her eyes.

When she reached the door of Taggart's apartment, she rapped sharply and Taggart answered within seconds. He was wearing a grey pinstripe suit and a grey silk tie, which Caley knew would upset William, simply because of how unimaginative it was. Still, Caley mused, it was better than golfing plus fours.

'Ah, Caley,' Taggart beamed, opening the door for her. 'Come in. I received your email and I have been waiting for you. The kettle has just boiled,' he added as he shut the door behind her. 'Can I get you a coffee? Black, no sugar,' he added as he headed towards the kitchen.

'Yes, thanks. That sounds great,' Caley replied.

'You can put your coat in the cloakroom if you want,' Taggart called as he opened the kitchen door, gesturing to a small room near the door.

'I won't, if you don't mind,' Caley replied, sitting down on the corner suite where she and William had sat the night before. While she was waiting for Taggart to return, she began to ponder the Genesis case and Max Favel: their prime suspect. She knew that she was missing something, but she couldn't figure out what it was. She then heard the telephone ring and Taggart stuck his head around the door.

'I will just be a minute; I will have to get that,' he called apologetically.

'Don't worry about it,' Caley replied, settling into the settee and admiring the view out of the window. The sky was as grey as Taggart's suit and as thick as William at five o'clock in the morning, she mused, as she looked outside. Rain splattered the window and as she watched, it grew heavier and faster. She sighed and turned away, and instead began to survey the room. Most of the rooms in Taggart's apartment were separated by doors, but the living room was large and spacious, with lots of doors leading off it, such as the one that led into the kitchen opposite the front door.

As Caley studied the room, with its minimalistic décor, and wondered how much the painting on the wall to the left of her (the door to the kitchen being on her right) had cost, she noticed a dark-green bag sitting on the floor in the corner of the room. The rest of the room was fairly sparse as far as possessions were concerned and Caley studied it, her brow furrowed. It was clearly a bag of golf clubs; so bulky and space-consuming that she was surprised she hadn't fallen over it, never mind seen it, when she first entered his apartment. Caley shrugged, and thought with a grin that it would be funny if Taggart knew Favel. As she thought, however, her brow creased further and she wondered if Taggart played golf at Domsville Park of a morning. Her mind began to race, as did her heart. She knew that something wasn't right and that she had to leave. She stood up and headed for the door, but then she hesitated – a mistake she later regretted – as she wondered what she should say to Taggart, if anything. And then it was too late. Taggart opened the door and strode into the living room, a tray in his hands.

'Is something the matter?' he asked as he set it down on the table.

'No,' Caley replied too quickly, hoping that Taggart couldn't hear her pounding heart from where he was standing. 'I've just had a call from William,' she lied, pulling her mobile out of her pocket. 'I need to call him back, explain that I'm here, with you. Maybe I should suggest that he joins us?' She stepped towards the door and Taggart took a step towards her. Her breathing uneven, Caley told herself to relax. Her suspicions were probably wrong. So what if Taggart played golf? She couldn't push the thought out of her mind, however, and she remembered that she had mentioned Max Favel the previous evening. Why hadn't Taggart said anything about knowing him? Maybe he didn't know him? Caley couldn't think straight and it didn't help that all she could think about was her dad. What if Taggart had attacked him? She started to tell herself that it was nonsense, when her blood suddenly froze. She remembered that Taggart was the investigating officer on the Genesis case after Baxter had been killed. What if he was the ringleader, not

Favel? Caley had to force herself not to scream. She maintained her poker face, which she had learnt from Andrew, as Taggart studied her suspiciously.

They stood a few feet away from each other, neither speaking nor blinking. But Caley was the first to lose her nerve. Her eyes darted to the bag of golf clubs in the corner of the room. It was only for a second, but it was long enough.

'I see,' Taggart spoke clearly and calmly, his educated voice not faltering once.

Caley decided that it was now or never. She dashed to the door and desperately pulled the door handle. It wouldn't open. She tried again, but in vain. When she turned back around, Taggart was standing in front of her, a golf club in his hand.

'I locked it,' he explained. 'Did I forget to say?' he asked sarcastically, swinging the golf club as he spoke. 'You might as well move away from the door; you are not going anywhere.'

Caley hid her fear, she strode over to the corner suite and sat down. Her mobile was still in her hand.

'I will have that please,' Taggart said, holding out his hand for it.

Caley hesitated, but Taggart swung the golf club threateningly. She may have been a lot younger and fitter than he was, but he had a golf club in his hand, he was dangerous and she was locked inside the apartment, so even if she did manage to get past him, where would she go? She handed over her phone, her expression composed and emotionless.

'Thank you,' Taggart replied coolly as he pocketed it.

'You killed Dominic Smith. You killed Daniel Jones. You killed Chief Inspector Dave Baxter. You tried to kill my father.'

Taggart raised his eyebrows at this brusque statement. 'You know, Caley, I think you need to stop beating around the bush so much; if you want to say something then just come out and say it.'

'Okay,' Caley replied with a shrug. 'You tried to cover up the murders of Daniel, Dominic and Baxter, but my father was too clever for you; he realised that you'd murdered them so you tried to kill him, but you couldn't even do that. Just face it, he has beaten you, and you know why? It's because he is better than you.'

Taggart's face flushed with anger. 'And I suppose that *you* think you are better than me too?'

Caley smirked. 'Naturally; I have his DNA.'

Taggart sneered in response. 'If your idea of winning is lying in a hospital bed in a coma then I would hate to see your idea of losing. Your precious father is going to die sooner or later and it is all because of me,' he gloated, emphasising the last four words.

Caley stiffened her jaw but maintained eye contact with Taggart.

'You are right though,' he added after a moment or two, his voice back to its usual composed tone. 'You always were clever, a good police officer.'

'Not good enough, obviously,' Caley muttered. 'Not to see what was right in front of me.'

'Maybe not, but even so, you had all the right ideas: the right motive, the right weapon,' he added, swinging the golf club as he spoke. 'You were just looking at the wrong person.'

'The right weapon,' Caley repeated. 'You hit him with a golf club, didn't you? Then you got changed into a clean set of golfing clothes, identical to the ones you were already wearing, so that you didn't have any blood on them, and you put the golf club back in your bag and walked away.'

'I did, yes,' Taggart replied calmly, 'Rather ingenious of me, don't you think?'

'How did you get him there?' Caley asked. 'He was supposed to be meeting me, but he arrived early to talk to you. Why? What did you say to him?'

'I knew that he was reinvestigating Genesis; I suspected it and I tried to check by going through his office, but everything was locked away. I went down to the archives, though, and I accessed the information about everyone who had looked at the file. Andrew's name was on it, which confirmed my suspicions. I called him and asked to speak to him. I told him that I thought he was investigating the Genesis case and that I wanted to help him. I told him what I told you and William, about not being happy with the outcome of the case, and wanting to know what actually happened. He agreed to see me before my game of golf and before your morning run.'

'Genesis wasn't a family feud, was it? It was a drug-smuggling operation and *you* were the ringleader.'

'Congratulations,' Taggart replied. 'Not that you could prove any of it.'

'The drug squad knew about the drug smuggling and that there had to have been a leader, and they know that it's still going on. They will find you out sooner or later.'

'Is that so?' Taggart asked. 'You have no idea,' he laughed. 'While they are all there chasing their own tails and following false trails and red herrings laid out by me, I am making my millions. By the time they *do* manage to – how did you word it? – see what is right in front of them,' he smirked, 'I will be long gone.'

'What, to the Caribbean?' Caley snorted. 'How original.'

'No, actually, not to the Caribbean; I rather fancy Italy. I love Italy: the history, the culture, the food,' he smiled dreamily. 'Rome, Venice, Pompeii . . .'

Caley started to move towards the edge of the corner suite and Taggart abruptly brought the golf club down onto the carpet with a resounding thud, mere millimetres away from the tip of her boots. Caley reluctantly shuffled back to her original position on the sofa and Taggart brought the golf club back to his side.

'I would not advise trying that again,' he recommended coolly, 'or anything else of that nature. You are not going anywhere and if you do move again then my aim might not be so fortunate next time,' he added menacingly. 'After all, I have experience in getting rid of nuisances with golf clubs,' he sneered.

Caley stared directly at him, determined not to display any emotion, but inside her was electric; she was beyond angry at his blasé remarks about attacking her father and killing Dominic, Daniel and Baxter, but she was also afraid. She knew that Taggart was going to kill her and she didn't know what she could do about it. Obviously, she was younger and fitter than him, but he was armed and dangerous and even if she did manage to get past him, where would she go? After all, the door was locked and she had no idea where the key was.

'Do you really think that you can kill me and get away with it?'

'I have done it before,' Taggart replied apathetically.

'What about William? He's investigating too.'

Taggart rolled his eyes. 'You have no proof. Besides, I am William's superior officer. I might just fire him,' he shrugged nonchalantly.

'How are you going to kill me without making it obvious that it was you?' she asked, her heart pounding too loudly for her to hear how bizarre the question was.

'There has been an awful outbreak of robberies in nearby apartments. Our apartment block has not been targeted yet, but it is only a matter of time,' Taggart replied. 'I am going to make it look like someone came in and began to burgle my apartment. You startled them, they attacked you with whatever came to hand,' he added, swinging the golf club in his hand as he spoke, 'and you were killed. A real tragedy. In fact, if I remember correctly, the back door to our building is broken slightly. It looks as if that was how they broke in.'

'You broke the door,' Caley's comment was not a question.

'That is correct. I did,' he replied. 'I have had some time to think about how this would happen.'

As he retrieved a pair of gloves from his pocket and pulled them onto his hands, Caley checked the time. It was ten past eleven, but she felt as if she had been talking to Taggart for a lifetime. Her mind was on overdrive. 'I have to stall him, delay him somehow,' she thought hysterically, scanning the room frantically, but not finding an escape route. 'He's going to kill me,' she thought, her heart beating furiously against her ribcage. 'No,' she thought. 'No, this can't happen. I can't let him kill me. Dad *is* going to wake up and I need to be there when he does. I have to come through this. I just need to delay him. I don't know what for, but I will when it happens. Something will happen. It must do. Come on, William,' she thought desperately. 'Where are you?' she sighed and pressed her lips together to retain her composure. Shaking her head furiously, she told herself to keep her cool, not to give up. 'Come on Caley, you can do this,' she thought to herself. 'You have to.'

As her thoughts diverted to William, she began to wonder what he would say in the same situation. With a smile, she heard his voice in her head as clearly as if he was sitting next to her. 'Giving up isn't an option. If one door closes, another one opens ... and failing that, break down a door.' Caley's smile grew into a grin as she thought of William and how she was convinced that he lived on a different planet to everyone else. 'It's all right though,' she thought. 'They know him there.' Shaking her head exasperatedly, she remembered William's constant stream of quotes and their authors. 'Who said that quote?' she wondered in her head. It was when her mobile rang that she remembered that it was Alexander Graham Bell who had originally said, 'If one door closes, another one opens.' The extra bit was William's own creation.

She watched as Taggart abruptly ended the call on her mobile phone and she sat in silence; the only sounds were her heart beating frantically and the rain splattering against the window behind her. 'Dad,' she whispered to herself, thinking of someone who would know what to do. 'Where are you when I need you?'

15

To the Rescue

Andrew heard Margaret's voice and the familiar tone soothed him, even though usually its tyrannical timbre would have had the opposite effect.

'I have tried calling her, but there is no answer,' she called from one side of the room and when Aziza answered, it was clear to Andrew that she was on the other side.

'It doesn't matter,' Aziza replied. 'She probably doesn't have a signal or maybe she's simply busy.'

'I hope she's found William,' Margaret commented.

Andrew heard footsteps: the clicking of high-heels from Aziza's side of the room, which informed him that she was moving towards Margaret. However, he also heard heavy, thudding footsteps moving at the same time as Aziza's but not as frequently, implying that their legs and therefore their strides, were longer.

'That will be Ray then,' Andrew chuckled.

A few seconds later, Andrew heard the door slam and he was left on his own once more. He sat in silence with only his thoughts for company, listening to the pouring rain, determined to figure out the puzzle. He now knew that whoever had attacked him was wearing brown leather shoes and he knew that he had seen them before. He also thought that they played golf. He shook his head and sighed. 'This is certainly not like any case I've ever solved before.'

As he thought about Margaret calling Caley, or at least he assumed that she had been calling Caley, because she was the only one missing, he remembered receiving a phone call on the morning of his attack.

'Who called me?' he wondered aloud, frustrated at his own memory, or lack thereof. 'Why did they call me in the morning? Was it to do with work?' There were a few minutes of silence as he thought.

'It *was* to do with work. It was to do with Genesis,' he thought excitedly as his blurred memories began to clear. 'They called me and told me that they had guessed that I was investigating Genesis, which I was,' he added, seeing the word 'Genesis' scrawled on the palm of his hand and automatically thinking about Baxter. 'And they wanted to investigate it too . . . because they took over the case after Baxter died. They were the investigating officer and they wanted to know what actually happened.' Andrew then frowned. 'Except he didn't want to know. He called me and he lied. He lied about Genesis and he lied about Baxter. When I met him, before my run with Caley and before his game of golf,' he thought with mounting excitement as he remembered where golf came into it all. 'He attacked me.' He clenched his fists and heard the incessant beeping accelerate. The beeping became faster and faster . . . as did Andrew's thoughts.

'Who did I meet? Who was the investigating officer? Whose are these brown leather shoes?' he asked in frustration, the beeping growing faster still. 'Taggart.' Andrew only uttered one word, but it was probably the most important word he had spoken since arriving in his armchair on that fateful morning. 'Taggart,' he repeated and then he opened his eyes.

Disorientated, Andrew looked around the room, his piercing green eyes not missing a detail. He was in a hospital; the mint-green walls gave it away.

'It's either a hospital or a morgue,' he chuckled and furrowed his brow as he heard the beeping once more, and it was getting faster. 'Where is that darn beeping coming from?' he growled.

He pushed himself into a sitting position, the effort exhausting, and looked around the room. It was empty, but Aziza's and Margaret's handbags were sitting on the floor beside vacant chairs. He smiled. He had missed his family. As he turned slightly, he saw the heart monitor standing beside him. He saw the green lines peaking furiously and heard the infuriating beeping emitting from it. With a growl, he pulled the wire from his hand and listened as silence fell upon the room. He then disconnected himself from various other monitors and pieces of equipment and slid off the bed. As he did so, he lost his balance as his head spun furiously. He managed to clutch a nearby table, however, and keep himself from falling. His usually strong legs felt weak, but as he looked down at them, he was glad to see his bare feet as opposed to brown leather shoes.

Chuckling, he stood up beside the bed and began to stretch his arms, legs and shoulders, the feeling in his body returning to him as he did so. He felt as if he had just awoken from a long, deep sleep . . . which he supposed he had. He then turned and looked at the empty bed, the white sheets rumpled and the cover pulled back.

'I must have been unconscious,' he muttered to himself. 'I wonder how long I have been here.'

Unsure of what to do next, he strode over to the vacant chairs, which had obviously previously been occupied by Margaret, Caley, Aziza and Ray.

'What about William?' he mused aloud as he strode among the chairs. That was when he saw a small piece of paper on one of the empty chairs with William's name scrawled onto it. He picked it up, recognising Caley's handwriting, so similar to his own, turned it over and read:

Hi,
I'm not sure where you are. I have tried calling you but
no response. As you can tell, I'm not here. I know we
said to meet here, but I need to bounce ideas off
someone. Hope your hangover isn't too bad! If you
want me, I'm at Taggart's.
Caley

His heart racing, Andrew gripped a nearby chair for support, as his knees buckled underneath his weight. His mind was racing and his head was spinning. He strode over to a wardrobe in the corner of the room and pulled the doors open frantically. To his relief, his clothes were hanging up inside it: the clothes he was wearing when he was attacked. He pulled on his running clothes and the note still on the chair where he had found it, started towards the door when he realised that he didn't know what to do. Obviously he had to get to Taggart's, but how?

He saw Margaret's handbag on the floor nearby and was about to search through it for her car keys when he saw a woman running towards the room. The woman had deep crimson hair secured loosely in a bun and her knee-length white coat flapped around her as she dashed towards him. He heard the sound of her plimsolls hitting the floor growing louder, the sound making him feel as though his head was inside a vice and was slowly being crushed. Dizzy and disorientated, he grabbed Margaret's handbag and ran out of the door, ignoring the cries of the doctor. He sprinted down the mint-green corridors of the hospital, other doctors and hospital staff assuming that he was a visitor because he was wearing his normal clothes, and therefore easily running past the hospital staff and security. He caught sight of his pale face and tussled grey hair in a dark window, but ran onwards regardless. There were only two things on his mind: Caley and Taggart.

As he sprinted through the car park towards Margaret's

cream Mini Cooper, her car keys in his hand, he could feel his head throbbing. He had had a headache since he had first woken up, but it had grown worse since then. He frowned in frustration at the pain. He didn't like admitting to pain as he saw it as a sign of weakness, but his headache was unusually painful.

'It feels as if I've been hit in the back of my head,' Andrew chuckled to himself as he unlocked Margaret's car.

Margaret's embarrassing sense of direction meant that she had a satellite navigation system in her car, which Andrew had bought for her birthday one year. Andrew didn't normally need to use it, not that he regularly drove Margaret's car as he had his own, because he had a highly accurate sense of direction, but his throbbing headache and dizziness meant that he was struggling to concentrate. He was glad of the help and furiously typed in Taggart's address. He then pulled out of the car park and almost drove straight into another car. Andrew waved his apology and continued to drive. Usually, Andrew considered himself to be a fairly good driver, despite Margaret constantly telling him that he was too arrogant when he drove, and he found that driving came quite naturally to him. However, today he was finding driving exceptionally difficult, something that probably wasn't helped by his headache, which he could now feel pushing behind his eyes, as well as in his head. Even the simple task of driving was exhausting him; his body ached and throbbed and as he drove he became aware of injuries that he hadn't known he had sustained. Some were old injuries, which usually didn't bother him, such as a stab wound in his stomach, but some were new injuries: most significantly the painful wound on his head, which he assumed was the cause of his headache.

Andrew was driving faster than he had ever driven before and he even thought that he was driving more recklessly than Caley, which took some doing. His right foot was practically flat on the floor and he wove in and out of cars and lanes, sometimes even in lanes where cars were driving at him as opposed to with him, as he frantically followed the instructions of the husky, male, satellite-navigation voice. If he hadn't been so scared for Caley, he would have found it amusing that Margaret had changed the voice of the navigation system from the smooth female voice to this deep male voice. However, he didn't find it amusing. He didn't even think about it; he didn't allow himself to think about anything other than Taggart and Caley.

After what had felt like a lifetime of driving, he pulled into the car park underneath Taggart's apartment block, parked Margaret's car illegally near the entrance, blocking several cars in, and sprinted into the reception area. Ignoring the frantic calls of the receptionist, Andrew raced up the stairs, remembering that Taggart lived on the top floor of the building. Hoping that he wasn't too late, he ran up the stairs three at a time. His head was spinning so much by this point that it was beginning to affect his vision, which was now blurred.

As he reached the top of the staircase, he could hear his heart pounding and his pulse racing. His head was throbbing, his body was aching, but still he persevered. He rounded the corner, almost running straight into a brick wall and sprinted through the door. He could see the door to Taggart's apartment right in front of him and had two options. Option one: he could knock on Taggart's door. Option two: he could break the door down. Option one would only work if Caley did not know that Taggart had attacked him; if she did know, then Taggart probably knew that she knew, which put her life in grave danger. In this scenario, if Andrew knocked on the door, then Taggart wouldn't answer and would probably kill Caley – unless he already had killed her. Andrew shook his head furiously, not allowing that to be an option. He thought all these things through so quickly that by the time he reached Taggart's front door, he had decided which option he was going to choose. As Andrew headed towards the door, his head and heart pounding, his hands shaking uncontrollably and his body sweating profusely, his vision blurred and his head spinning, he gained speed. He ran straight into the door with all of his strength, all of his weight, all of his power, with everything that he had in him. The door crashed to the ground, but Andrew kept running. He saw Taggart standing in front of Caley with a golf club in his hand. Taggart turned around in the direction of the noise. He was about to see Andrew. It was about to be too late. Andrew's vision started to fade. Everything was going black. He could feel the bruises on his body from where he had made contact with the door, but he kept running. He ran straight into Taggart, tackling him to the ground, then raised his fist in the air and ploughed it straight into Taggart's face.

Taggart lay unconscious on the ground. The golf club lay beside him. Andrew staggered to his feet and saw Caley, her expression a mixture of shock, fear and joy, all at once.

'Dad,' she cried out, noticing with worry how pale his usually tanned and ruddy face was.

It was all over. She was safe.

'What are you doing here?' she asked, her worry evident in her voice.

'To the rescue,' Andrew whispered with a chuckle. Then everything went black.

'Dad,' Caley called once more as Andrew collapsed at her feet. Trying to comprehend what had just happened, she grabbed her mobile phone out of Taggart's pocket and dialled 999.

Caley was frantically reciting the address of Taggart's apartment building when William strolled in. William saw Taggart lying on the floor and noted the large, deep purple bruise blossoming around his eye, his unconscious state, and his grey pinstriped suit, which did *not* match his brown leather shoes (providing William with another reason to dislike him). He then saw, with shock, that Andrew was lying beside him; his face was pale, his thick, steel grey hair was rumpled and he was wearing his running clothes. Next to Andrew lay a golf club. That was when William realised what had happened. A bemused expression on his face, he meandered over to where Caley was knelt down next to Andrew.

'Taggart,' he pondered aloud. 'I knew that he was up to something; I've been down at the Labyrinth and I've found out some pretty interesting stuff, but I thought that Favel had bribed him. Taggart,' he repeated. 'He was the ringleader of Genesis, wasn't he?'

Caley nodded sombrely.

'He killed Dominic, Daniel and Baxter . . . and he attacked Andrew.'

Caley nodded once more, blinking back tears as she clutched Andrew's hand in her own, needing to use both of her hands because of how big Andrew's hands were.

William moved slightly closer to Caley and Andrew, kicking Taggart sharply in the ribs as he did so. 'Oops,' he said, taking a cigarette out of the inside pocket of his suit jacket and casually lighting it.

There was a noise behind them and William turned to see a small team of security standing, dumbfounded, in the doorway. He held out a hand to them. 'Don't come any closer,' he ordered, producing his police identification badge. 'We've got everything under control.'

The men stepped back slightly.

'Erm, you shouldn't really be smoking in here,' one man called out nervously. 'The owner really wouldn't like it.'

'I don't think he will mind; he's going to prison for a *very* long time,' William replied coolly.

There was silence for a few seconds while the men looked at each other in confusion.

'A man charged through reception and came up here,' one of the men explained. 'We have received instructions to find him and escort him out of the building. We even thought that the police might have needed to be called.'

Another man added, 'Apparently he looked very threatening.'

'This man,' William asked, 'was slightly taller than me, piercing green eyes, thick head of steel-grey hair, wearing running clothes?'

The second man nodded. 'Do you know who he is?'

'Is he a criminal?'

'Worse,' William replied. 'He's a police officer.'

Epilogue
Brown Leather Shoes

'Morning,' Caley called out cheerfully as she strode into the hospital room.

'Shhh!' Margaret hushed her, gesturing to Andrew who was still asleep. The door slammed shut behind Caley, however, and Andrew began to stir.

'Sorry,' Caley whispered as Margaret glared at her.

'It's a bit late to whisper,' Andrew chuckled. 'I'm awake now.'

Margaret's death-like glare melted away as Andrew's laughter made its way around the room; his infectious, booming chuckle making everyone else laugh.

'Do you know anything more?' Andrew asked Caley when he finally stopped laughing.

'Anything *more*?' Margaret repeated. 'Why do you know anything at all?' she demanded, glaring at Andrew and Caley in turn.

Andrew and Caley exchanged a guilty look.

'Andrew,' Margaret said threateningly.

'After you left yesterday evening, I wanted to know what had happened,' Andrew began.

'Yes, but you needed your rest,' Margaret interrupted. 'You have been in a coma in case you have forgotten, after being attacked and seriously injured. It's bad enough that you woke up yesterday, left the hospital and confronted Taggart,' she scolded, but she did so in exasperation not annoyance, and although her voice was cold, her eyes were warm and her lips were twitching into a smile: a result of the puppy dog eyes that Andrew was fixing on her.

Margaret sighed exasperatedly. 'Let me guess, Caley came round after we left and you two stayed up half the night discussing what happened?'

Caley and Andrew exchanged another guilty look and Andrew smiled sweetly at Margaret. 'I missed you,' he simpered at her, causing her to laugh exasperatedly.

Andrew looked around the room and beamed at the familiar faces of his family: Margaret, Aziza, Ray, Caley ... 'Where's William?' he asked, his face creasing into a frown.

'I'm here,' William exclaimed, strolling into the room and holding his arms out as if to say 'Ta dah!'

Caley and Margaret rolled their eyes simultaneously and William meandered over to a vacant chair beside Caley.

'It's good to have you back,' William grinned at Andrew.

'It's good to be back,' Andrew returned.

'Have you been smoking?' Margaret demanded, turning to face William suspiciously.

William smiled innocently as the smell of tobacco diffused into the air.

'You should give up,' Margaret scolded.

William shrugged. 'I was *going* to give up smoking ... but then I decided that I'm not a quitter,' he winked.

Margaret smiled despite herself.

'I'm glad you're looking more like yourself again, William,' Aziza smiled. 'You didn't look like yourself at all yesterday. I mean, you were wearing a *black* suit ... even if it *was* a stylish black suit,' she laughed.

William was wearing an emerald-green suit with black buttons and black leather lapels. Underneath the suit, he was wearing a crisp white shirt, a deep green tie and black leather shoes.

'Thanks,' he grinned, straightening his lapels. 'That means a lot coming from someone as gorgeous as you,' he winked.

Aziza laughed and Ray replied with a grin, 'The only reason that you're still conscious is because I know you're no competition.'

Andrew interrupted the laughter. 'I've just realised I didn't get an answer. Caley, do you know anything more?'

'Obviously, Taggart has been arrested and he's unlikely to get bail. His lawyer's advised him to plead guilty. Between what happened yesterday, what we found out in our investigation and what you found in yours, plus what William found out about Taggart's accounts, even if it *was* illegally,' she added, 'he doesn't stand a chance. He's going to jail . . . for a *very* long time.'

Andrew grinned. 'That is going to be one long list of charges.' He then turned to Margaret. 'What's wrong? You're the only one who doesn't look as if your mouth is hooked onto your ears.'

Margaret smiled softly. 'It's nothing. I'm just worried,' she replied.

'Worried about what?' Andrew asked.

'You, of course, and Caley,' she replied, glancing sideways at Caley. 'You could have been killed . . . twice,' she added, shaking her head despairingly at her husband.

'It's part of the job,' Andrew replied with a shrug.

'I know. I understand . . . It doesn't mean that I don't worry, though.'

'I have an idea,' Aziza added, in her gentle voice. 'I could rent Ray out, you know, as a bodyguard.'

Ray grinned and his boulder-like shoulders moved up and down as he laughed: a laugh that sounded as if he laughed easily and often, which he did.

'Well, it always works for me,' Aziza laughed.

'No, sorry, I'm taken,' Ray laughed, wrapping his huge, muscular arm around Aziza's petite shoulders.

The laughter gently faded away as the door opened. Standing in the doorway, and filling it, was Deputy Chief Constable Steinmann. Steinmann stood in the doorway for a moment as he met Andrew's eyes then he inclined his head briefly. When Andrew returned his brief nod, Steinmann stepped into the room. He was dressed in a dark-blue, pinstriped suit, a white shirt and a dark-blue tie (the same shade as his suit) and as he strode across the room to Andrew, William nodded his approval at his attire.

'What are you nodding at?' Caley whispered to William.

'His suit,' William replied, as if it was obvious. 'Naturally, he doesn't look as good as me,' he continued in a whisper, adjusting his emerald-green cufflinks as he spoke, 'but who does?' he winked. 'I mean, no one has my pizzazz.'

'Pizzazz,' Caley repeated incredulously. 'As if that's a word!'

'It *is* a word,' William replied, visibly insulted. 'It's in the Oxford English Dictionary and therefore it *is* a word.'

Caley rolled her eyes, but William continued, in a whisper, 'Pizzazz is an attractive combination of vitality and glamour . . . just like me.'

'May I?' Steinmann asked Andrew, gesturing to an empty chair beside the bed.

'Of course,' Andrew replied.

As Steinmann sat down, he glanced around the room and his burnet-coloured eyes rested upon Caley and William momentarily. Caley and William exchanged a guilty glance as Steinmann turned his attention back to Andrew.

'I hope that you are on the mend,' he began, his voice as formal as ever.

'Naturally,' Andrew replied easily. 'I am sure that I will be back to work in no time.'

Steinmann allowed himself a brief smile, which William acknowledged with a gentle elbow in the ribs to Caley.

'I have no doubt about that, which is partially why I am here.'

Andrew did not reply, but instead waited for Steinmann to elaborate. The room was silent as everyone unashamedly listened into their conversation.

'I won't go into details here, but I just wanted to let you know, on behalf of the Domsville Police Force, that you have done a good job. Chief Superintendent Richard Taggart is under arrest for a number of crimes and is likely to go to jail for quite a considerable stretch of time.'

'Justice has been done,' Andrew added softly.

'Quite so,' Steinmann agreed, acknowledging Andrew's statement with an inclination of his head, 'and as I am sure that you are aware, that leaves us with a problem. We are a police officer down; we need a new Chief Superintendent.' Although Steinmann didn't actually ask a question, he waited for an answer.

Andrew waited for a few seconds, his poker face straight, and then it split into a huge grin. 'I would, of course, be delighted,' he replied and held out his hand towards Steinmann, 'Deputy Chief Constable Steinmann.'

Steinmann smiled back and although it was a smile and not a grin, unlike Andrew's, William elbowed Caley so excitedly that he almost pushed her off her chair. He then shook Andrew's hand firmly and said, 'Chief Superintendent Arling.'

After Andrew and Steinmann had exchanged a few words, Steinmann stood up and began to leave the room. Before he did, however, he turned to address Caley and William.

'Inspector Arling, Sergeant Aaron,' he acknowledged them with a brief inclination of his head, which they returned. 'I would also like to, once more on behalf of Domsville Police Force, congratulate you on your effort in the arrest of Richard Taggart, even if it *was* carried out against orders and even if some of it was conducted through … *unorthodox* methods,' he added with raised eyebrows.

Caley and William exchanged a brief glance, but no one noticed as they had all turned to look at Andrew who was chuckling.

'Even though we would appreciate it if you actually followed orders and rules and regulations, after all they are there for a reason, we will let you off this once,' he smiled. 'And you never know, there may be room higher up in the ranks now.'

Steinmann scanned the room one last time with a rare smile on his face, and with one last brief nod to Andrew, he turned and left.

Margaret turned to face Caley and William and shook her head in exasperation.

William smirked. 'Rules are made to be broken.'

'You are definitely your father's daughter,' Margaret smiled at Caley, still shaking her head as she did so.

'Talking of which,' Margaret continued. 'Congratulations *Chief* Superintendent,' she grinned, striding over to Andrew and perching on the edge of the hospital bed.

Andrew grinned and wrapped his arm around her shoulders. 'We are definitely celebrating when I get out of here,' he replied.

'It sounds like a plan,' Aziza agreed.

'It sounds like my kind of plan,' William laughed. He suddenly stopped laughing, however, and his eyes widened with shock.

'What's wrong?' Caley asked.

'I've just thought; if I get promoted I'll have to change my registration plate!'

Caley snorted and William called out over the laughter, 'I need to use alliteration. What begins with 'I' for Inspector?'

'Idiot,' Caley replied.

William looked around the room and saw that Ray had his arm around Aziza, and Andrew had his arm around Margaret. 'I feel left out,' he frowned, reaching out and wrapping his arm around Caley with a grin.

Caley laughed and rested her head on his arm. 'That's as far as you're going,' she laughed.

'Yes, sir,' William replied with a wink.

*

Andrew looked around his hospital room and his mouth curved into a smile, which grew until it completely engulfed his face and became a deep, contagious chuckle. He smiled at his wife, whose exasperated expression had transformed into a smile despite herself, and then at his eldest daughter with her fiancé, and his youngest daughter who had followed in her old man's footsteps and was sitting with William.

'It's good to be conscious to witness this,' he laughed, 'and it's all thanks to those darn brown leather shoes.'